Cursed

Beauty

The True Story of Sleeping Beauty

M. Lynn

Edited by Melissa Craven
Proofread by Patrick Hodges
Cover by Covers by Combs

This one is for the readers who've been with me on the journey through this entire series. Aurora wouldn't exist if you hadn't loved Etta, Helena, and Amalie. Thank you.

And for Melissa - you're a part of this series too. Thanks for helping me create something I'm proud of.

ABOUT CURSED BEAUTY

So, if you've read the rest of the *Fantasy and Fairytales* series, you know that this is the seventh book.

Aurora and Phillip were such a pleasure to write. I was worried, like I know some of you will be, that I wouldn't be into it as much because it happens 200 years before the events of the other books, meaning it doesn't feature any known characters.

BUT, I was wrong. This book quickly became my favorite. Just don't tell Etta and Edmund.

Here's the skinny. In Golden Curse, Etta suffers under a family curse tying her to the Durand heir. You get a little bit of the back story and a few mentions of her ancient ancestors, Aurora and Phillip, but nothing more than some cursory information.

Well, tada! This book explains everything. It's the only true standalone in the series because it's its own story with no influences from the others. In fact, it's the other way around. Cursed Beauty shapes everything that happens in the first six books. And we get to see what makes La Dame such a big bad!!

This is the story of the Basile curse and how it came to be. I hope you love it as much as I do.

If you haven't read the others in the series, hopefully this will leave you hungry to start from book 1, *Golden Curse*.

Sometimes to understand the end, you have to go back to the beginning.

Welcome to Bela, 200 years before the events of Golden Curse.

PART I

CHAPTER ONE

PHILLIP

The drums of war held a foreboding rhythm Phillip Basile would never forget. The general prince—as they called him—had stood on bloodstained fields many times before. This time was no different. He still saw no end to the continuous wars between his kingdom of Bela and their greatest enemies, the hordes of Gaule.

Phillip stood atop the eastern tower of one of the border fortresses watching the savages streak across the hillside in the distance. Gaule was a crude land led by a cruel king who had attacked Bela's border villages for too long. They lacked Bela's sophistication and common decency.

Shaking his head, Phillip turned to the men at his back. They'd die for him. He knew that. The warriors of Bela had always been loyal to the crown, and the crown was loyal to them as well.

"Call the archers to line the walls. This fortress will not stand another assault. I want my best magic wielders to meet me at the gates. We will ride out to face them. Once the fight begins, prepare those inside these walls to make for the forest."

One of the armor-clad men dipped his head. "Yes, General." Among his men, Phillip was not a prince, not royal. To them, he was a seasoned fighter, one of their comrades. The general.

He strode back into the tower and thundered down the stairs with his guards following behind. Alfred and Chandler were magic wielders who'd been with him since they were all young boys spying on soldiers in the palace.

"General," Chandler called as Phillip marched across the courtyard. He didn't pause, so Chandler tried again. "General."

"Phillip," Alfred barked. "Stop for a damn minute."

Phillip turned, his jaw clenched. "There is no time. Within the hour, they will overrun us."

"You can't ride out. What will protect you?"

Chandler nodded in agreement. "Phillip, the entire Gaulean force is out there. Even with our magic, we can't match them. You're the heir to the Basile magic. We can't risk you."

Bela was the least populated of the six kingdoms by more than half, but each person born in their land held magic in their blood. The only other kingdom that could boast such a feat was Dracon. Magic had protected Bela for centuries, yet only when the ancient power of the kings was also present. Each Basile king possessed a magic matched only by that of the dark sorceress of Dracon.

And the king was dying. Phillip thought back to the last time he'd spoken to his father. The old man had wanted to make the journey, to ensure they won the day, but he wasn't even able to stand. He wouldn't have had the strength to travel, let alone wield his own magic. If he died, Phillip would inherit the power, allowing him to protect Bela.

What would his father do now? Would he abandon the last remaining border fortress? Would he try to protect the few people Bela had left?

No. Phillip stood taller. His father would fight until he couldn't any longer. He met the worried gazes of his two oldest friends. "I won't force you to join me, but I'm not allowing those savages to cross into Bela."

He turned on his heel and marched to the stables, barking orders as he did. "Ready the horses." All those who wished to fight gathered their weapons. Steel flashed in the early morning sun, but it was only a tool, a ruse. Their greatest weapons lay inside them.

Each magic-wielder's power was different. Some could call on the heat of the sun, others forced the winds to obey their commands.

And Phillip? His greatest weapon was his protective shields against the enemy. A king should have been able to do more in battle. He'd always thought it ironic that his gift wasn't more.

One day, it would be. One day, he'd know what it felt to be invincible, to harness the power of his ancestors, the magic that belonged to the Basiles, transferring to each new generation as they stepped up to rule.

And when that time came, Gaule would regret the day they made an enemy of Bela.

PHILLIP KNELT DOWN in the middle of the battle, digging his fingers into his thighs as he tried to hold the parts of his invisible shield that hadn't already fallen. An arrow sailed for Alfred's back. Phillip clenched his teeth, pulling in his little remaining energy to expand his shield, throwing it out toward Alfred. The arrow hit the invisible force and snapped in two, sending a tremor through Phillip. The prince slumped forward.

"General!" Chandler ducked away from the arc of a sword before slicing his attacker across the back—not with his own blade, but with his magic. His power was an extension of his sword.

He sprinted toward Phillip and grabbed his arm to haul him to his feet. "I told you not to use your shield to protect all of us. You can't hold it that wide."

"You don't give me orders." He sucked in a breath, and it rattled painfully in his chest.

Chandler scanned the battlefield where many of their comrades had fallen. Horses darted from the fight. The Gaulean savages continued to come.

"You need to order a retreat." Alfred joined them, wiping his dripping blade on the grass.

Phillip shook his head. A retreat meant defeat. It meant allowing their enemies to have a piece of Bela, to encroach upon their land. He lifted his eyes to the hill where the Gaulean king sat atop his horse, never joining the fight. Such was the way of the Durands.

Alfred gripped Phillip's shoulder. "We've already lost. Now is the time to save what little we can."

He was right. There was no denying it. Enough people had died this day. Phillip nodded and Alfred lifted his chin. "Retreat." His voice carried on the strength of his magic. He could make himself heard at great distances. Those on the battlefield and in the fortress would hear his call. "Retreat."

"We have to get to the woods." Phillip looked toward the Gaulean king once more, and the man's dark eyes turned in his direction as if he could see the Belaen prince amidst the chaos.

The woods were their only chance. The Gauleans were a suspicious sort, fearing the dark forests that stretched across Bela.

Phillip tried to pull his magic forth, to shield them as they ran, but it was no use. He had no strength left for it. His feet thundered across the open land. His head turned each way to make sure the rest of his army followed. The remaining Belaens fled for their lives, abandoning a fortress they'd held for centuries.

But some things were more important than buildings and land.

A man collided with Phillip, knocking him to the ground. The prince tried to roll him off, but the Gaulean was too strong. He held a knife in one hand and slashed it across Phillip's stomach. Pain radiated from the point of attack, and then someone hauled the man off him. Chandler stabbed his sword through the savage and pulled it out in one movement. As the dead man collapsed to the ground, Alfred pulled Phillip back to his feet.

Phillip pressed a hand to his wound, trying to stem the bleeding. Crimson life seeped between his fingers.

Chandler and Alfred both yelled his name, but he didn't hear them as he fell to his knees. Agony seared through him.

The end. It comes before you're ready. It never takes into account how much you have left to accomplish.

Death cares little if you're the prince, if the Basile power should one day belong to you.

It takes everything and leaves you with only darkness to call your own.

CHAPTER TWO

AURORA

Aurora Rose Brynhild never imagined the kingdom's battles would come so close to her home. Since she was a child, she'd lived among the trees with only her grandmother for company. But her grandmother was gone now, and she'd been alone for over two years. Had it really been that long since she'd spoken to anyone other than the dark sorceress?

Her grandmother told her people were dangerous. When she was a child, the subject came up frequently in conversations with her father. He would leave her for weeks, and then one day he never returned.

She knew who'd taken him. The sorceress over the wall— the Draconian queen. She held Aurora's life in the palm of her hand, never letting her experience true freedom.

Aurora pressed herself against the tree in her perch high in the branches as men trampled through her beautiful woods, leaving blood in their path. Most weren't followed. Those they'd fought stayed at the edge of the forest.

Something caught her eye, and she leaped from one branch to another until she could get a closer look. Two men huddled over a third, trying to lift him. Their voices reached her.

"He's dying." One looked to the other.

A scream tore through the air, followed by a mass of large men in leathers breaking through the trees at the edge of the woods. Soon, they'd spot the dying man and his companions.

"They can't find him." The first man lifted his eyes. "We have to lead them away."

The second shook his head. "And just abandon him?"

The first stood and gripped the injured man under the arms, hauling him into the thick underbrush. He covered him.

"He needs a healer." The second man gripped his sword.

The first man met his eyes. "And we'll get him to one. We won't let him down. But we won't be any good to him if we're overrun. Don't you think the Gaulean king would love to have him as a prisoner?"

Together, both men turned and ran back the way they'd come.

Aurora leaned against the tree, listening to the sounds of battle, waiting for the men to return.

After a few moments, she gripped the branch in front of her and dropped down onto a lower one before jumping to the pine-covered ground. She approached where they'd hidden the man and ripped aside the bush covering him.

The face that greeted her was younger than she'd expected. Dirt and blood streaked across his tanned skin and into his sun-bleached hair.

His eyelids twitched but didn't open. Aurora bit her lip, considering the man. She felt for injury, finding a hole in his leather tunic. Wadded fabric lay pressed against his skin, bulging behind his shirt. Yet, blood continued to run free.

They were right about one thing. This man needed a healer, and he needed one fast. Glancing up to make sure no other soldiers remained in this part of the woods, she made a decision. Her father would scold her for her compassion. Her grandmother would worry, trying to hide the pride on her face. She could picture them now, waiting for her at the cottage. Tears threatened to prick her eyelids, but there was no time for sentimentality. She dragged the man into the open, past thick pine trees, and across the clearing to where she'd hidden her only friend. Lea's soft brown eyes bore into hers. The mule shifted as Aurora dug through the bags on her friend's back, looking for the length of rope that was an ever-present companion to the girl who spent her days climbing trees looking for the freshest fruit and setting snares for rabbits.

She pulled the rope free and tied an end to each of the man's arms before looping the middle around a hook on Lea's saddle.

"Come on, girl." She patted Lea's neck before untying her. "I couldn't just leave him." She took the reins and led Lea into a deeper part of the woods where very few people ventured. It was too close to the walls of Dracon, and the only thing that frightened Belaens more than the hordes of Gauleans was the Draconian Queen, La Dame.

Aurora grimaced as the man's body hit a bump in the road, but she reminded herself there was no other way home. It took the better part of an hour to reach the small cottage where she lived alone. Thick pine trees shielded it from anyone who didn't know the way. A field of white lilies came into view before the stone structure.

Aurora breathed out a relieved sigh as she pulled Lea to a stop and got to work untying the man she'd brought to her sanctuary. It was probably a mistake. Her family wouldn't have approved, not with the curse inside of her. They'd claim it was too dangerous, that she risked activating La Dame's threat. But wasn't it also dangerous to leave a dying man alone in the woods? Soon after she was born, her mother grew ill, and her desperate father turned to the dark queen of Dracon for help.

But her aid had come at a cost, a curse on the family.

On Aurora's eighteenth birthday, she would fall into a magical slumber that would end when one hundred winters had passed.

She only had one short month remaining of her young life. Slumber wasn't death, but the uncertainty of it might prove to be much worse.

Aurora looked to the stranger once more. At least with her final act, she could do something good.

AURORA STEPPED out her front door and turned to examine her home. The magic pooled in her fingertips just as it did for all Belaens. She'd inherited the same power her grandfather once had. Not all types of magic ran in families, but the power of growth lived strong in their line. Her grandmother called it a power over life. She didn't know if she believed that, but it allowed her to remain hidden in the woods.

She curled her fingers in, pressing them against her palms as vines snaked up the sides of the cottage until she could only see the door. Someone would have to be looking for it to find it. The solitude suited her. If she had nothing in her life, then sadness couldn't overwhelm her. No one would miss her while she slept, no one besides her would live with the anguish of her curse.

With a sigh, she brushed her hands down her pale pink

dress. The laces frayed, but each time they broke, she repaired them. The only clothing she owned was that which she made herself or that which belonged to her long-dead family.

She picked up a bucket she'd left by the side of the house and smiled at Lea as she passed her. The walls of Dracon stood ominously close, but they'd never frightened her as they had most other people. Not even La Dame herself scared Aurora. She'd already done her worst when she set the curse on a newborn baby girl.

Aurora had resigned herself to her fate. Nothing in life could hurt her now.

The best berries hung on the bushes at the base of the wall. Purple and juicy, they were one of the few pleasures she had left to enjoy in her remaining days. She walked through the woods until a line of thick and thorny bushes stretched out before her.

A small smile played on her lips as she pulled the first berry and popped it in her mouth. An explosion of sweet juices had her closing her eyes. It had never taken much to bring Aurora joy. She didn't need fancy clothes or a handsome prince to show her how lucky she was to be alive.

The fresh breeze stopped, and she snapped her eyes open. It was the first time she noticed the absence of birds singing overhead. The berry she chewed turned sour, and she spit it out before pivoting on her heel and coming face to face with the tormenter who'd become a frequent visitor in the woods.

"Oh." Aurora crossed her arms. "It's you."

La Dame flashed her a smile. Aurora always got the impression she amused the sorceress, and it always irritated her.

"What do you want?" she asked.

La Dame's long inky hair hung in waves down her slender

back. Her beauty was no secret, but the stories said little else about her. She continued to stare.

Aurora bristled. "I asked what you wanted. You've already set my curse. Can't you leave me alone and let me enjoy the little remaining life I have left?"

La Dame reached forward, and her icy finger wiped at Aurora's chin. "It isn't proper to let the juice dribble down your skin, my dear."

Aurora pushed her hand away. "I'm not your dear. If you have no important reason for infringing upon my solitude, then I'll be on my way." She turned and walked away.

La Dame followed her. "But I'm not the only person interrupting your peace, am I?"

"Go away."

"I think I'll stay and meet your visitor."

Aurora froze. "He's not capable of conversation right now. Go get your entertainment somewhere else."

For a moment, she wondered if the sorceress had listened to her because she heard no further pursuit. When she reached her home, however, La Dame stood at the door.

"How did you...?"

La Dame's eyes danced. "You have no idea what I'm capable of, Aurora." Without another word, she ducked her head and pushed through the door.

Aurora ran after her, stopping inside when she saw the strange man struggling to sit up in bed. When she'd brought him to her home, she'd removed his dirty, blood-soaked clothing and cleaned him as best she could.

He stilled when he saw them. "Who are you?" His voice was deep and rich and so utterly male it took Aurora a moment to realize he'd asked a question.

He didn't wait for an answer as he lifted the blanket she'd covered him with. "And why am I naked?"

A blush crept up her cheeks. "Umm..." She rubbed the back of her neck. "You..."

La Dame laughed. "I think what my dear Aurora is trying to tell you, young man, is that she found you injured and alone in the forest before bringing you here where she had to cut away your shirt to tend to your wound. And the rest of your clothing was wrecked from the battle."

Aurora snapped her gaze to La Dame. "How do you know all of that?" The sorceress hadn't been there when she'd brought the stranger home.

La Dame shrugged and stepped closer to the man. "I am watching you, young man. Nothing you do goes unnoticed in Dracon." Before Aurora could stop her, La Dame uttered a few unintelligible words and placed her hand against the man's head. He struggled against her touch, uttering a few curses that only made La Dame laugh.

"No," Aurora gasped.

The man slumped back on the bed, his eyes closed.

"What did you do to him?" She dropped to her knees beside the bed.

La Dame walked toward the door. "He wasn't needed any longer. Be careful, Aurora. One month." She glanced back at the man. "This one might be the one."

"What are you talking about?"

La Dame tapped her chin. "You'll soon find out, I think." Without another word, she disappeared as if she'd never been there at all.

A tear slipped down Aurora's cheek. "I'm so sorry," she whispered, leaning over him.

When his chest rose, she sucked in a breath. Not dead. She closed her eyes, thanking the stars La Dame hadn't taken this stranger's life. He was only here because of her, and Aurora couldn't stand to see La Dame take someone else's life.

She already had hers, but it gave her some comfort knowing the people of Bela would go on with their lives, never knowing she'd been there, never missing her.

La Dame required payments for deals she made. She didn't want deaths. No, nothing so simple as that. She wanted lives. Aurora would sleep for one hundred years, and when she woke, she'd become just another servant of La Dame's.

Sometimes, Aurora wondered if La Dame only wanted the entertainment her curses provided.

Aurora sighed. "Only one way out," she whispered to herself. La Dame's curses always held something twisted. There was a way to break the curse, but it was up to the curse bearer to figure it out, and, once she did, she was sure she'd regret it. No one ever liked the consequences of breaking a curse.

La Dame's cruelty knew no ends.

She sat back on her heels, watching his chest rise and fall and wishing the world had let her fade into the sleep as her curse demanded. Instead, it had given her one final test.

CHAPTER THREE

LA DAME

A cry pierced the solitude of La Dame's slumber. How dare the child wake her at such an hour? She rolled from her bed, planning to yell for one of her servants to care for the baby down the hall. Rapunzel. What a stupid name.

What possessed the sorceress to bring the girl back to her palace? Images from the night before flickered through her mind, moving pictures she cared little for. A fire wound through one sector of the village nearest the palace. The commotion pulled their queen near to see what was happening.

She could have stopped it. She could have saved the people who didn't survive the raging flames.

But no one in Dracon would have been surprised at her inaction. Then she found her. A tiny baby someone had thrown from an upper balcony. La Dame caught the child and hadn't let go until she returned to her home. No one would miss the babe. Her parents were now nothing but ashes.

All La Dame remembered of them was a woman wailing for her Rapunzel.

Where were the damn maids? Didn't they hear the obnoxious piercing wail? La Dame pushed out with her magic, forcing the door to Rapunzel's room open. The child thrashed in the crib one of the servants provided.

As soon as La Dame hovered over her, crystal blue eyes popped open, and the wailing ceased.

"It's been a long day, little one." She sighed. "You interrupted my sleep." She'd spent the day on the other side of the wall in Bela visiting Aurora, the girl who would one day be hers. When she'd first placed the curse on the Brynhild family, she hadn't imagined the relationship she'd develop with the Belaen.

Aurora hated her, but that was nothing new. La Dame couldn't remember a day in her life when she hadn't been hated.

One day, Aurora would be like a daughter to her, a family she'd never had. But only after the curse played itself out.

"Rapunzel." She tested the name out. The girl looked up at her like she understood. "I don't like having anyone else living in my palace." She expected her servants to be mostly unseen unless called for. "Your parents died a horrible death, I'm afraid." Yet, the baby was here. "So did mine."

The difference was La Dame held full responsibility for what happened to her family. She angered her father every day of his life. He'd been a revered and loved king in Dracon decades ago, but when it came time to choose the successor for his magic, he'd chosen La Dame's younger brother. The only way for him to inherit the magic was for her to die.

Her mother tried to stop the events that happened next. She tried to save her only daughter as a mother should, warning her of her brother's treachery. But in saving one child, she doomed the other.

"I drove my brother's own knife through his back, severing

his spinal cord." She smiled at the memory. "He couldn't even move in his final moments. Then I went for my father."

Her family was torn apart by their lack of love, as many families were. Her mother eventually succumbed to self-inflicted injuries, leaving La Dame alone in the world with untold power in her hands.

And a promise.

She'd take care of children whose parents chose themselves over their kids.

Which brought her to Aurora and Rapunzel. Leaning in, she dropped her voice. "You're mine now, Rapunzel. And one day, once her curse has finished, you will have a sister."

CHAPTER FOUR

PHILLIP

A dull pain throbbed in Phillip's chest as he opened his eyes and took in his surroundings. Right, he'd been injured. He remembered nothing other than seeing Alfred and Chandler jump into a fight with Gaulean savages. After that, everything went dark.

No light lit the room save for a fledgling fire in a small stone hearth. He scanned the room, noting the windows were covered with what looked like... branches? He lay on the only bed, but a small form huddled under a blanket in front of the hearth.

Phillip tried to ignore the intensifying pain as he slid from the bed. The blanket fell, revealing his state of undress. He picked it up and wrapped it around his waist before walking across the tiny room. A privy sat to the right with a small simple kitchen to his left. Whoever lived here had everything they needed in this one room.

His brow creased as he moved close enough the see the girl. An orange glow from the fire lit her pale face. Straw-colored hair fanned around her head. She mumbled something and pursed her full lips.

Phillip's blood rushed in his ears as he watched her, unable to look away. This was his savior? He bent down to get a better look at her high brows and rosy cheeks.

Memories flashed through his mind. Had he woken before? Had he met her? An image of a tall, dark-haired woman came to him. What had she said?

She'd called her Aurora. That was all he remembered.

His legs wobbled beneath him as he breathed deeply. Blood dripped down his chest, and he looked down to see his wound had opened up and soaked the bandage. He stumbled back, crashing into a small table. A chair clattered to the floor.

The girl he'd been watching only moments before shot to her feet, her eyes wide. "You're awake." Her voice had a breathless quality he wanted to hear again.

He nodded. "I can't sleep forever."

A dark look crossed her face, but it was gone so quickly, he thought he'd imagined it.

She shook her head. "No, but you can sleep this night. You shouldn't be out of bed." Her eyes drifted to his bare torso. "And you've opened the wound. Go lay down. I'll get a new bandage."

He obeyed her without question, lowering himself to the bed. "I'm really okay."

"No, you've lost a lot of blood. You need a few days' rest."

"What I need is to return to my men. They'll be searching for me." He tried to sit up, but she pressed a strong hand against his shoulder.

"You're not going anywhere."

He narrowed his eyes. "You don't know who I am. I will go where I please. There's nothing you can do to stop me."

She raised an eyebrow and lifted her hand. After a moment, she met his eyes again. "Go ahead. Try to leave."

He pushed her away and got to his feet, holding the blanket around his waist, and stumbled to the door. He gripped the handle and pushed. The door didn't budge. He rammed his shoulder into it, mustering every bit of strength he could. Pain shot through him, but still, the door didn't open.

He turned back to her, leaning against the door for support. "What did you do?"

"The trees and grasses and vines all obey my magic. You won't be going anywhere until I've decided you're recovered enough. Now, sit back down and allow me to change that bandage."

When he sat without further argument, she pressed a palm to his chest. Her touch warmed him. She cleaned the blood from his skin with a rag she pulled from a bowl of warm water beside the bed. When she finished wrapping a new bandage around his chest, she sat back to examine her work.

He used it as an excuse to study her. She looked so fragile, yet had a surprising amount of strength, both physically and in strength of will. He couldn't remember the last time someone contradicted his demands.

She ran a hand through her wild hair and smiled. "You're going to live."

He relaxed, his earlier anger dissipating. "I... you saved me, didn't you?"

She bit her lip. "Really it was Lea. She dragged you all this way."

"Lea?"

"Oh... um, my mule."

He couldn't help the laugh escaping him. She credited her mule with saving his life. "Well, thank Lea for me."

She tucked her hair behind her ear, a dimple appearing in her cheek. "I don't know your name."

"Phillip," he said quickly. He didn't know why he needed her to have his name so badly. Names held a power, and he wanted her to have a piece of him, even if it was just in thanks.

"Phillip," she repeated in her soft lilting tone. Her eyes widened and when she spoke next, he got the distinct impression she spoke only to herself. "Phillip. The battle. Please, Aurora, tell me you didn't trap the crown prince of Bela in your home."

Phillip waved a hand in front of her face. "Uh, hi. Yes, crown prince here. The kingdom will forever be in your debt for saving me."

She distanced herself from him. "I don't need the kingdom's gratitude." She hugged her arms across her chest. "But I'm still not letting you go. You wouldn't make it across Bela to the palace in your condition. I'm sorry, your Highness. I have the power to keep you here, and I'm using it."

Phillip grimaced. His friends would tear the kingdom apart searching for him if they didn't already mourn him as dead. His father was ailing, and his mother ran the kingdom on her own. She needed his help and yet, here he was trapped with a strange girl he couldn't take his eyes off.

"At least tell me your name."

"Aurora." She blushed. He'd already realized she did that a lot. In his mind, he heard La Dame speaking her name. Maybe she had been here after all. "Please don't call me Highness, Aurora. Just Phillip."

She frowned. "But that's what you are. A prince. I don't..." She brushed a hand through her hair. "I don't have experience with people. I may be simple, but that doesn't mean I don't know how to treat royalty."

Her words brought a smile to his lips. She said she was simple, but he could already see there wasn't a simple thing about her. "Please." He met her gaze. "Just Phillip."

She sighed and got to her feet. "Fine, but Phillip, you need sleep. So, rest."

"You should have your bed."

"Are you going to question every decision I make?" She turned away from him, mumbling to herself. "This was a mistake. You don't have any right to be in the presence of a prince."

He grinned as she continued talking to herself. This girl was one stop short of crazy. She lived alone in the woods, talked to herself constantly, and locked people in her cottage.

Yet, her soft murmuring allowed him to drift into a peaceful sleep with only one question on his mind.

If it had been real, what association did a girl like Aurora have with the dark sorceress?

CHAPTER FIVE

AURORA

Lea whimpered from her place in the yard as Aurora let herself into the dim morning light. "It's just me, buddy." She patted Lea's neck and bent to pour grain into her bucket at the side of the cottage. When she straightened, she looked to the sky. "It's going to storm today, Lea." Swirling dark clouds hung overhead, visible through the swaying tree canopy. Wind whipped Aurora's hair away from her face. "Once you eat, go find your shelter, okay?"

Lea only shook her head and lowered it to begin eating. The beast hadn't understood a word Aurora said, but she'd sense the storm and find the cave she retreated to whenever the weather turned bad.

Glancing back at the cottage, Aurora hoped Phillip wasn't awake yet. She'd have to trap them inside again once he could move about. He'd been injured and unconscious when she brought him here three days ago. He still had quite a bit of healing to do before he could journey back to his home, his life. And by then, Aurora would be preparing for perpetual slumber. One hundred years. That was the curse.

By the time she woke, she didn't know what kind of world she would find.

A raindrop hit her cheek, and she didn't bother to wipe it away as more fell from the sky, soaking into the faded yellow skirts of her dress. "Aurora." She sighed. "This is not your life. You don't mingle with a prince. He isn't even supposed to know your name."

Why not? A voice in her head asked.

"Because." She turned back to the only home she'd known since she was a child. "You belong to *her,* and soon, she will claim her prize."

She trudged across sopping ground to push open her door. As soon as she shut it, her magic pulled vines to hold it in place, keeping her inside with Phillip and the rest of the world outside.

Phillip still slept as she toed off her wet boots and made her way to the kitchen. She gripped the handle of the cast iron teapot and hung it over the flames before twisting to the side to reach for more wood to keep the fire going.

She cast another look at the prince to make sure he was still asleep before pulling her dress off over her head, laying it on the back of a chair to dry in front of the flames. Digging in her single trunk at the end of the bed, she found a comfortable pair of worn trousers and a tunic that was two sizes too big. They were her father's clothes. She didn't wear them outside the cottage, fearing the damage that would come to the last remaining parts of him she had. But she wouldn't be going anywhere today.

As if to punctuate the thought, a crack of thunder shook the cottage. She closed the trunk and stood to find Phillip watching her from the bed.

She clutched the clothes to her chest, uniquely aware of how her underclothes left her stomach exposed. Her muscles rippled like no woman she'd ever seen and shame filled her. Since she was a child, Aurora spent her days traipsing through the woods, hunting and climbing trees. The activity had made her strong, but ever since her grandmother died and the curse grew closer, she hadn't wanted to stop moving, to stop using her body. Now, it was hard where a woman's should be soft.

Phillip's eyes blazed into her.

"Um," she stuttered. "Can you..."

He coughed uncomfortably. "Yes, of course. I'm sorry." Red tinged his skin from his cheeks to the tips of his ears.

She turned away from him and slipped into the clothes. The whistling of the kettle gave her the excuse she needed not to look him in the eyes.

He sat up, his fingers probing his wound.

"Don't get out of bed." She didn't even turn to give him the order.

His chuckle vibrated through the cottage. "Wouldn't think of it, but... uh... do you have my clothes somewhere?"

She focused on pouring water over the tea leaves in two chipped cups. It wasn't the finery he was used to, but it would have to do. "I tried washing your clothing but gave up and burned them instead."

He choked. "You burned my clothes?"

She shrugged. "They were disgusting, and I didn't want them in my home." Her voice lowered. "I couldn't get the blood out." In truth, it had reminded her too much of her grandmother's death. She closed her eyes as images of blood returned to her.

"Breathe," she muttered to herself. "Just breathe."

"Do you always talk to yourself?" His voice held no judgment, only curiosity.

She turned, two cups in hand, and crossed the room to him. "Who else would I talk to?" Her question seemed to catch him off guard because he didn't say another word as he accepted the tea. She set hers on the bedside table and returned to her trunk. "Some of my father's clothes will most likely fit you."

"Your father?" Panic entered his gaze. "Will he return to find me here with you?"

With that statement, Aurora saw him as just a boy, not the prince who led the kingdom to war. But it didn't lessen the stab of pain she felt at the mention of her father. "He's dead."

Sympathy entered Phillip's eyes, but Aurora didn't want his pity. She could survive on her own. She was strong enough to walk into La Dame's curse with open eyes. She didn't break so easily.

With a shrug, she procured long trousers and a tunic with holes in the bottom of it.

A TENSE SILENCE filled the cottage for most of the day. Phillip slept a lot, regaining his strength. Aurora busied herself mending clothes and making bread between periods of watching the prince sleep. He thrashed about the bed, his eyes shifting beneath his lids. She'd found him at the end of a lost battle. What kind of horrors had he witnessed?

He was right when he said the entire kingdom would be searching for him, but they'd never find him this close to the Draconian wall. At that thought, her brow scrunched. La Dame's words returned to her. *He might be the one.*

The one to what?

She shook herself. She had no right to think of the prince, let alone be in the same room as him. "I'm just a forest girl." And one normally only in the company of a mule. She knew she came off rough sometimes, issuing orders when it wasn't her place, but she'd had so little experience with people in recent years.

Digging her hands into the dough, she folded it and kneaded it, taking out her frustration. Why did she have to help the prince? She should spend her final month of freedom alone as she preferred. She should be racing Lea through the trees and feel the sun on her face, not staying trapped inside her cottage until the curse finally took her.

She worried what would happen to Lea when she was gone. Maybe the prince could take her back to the palace where she'd have every luxury.

Aurora set the dough aside to rise and wiped her hands on her apron. She stepped up to the window, allowing her magic to pull back the vines covering it. The storm continued to rage outside. Wind thrashed the rain against the window and the water leaked through. She let the vines settle back into place to keep the weather from entering their dry space.

"Aurora." She twisted her hand through her tangled hair. "Enjoy even the rainy days now. Soon, they will no longer exist to you."

"Why wouldn't they exist?"

Phillips voice made her jump. For a moment, she'd forgotten he was there. Ignoring his question, she turned. "You're awake. Would you like some tea?"

He studied her but didn't ask the question again. Instead, he settled on one that was almost as complicated. "How do you acquire items such as tea and wheat when you live so far from town? Do you travel often?"

She wrung her hands together. How did she tell him that she relied on the dark sorceress' good will since her grand-mother died? Belaens were supposed to hate La Dame—to fear her. Aurora had never known why La Dame took care of her, provided for her, but she never questioned it when she had so few other options.

Aurora moved past the bed and poured two cups of tea from the steaming kettle. Handing one to Phillip, she moved to sit across the room.

He shook his head. "Am I not to know anything about the girl who saved my life?"

She sipped her tea. "There is nothing a prince needs to know about me."

He set his tea aside and struggled until he sat on the edge of the bed. "Why not?"

It was a challenge, but she knew her place. She shrugged. "Because soon I won't matter."

"What does that mean?"

"Nothing. It means I am nothing. Please, your Highness, do not ask me more than I am willing to tell. You don't deserve to carry the burdens of my truths. Your shoulders are already heavy enough from your own burdens."

He let out a frustrated huff. "You are Belaen. When I am king, you will be my subject. I would like to know what troubles you."

"I may live on this side of the wall, Highness, but make no mistake. I do not belong to you." She stood, moving toward the door. "I am hers."

Speaking to the vines with her magic, she forced them to let her through into the storm. Her cottage was too small for two people, especially when one of them demanded answers. As soon as he recovered, the prince would return to the palace and forget about the girl he'd met in the woods.

Rain pelted her as she made her way to the cave she knew Lea would have taken shelter in, plastering her hair to the side of her face. The mule was her only friend, and she needed to make sure she was okay. Lightning lit the dim gray sky as she found the mouth of the cave.

Lea lifted her head when Aurora entered.

For the first time all day, Aurora smiled. "Hi, buddy." Her entire body relaxed as understanding eyes bore into hers.

"The prince sure takes up a lot of room, doesn't he?" A chill raced up her spine, and her limbs shook. She sat and curled against Lea, trying to protect herself against the cold. Her sopping clothes only added to the ice snaking over her skin.

She leaned back against the wall. "I'm going to have to leave you soon, Lea." She hadn't yet had the conversation with her friend, but it was time. The mule wouldn't understand, but it felt necessary anyway. "I promise you I'm not abandoning you. You're in my every thought, and I don't want you to be alone in this world with no one to take care of you." A tear slipped down her cheek.

Aurora spent years preparing for her slumber, rarely letting herself feel the impending fate. Maybe it was La Dame's visit the night before, maybe it was something else, but she couldn't stop thinking about the world she was leaving behind. Would someone find her cottage? Would everything she owned belong to someone new? Maybe La Dame's next victim? She wasn't the first, and she wouldn't be the last.

She hugged her knees to her chest to calm her shivering as a sob wracked her body. "I'm so sorry, my friend. I don't want to go, but La Dame has always owned my future." She'd never stood a chance in life.

Her words drifted away, drowned out by pounding rain, but her tears remained.

Lea whinnied, and Aurora lifted her eyes to the mouth of the cave where a soaking wet Phillip stood, sword in hand. Her eyes widened when she saw the sword.

He glanced at it. "Oh, sorry. I used it to hack my way out of your trap of a cottage." He set the sword leaning against the wall of the cave and approached her. "Are you okay?"

Phillips shirt clung to the ridges of his stomach. A small patch of red seeped through. He must have overdone it looking for her in this storm.

She wiped her face and stood. "You shouldn't be out here." She had to shout to be heard over the rain.

"I had to make sure you were okay."

"Why?"

The question seemed to confuse him, but he answered anyway. "You saved me. I'm not going to let something happen to you." He cocked his head. "I don't let women just wander into storms on their own."

"Just great, Aurora" she mumbled to herself. "You had to go and save a noble fool, not some man who'd just leave the first chance he got."

A grin appeared on his face, and she didn't know if she should feel irritated he found her amusing.

She stood, her eyes flicking to where his wound was obviously bleeding again. "Bloody fool." Grabbing his arm, she dragged him back into the rain. "Come."

She didn't bother with the vines this time when she shut her door. He'd leave if he wanted to leave. It wasn't her business.

She shoved him toward the bed. "Remove your clothes."

He lifted an eyebrow.

She put her hands on her hips. "I need to see your wound. Besides, I don't want you soaking my bed just because you're an idiot."

Laughter sparked in his hazel eyes. Did anyone ever tell this man what they truly thought of him? She guessed not.

Phillip pulled the sopping tunic over his head and

dropped his trousers until he only stood in his underclothes. "Would you like me to keep going?" One side of his mouth tilted up.

Heat rose in Aurora's cheeks, and she pivoted away to grab the bandages. "Sit on the bed. You shouldn't be on your feet."

"As you command."

The pile of bandages were just strips of cloth Aurora had cut when Phillip was sleeping. She may have regretted bringing him into her home, but now that he was here, she would make sure he didn't die. It was past that point now. If he managed to rest, he'd be out of there in no time and she'd be left to fall into her cursed slumber alone, just as she'd always expected.

But, if there was one thing she already knew about the prince, it was that sitting still was not easy for him. He wanted to be up and off protecting his kingdom. It killed him to sit in some strange woman's home while his people searched for him. At least, she assumed that was the thought entering his mind.

He could have left. When he hacked his way through the vines keeping him in, it was his chance to escape her and her crazy idea to abduct the prince. He hadn't though. Instead, he'd come to find her.

She turned, surprised to find him watching her, curiosity sparking in his gaze. She brushed a hand over her face, thinking something odd had caught his attention. Wet tendrils of hair stuck to her cheeks, and she could only imagine how she appeared.

She leaned forward to examine his wound. Blood no longer flowed from the gash, but instead only seeped out at the corners around the crusted skin and the beginnings of a scab. That was a good sign.

"This would heal a lot quicker if you didn't do idiotic things like walk out into a storm." She didn't meet his eyes as she dabbed at the wound. "Does that hurt?"

"Would you think less of me if I said yes?" He grimaced.

"No. I'd think less of you if you lied to me rather than admitting there was something human about you."

He sucked in a breath as she continued to probe the wound. "You're lucky I didn't have to stitch this."

He chuckled humorlessly. "Don't tell me you didn't want to stick a needle in me."

She finally snapped her eyes to his. "Only a little."

He closed his eyes against the pain. "To answer your question about the storm—"

"I didn't ask a question."

He continued without missing a beat. "I wouldn't have gone out into it if you'd stayed safe inside."

She turned, pulling a strip of fabric free. "Sit up."

He did as she asked.

"I've lived here on my own for a long time." She scooted closer to wrap the bandage around his torso. "I don't need a man showing up with some misguided idea of protecting me. You don't even know me." She jumped when a crack of thunder shook the cottage.

"You're right. I'm sorry."

His words surprised her, and she waited for him to say something else. She twisted her arms around him to grab the end of the bandage and only then realized how close her face was to his bare chest. Her eyes drifted to his as she tilted her head back. Gone was the curiosity and the laughter. Instead, the intensity took the breath from her lungs.

He brushed wet bangs out of her face as she sat frozen, unable to move away, unwilling to close the final distance between them.

"When I found you in that cave," he whispered. "You were crying. Why?"

His words were what she needed to break her trance. A sigh pushed past her lips, and she sat back to finish tying the bandage and examine her work. Satisfied, she rocked back onto her heels and stood.

"Tea?"

"Do you always use tea as a way to avoid uncomfortable questions?" He leaned back against the pillows.

"Do you always ask uncomfortable questions?"

He chuckled, and the sound shot straight through her, sending goose bumps racing down her arms. "I'm trying to understand you. To understand why a young woman would choose to live in isolation rather than among her own people. Why she'd easily associate with La Dame, but only show scorn for Bela's prince."

She crossed her arms over her chest, a chill piercing through her still-wet clothing. "I haven't only shown you scorn."

He raised an eyebrow.

"I need to change into something dry. Turn away." She paused. "Please."

He rolled over in the bed as she struggled out of her tunic and pants, replacing them with a simple green dress. "I'm finished." She pulled her wet hair into a high tail to keep it from soaking her shoulders.

He studied her for a moment. "Why is it so wrong of me to want to know one of my subjects?"

"I'm not one of your subjects." She plunked herself down in a chair facing the fire.

"My father is dying." A sad tone entered his voice. "I will be your king soon."

She shook her head, pulling her knees up to her chest.

"Aurora—"

"I belong to her!" She hadn't meant for the words to slip out, but she couldn't call them back. She buried her face in her arm. "I'm sorry, Phillip. I may live on Belaen soil, but you can never be my king."

CHAPTER SIX

PHILLIP

Bela wasn't like the rest of the Six Kingdoms. There was no inner turmoil, no plotting or deceiving. The people had always been loyal to the Basiles, their ruling family. Some claimed it left them vulnerable to the day when someone betrayed them because it meant the king trusted his people. Phillip and his family were as loyal to the Belaens as they were to the crown.

And it worked. They banded together to fight invading forces, protecting the special kingdom they'd built.

Phillip didn't have to draft men into his army because they came willingly.

But now, this strange girl's words echoed in the hollow spaces of his mind, trying to take root but finding no place to settle. He didn't need to ask who this "her" was Aurora claimed loyalty to. He'd seen the dark sorceress with his own eyes.

It made so much sense now. Why a young girl would live out her days in the forest alone. Why the Draconian queen had any kind of interest in someone of no import.

His gaze hardened as Aurora stared into the flames. "Is that why you've trapped me here?" La Dame had never made a move against Bela—or at least against the ruling family. For years, people disappeared from their families, and it was well known they were on the other side of that ominous wall. Why did she want him now? "Is that why you saved my life?"

Aurora's head snapped up, and her tear-stained cheeks shimmered in the orange glow as she turned to him. "No. I saved you because you needed my help."

He scrubbed a hand over his face. "No one helps someone just because they need it. Belaens are beholden to me, but you claim you're not. Why did you bring me here?"

She crossed her arms over her chest. "I'm sorry for the kind of world you live in, Prince, but not everything is so damn complicated." She held out one palm face up. "Man in the woods with guts falling out of his stomach." She turned over her other palm. "Girl in the trees with the ability to save him." She clapped them together, making him jump. "Decency." Leveling him with a stare, she continued. "I said I belonged to La Dame not that I am loyal to her or worship her. Trust me or not, I don't care, but listen to me Phillip Basile. I didn't save you so you could leave here and collapse on the journey back to the palace."

She turned away from him. "You don't have to speak to me, but you have to stay. At least for a little while longer."

His voice was quiet when he spoke next. "And if she comes again? If she demands you turn me over to her?"

Aurora's eyes blazed with a type of fire he'd never seen before. "La Dame owns my future, but the present... that is still mine. At least for now. You're safe here. I can promise you that."

AURORA DIDN'T SPEAK to him again that night, so he lay listening to the rain patter against the roof, muffled by the vines covering the thin wood. Memories of battle flashed through his mind with an almost comforting rhythm. Fighting was something he knew how to do. No one in Bela could lead an army better than he could. It was why his father put such faith in him.

That was what he was meant to do. He'd been injured before, but never felt so weak, so like a burden, before now. Aurora lay curled on the floor, not issuing a single complaint. Phillip wished he'd had the strength to rise and make her take the bed, but he found his eyelids drooping instead.

FIRE. It burned through Phillip, charring his skin. Sweat dotted his forehead. Was the cabin burning to the ground? Alarm shot through him, but he couldn't lift his head. Why was it so heavy?

"Phillip." The voice sounded far away. He tried to latch onto it, to let it pull him out of the fog, but like an unraveling thread, it drifted just out of reach.

"Phillip." There it was again. The sound settled around him until all he heard was his name again and again.

Something pressed down on his shoulder, jostling him out of his own thoughts. "You need to wake up." He recognized the person speaking to him as he pried open a heavy lid.

"Aurora," he whispered, unable to infuse more strength into the word.

Kind eyes stared down into his, so unlike the hard gaze she'd given him the day before. Her lips moved, but the words didn't reach his ears. She shook his shoulder again.

As his glazed eyes stared at her, he realized he'd never

seen anyone so beautiful. Wild straw-spun hair, skin tanned by the sun, wide eyes. He wanted to touch her, to run a finger down her delicate cheek and over her full lips.

"Beautiful." He closed his eyes. "So beautiful."

Aurora sighed and shook him again. "Just the fever talking."

He didn't know whether she meant those words for him or herself. He could never tell.

"Phillip, you need to drink some tea."

What was happening? He tried to sit up, but his limbs wouldn't move. "Aurora." The weakness in his voice didn't escape him, but he was too tired to care.

When he opened his eyes again, worry creased her brow. "I think your wound is infected."

Infected. He'd seen many men lose their lives not to the battles, but to infection as their wounds were treated. Was this the end? Would his family, his men, ever know what became of him?

They'd assume he died in battle. Who would lead the army now? Gaule now held a piece of Bela, pushing the borders farther in. That couldn't be allowed.

Aurora slid a hand under Phillip's neck and tilted his head up while she held a cup to his lips. The bitter liquid hit his throat, and he sputtered. "What..."

"Just drink it. It will help you heal." After he'd choked down a few more sips, she set the cup aside. "Now, I need to open up your wound."

His eyes widened, but she put a finger to his lips.

"It needs to be drained of infection."

He didn't have the energy to argue as she went to the washbasin and scrubbed her hands. He couldn't watch her prepare, so his eyes drifted to the window that was no longer covered by vines.

The storm must have passed in the night because sunlight streamed in through the open windows. He focused on the fresh air as Aurora returned to his side and gripped his jaw, prying it open. She stuffed a wad of cloth in his mouth.

"Bite down. This is going to hurt."

She had no words of comfort for him, only cold honesty. She pushed up his shirt until it was bunched under his armpits, removed the bandages, and set a cool cloth against his heated skin. Scrubbing circles around the wound he'd thought was healing, she hummed to herself. A quiet song at first as if it was meant for no one but her.

Her lilting voice rose to a crescendo as she set aside the cloth and pulled a knife free.

With steely eyes, she dug the tip into his skin.

Phillip bit down so hard his teeth crashed into each other through the cloth. His howl of pain reverberated around the room, but she gave no indication she'd heard it.

Her melody didn't falter, and she didn't spare him one glance as she tore through his flesh.

Blackness encroached on his vision, and he welcomed it with open arms. One final thought flitted through his mind before he fell over the edge of consciousness.

This girl was insane.

CHAPTER SEVEN

AURORA

Aurora spent the next few days by Phillip's side, worried if she left, all her efforts would have been in vain. She didn't want him to die. Despite what she'd said about not being his subject, she wished she was. She wanted more than anything to be like any other Belaen, protected by the crown. But they'd never been able to protect her or many of their people, and soon she'd pay the price.

Each time Phillip mumbled in his sleep, she shot up from her place on the floor beside the bed, but he didn't wake. The only time he opened his eyes was when she forced tea or broth into him.

She hadn't meant the tea would truly help him heal, but it was a trick she'd learned from her grandmother. She'd placed bitter herbs in it to sell the effect, but in truth, it was normal tea. The healing part was in the hope it provided. When she was young, her grandmother would give her the tea, telling her it would make her well, giving her a belief that something could help.

She didn't know why she'd tried to do the same with the

crown prince of Bela. Now, as she watched him, it seemed a silly act from a silly girl.

She leaned up on her knees, examining his flushed cheeks and sweat-soaked hair. Each morning, she lingered longer than necessary in her pallet on the floor, not wanting to rise, worried she'd find him dead. And each morning, relief flooded her.

After forcing some broth into him, she couldn't stand to be in that room any longer. Waiting threatened to clog the breath in her throat. Waiting for what? For the prince to die? For Aurora herself to fall into the deep slumber awaiting her?

Sixteen days. That was how much time she had left of this existence. It wasn't enough time.

She yanked open the front door, walking into the bright sun that broke through the trees. It warmed her face, and she tilted her head back. She would miss the sun.

Lea stood at her food bucket, and Aurora laughed. "Waiting for me, are you?"

She took the bucket to the side of the cottage where she kept the grain for Lea and filled it. When she rounded the house again, she froze.

La Dame stood next to Lea, rubbing her between the eyes as if they were old friends. "I quite like this mule. I think I'll take her when you can no longer care for her."

Aurora clenched her jaw. "She's already spoken for, I'm afraid."

"Dear." La Dame cocked her head. "I don't believe you're afraid of anything. Sad, maybe. But fear? There isn't an ounce of that in you. It's why you and I get along so well."

Aurora set the bucket of grain down. "Fear only exists when you have something that can be taken away from you. There is nothing I will leave behind."

La Dame's smile stretched across her face. "And the prince?"

She swallowed. "What about the prince?"

"Is he afraid?"

"Why would he be afraid?"

"Because he's dying."

Aurora stumbled when she stepped back, but La Dame grabbed her arm to keep her upright. Aurora ripped her arm away. "He's not going to die."

La Dame tapped a finger against her chin. "No, he won't. I'm here to save him."

Shaking her head, Aurora positioned herself between La Dame and the front door. "No. You won't use your healing magic on him."

She stared at the dark queen, recalling everything she knew about her. It was true. La Dame had the power to heal – just like all Draconians. It was how she'd saved Aurora's mother. But what was her true motivation? Why would she offer to save the prince of Bela?

Long before Aurora lived, La Dame took control of Dracon from her own father, killing him for the magic he possessed.

"Aurora, dear, do you want him to die? That is so unlike you, but I can't say I don't like this side of you."

Aurora narrowed her eyes. Since the first day she met La Dame when she was a child, she refused to be intimidated. She wouldn't fear the sorceress as the rest of the Six Kingdoms did. She wouldn't give the dark queen what she wanted.

All laughter drained from La Dame's face. "Let me pass, Aurora."

"No."

"If I don't go in there, the boy dies."

"I know what the price is for your help and I won't let him pay it."

La Dame brought her hand up and with a flick of one finger, she threw Aurora to the side as if she were no more than a doll.

Aurora grunted as she hit the ground and rolled back to her feet. By the time the ringing in her ears ceased, La Dame was already inside. She ran in after her to find Phillip more alert than he'd been in days.

His wide eyes stared at La Dame in apprehension. He feared her because he did have something to lose. If she ended him, he'd leave behind a life worth living.

His chest rose and fell frantically as his breath came out in gasps.

"You're dying, young prince." La Dame bent over him. "I can help you."

"No!" Aurora's cry had Phillip snapping his eyes to hers. "You can't."

La Dame didn't turn. "Ignore her, young man. Tell me, do you wish to live?"

All he could manage was a nod.

"In Bela, you know little of the magic I possess. You've heard stories, I'm sure. I can heal you. Would you like that?"

He nodded.

Aurora rushed forward, shoving La Dame out of the way. "You don't want to do this."

His eyes scanned her face, the only part of him he could move. "Don't want." He sucked in a breath. "Die."

She reached forward to place a palm against his cheek. "You might still get better. I won't stop trying to help you, but Phillip, nothing La Dame does comes without a cost. She's going to heal you now, but demand something unimaginable later." A tear slid down her cheek. "You have to believe me.

You have to trust me. You don't want to live with the consequences of her aid."

Through all of this, La Dame hung back. She took pleasure in people succumbing to her curses—like Aurora's father. He'd allowed his wife to be healed, not knowing it would curse Aurora to a shortened life.

She wouldn't let Phillip go through that. The guilt had destroyed her father until she no longer recognized him. It eventually killed him.

Aurora's tears fell freely, and she leaned forward to rest her forehead against Phillips chest. "Please. Don't do it to yourself."

A hand brushed her hair, and she lifted her eyes to peer into Phillips. His lips formed words she couldn't hear, but knew all the same. *Trust. You.*

"I need an answer, Phillip." La Dame set a hand on Aurora's shoulder and pulled her away. "Do you want to live?"

"Yes." He forced out the word. "But not with your magic."

She raised an eyebrow in surprise. "Well, then I guess Aurora may gain some fear inside of her yet." She turned to Aurora. "Sixteen days, my dear. Enjoy them."

Then she was gone.

Phillip seemed to sink further into the bed, but his eyes didn't leave Aurora's face. Many questions lay in their depths, but he didn't ask them. Instead, his eyes slid closed and silence was once again Aurora's greatest friend.

Her hands shook as she pushed herself up from the ground. She let her mind rest as she walked the length of the cottage to stoke the fire and clean up what she could. Wrapping her fingers around the handle of a broom, she swept, enjoying the mindless motion.

La Dame left a chill behind her that had nothing to do with the late autumn freezes. Aurora stopped moving and leaned against the broom for support, her chin resting against her chest. She breathed in deeply, trying to will away La Dame's words ringing in her mind.

Aurora may gain some fear inside of her yet.

Her eyes settled on Phillip of their own volition. He'd risked his life in turning down La Dame. There was no guarantee he'd recover. She'd drained as much of the infection as she could, but the fever persisted, and she didn't know what else to do.

Yet, he'd said no. It would have been so easy for him to accept La Dame's healing magic. She wouldn't have only made the infection disappear, but also the wound itself. He'd have been able to return to the palace, to his family, his friends.

He'd have been able to escape the crazy girl living alone among the trees. Sometimes, she wished she could escape herself as well.

"He trusted you," she said, needing to hear the words out loud. "Why?"

Phillip probably thought something was loose in her brain when she spoke to herself, but she wouldn't burden him with the truth. She'd lived in silence for so long, speaking to no one other than her mule, that she said thoughts out loud just to fill the empty spaces.

With a sigh, she put the broom away and prepared her own simple supper—dried rabbit she'd caught weeks ago and the remaining berries from the trees near the wall. Soon, she'd have to venture out to her traps to check for more food.

Before Phillip arrived, she'd had a routine. Every day, she woke with the sun and walked to each of her traps, some more than a mile away. She used Lea to haul back anything she caught before hanging the animal carcasses behind her cabin to drain them of blood.

Some afternoons were spent butchering those she'd caught days before or collecting the various fruits and herbs that grew in the woods.

When time allowed, she walked through the trees, sometimes climbing them to get a better look at the forest she called home. She rarely saw or spoke to other people. Until Phillip.

She finished eating and sat beside his bed with a bowl of broth she'd boiled from animal fat and vegetables. When she tried to wake him, he only mumbled something unintelligible like he'd been doing since the fever set in.

She set the bowl aside and checked his wound. It was healing again, but his body still had to fight off the infection.

Lowering his shirt, she rested her elbows on the bed and leaned forward. This time, when she spoke to the darkness, the words weren't meant for her alone. "You have to fight this, Phillip. If you die, my last act was in vain. I don't know why you said no to La Dame, or why you trust me, but I believe in you. Even if I can never be your subject, I know you'll make a great king. I wish I was going to be around to see it." A tear slipped down her cheek.

Phillip's hand brushed her cheek, but she wasn't sure he'd heard any of her words. His eyes remained shut as she took his hand in hers.

She stayed by his bed into the night, falling asleep with her forehead leaning on the mattress.

THE SUN nearly blinded Aurora when she opened her eyes the next morning. Pain inched up her neck from sleeping at such an odd angle. It took her a moment to realize she was still sitting beside the bed, Phillip's long fingers entwined with hers.

She lifted her head to find him staring at her, the flush gone from his cheeks.

"Morning." His voice still sounded rough, but the word was said with little effort.

She slipped her hand from his, embarrassed he'd found her holding it. Words escaped her, and a small smile tilted his lips, transforming his sickly face into that of the handsome prince she'd met.

Pressing the back of her hand to his forehead, she released a breath when it was cool against her skin. "The fever."

"Gone." His eyes crinkled, the first sign of true life she'd seen from him in a week.

Her heart leapt into her throat, and she could no longer control her emotions as she leaned down, pressing her lips to his. The act was so fast, she hadn't known what she was doing.

He froze beneath her, and she tried to pull back, mortified.

Before she got too far, he reached up, pulling her back to him, taking control. Aurora had never kissed anyone before, but all insecurities floated away as Phillip released a growl deep in his throat. His lips moved expertly against hers. It wasn't until his tongue slipped past her lips that the nerves got the best of her. She clamped down, accidentally biting his tongue in the process.

He yelped in surprise, and she jumped back, her chest heaving. "I'm... I'm sorry. I shouldn't have done that."

"No," he agreed. "You shouldn't have."

Embarrassment washed through her until he smirked. "The tongue biting part. The kiss was unexpected, but I can't say I regret it."

It was the most he'd been able to say in a week, and she should have been glad to see light enter his eyes, but instead, she wished she could take it all back. She'd been so relieved to see the first sign of a recovery, her body had taken over.

But Phillip Basile was a prince. A prince who deserved happiness. And her? She was just a girl running out of time.

As if sensing her discomfort, Phillip's grin dropped. "Aurora, look at me."

She shook her head.

"Please."

"I need to check your wound." She didn't meet his eyes as she lifted his shirt like she'd done so many times before. She knew his chest better than she'd known any man's. The scar was warm against her fingers. "I had to put in a few stitches this time, but you weren't conscious, so I figured you wouldn't mind." She lowered his shirt. "The fever has broken. That's a good sign. You're over the worst of it. Now you just need to regain your strength and then you can leave and return to your life."

She rocked back on her heels to stand and wiped her hands on her skirt.

"Aurora," Phillip said again, this time more forcefully.

She turned away from him and stepped into the kitchen. When she returned to his side, she handed him a cup of water and a plate of bread. "You need to eat to regain your strength. If we are to have meat, I must go check the traps."

Without another word, she pulled on her boots and cloak. As she stepped out the door, Phillip's words followed her. "Thanks for taking care of me."

She shut the door, putting the barrier between them. Leaning against the outer wall of the cottage, she ran a hand through her hair, knowing it needed a wash but only able to focus on what happened moments before. She touched her lips, still feeling the whisper of his kiss.

She didn't want this. She didn't want to care. Not now. Not when her life was so close to its end.

She closed her eyes, wanting to feel him against her again.

"You're an idiot, Aurora," she whispered. "He's the prince of Bela, and not even he can save you from your fate."

With a resigned shake of her head, she walked away, not allowing herself to look back.

CHAPTER EIGHT

PHILLIP

Phillip couldn't help the smile crossing his face as he tucked one arm behind his head. He was alive. Each time he'd started to fall asleep over the last few days, he'd worried he wouldn't wake, but she pulled him back time and time again.

He was a Basile. He had an entire Kingdom who'd do anything for him. They fought wars for him, sacrificed themselves. Yet, no one had ever just been there. Not even Chandler or Alfred during their childhood. They'd always lived their lives at such a fast pace. Wars. Festivals. Never a spare moment. His parents were busy with the running of the kingdom and over the last few years, his father slipping further and further away from them into illness.

He'd watched his mother rule the kingdom when his father could not, but he didn't remember her ever just sitting by the king's side. He couldn't picture her holding his hand. Theirs had been a marriage of convenience, one that strengthened the ties within Bela. Belaens never married those without magic for fear of diluting the power for future generations. Yet, they'd grown to love each other.

Before Phillip left for battle, the queen had spent a great deal of time searching for her only son's future wife. She'd paraded him around at balls and dinners. He wouldn't lie. Phillip enjoyed every moment of the attention. The beautiful women who threw themselves at him. The rich foods and lavish gifts.

But now, as he lay in a stranger's home, the stillness surrounding him, he saw all of it for what it was. Fake.

He struggled to sit up, needing to feel the sun on his face, the wind against his skin. He'd been stuck inside for too long.

He wasn't surprised to find the door unimpeded by weeds and vines. Aurora no longer held him prisoner with her magic. Now, his body kept him there with its weakness. He smiled as soon as he felt the chill of the outdoors.

He could have searched for a spare cloak in the trunk Aurora was always digging in, but he wanted to feel everything. After days of nothing but a burning fever and icy chills, he needed to sense what was real.

He walked around the side of the cottage, noting the two small animals lying dead against the wall, and a thick crop of trees standing across the clearing. His gait faltered as he pushed his body as far as it could go. Pain seared into his stomach at the movement, but he didn't turn back. He wasn't ready to return to the bed he'd been confined to for so long.

Unbuckling his trousers, he sighed as he emptied himself. When he was finished, he ambled back the way he'd come, wanting to lay down before his legs gave out beneath him.

A soft humming reached his ears, and he smiled at the sound, recognizing it immediately. He didn't know if Aurora even knew she made the sound, but it had been the only thing to keep the pain from overwhelming him as she cut into him.

Her hard eyes flashed through his mind. Did anything

scare her? He was used to brandishing knives in battle, letting them bite into flesh, but she couldn't have been.

Aurora carried a small wooden bucket in each hand. Her hair was wet and twisted up away from her face.

Her face showed no emotion.

Forgetting his current state, Phillip stepped forward. "Let me help you."

She smirked, still not taking her eyes from him. "He thinks he can help, even in his state. Men." She rolled her eyes to the heavens, and he grinned, wondering if she knew he could hear every word.

He walked forward, a rock on the ground throwing him off balance. Before he fell, Aurora dropped the buckets and jumped forward, looping an arm around his waist. "I've got you."

She shook her head, turning him toward the cottage. "You shouldn't be out here."

He let more of his weight rest on her than he liked but he couldn't hold himself up. "You're probably right."

She tilted her head back, giving him a look he couldn't quite understand.

"What?" he asked.

"I think that's the first time you've acknowledged I know what I'm doing."

He grunted. "Is not. It can't be."

"Yes. You usually argue with me until you give in, but not because you agree, only because you lack the energy." She shrugged and helped him limp forward. "You're a very difficult person to get along with, Prince."

He grimaced. There was no laughter in her tone, no teasing, only a calm acceptance. Yet, one word stuck out to him. "Can you do something for me?"

She pushed open the door and helped him through. "Depends on what it is."

He lowered himself onto the bed, his muscles relaxing as if they'd just run through the woods rather than a simple walk across the yard. He leaned back with a sigh. "Please stop calling me prince."

She'd been about to turn away, but she froze. "Why?"

"Do you have to question everything?"

She nodded. "Yes. I do."

"I don't have an answer for you other than I don't like hearing that word come out of your mouth."

She frowned. "Look, Pr-Phillip, about this morning. I'm sorry. I kind of attacked you. I was just so glad you were still alive that I stopped thinking altogether. I shouldn't have done it, but I'd have felt so guilty if you died. I don't want anyone else to die in my care."

He wanted to ask her who else she'd taken care of and lost. What was the weight she carried around? But, she'd already turned to busy herself in the kitchen, so he only uttered one thing. "I kissed you back."

Her shoulders tensed, but she otherwise acted as if she'd heard nothing at all.

Phillip didn't know how he could be drawn to a girl who showed him so little of herself. A girl hiding from the world among her trees. He thought of the women at court, the ones who'd never apologize for kissing him. Who'd never given a thought to whether or not he wanted their advances in hopes he'd pick them. All they wanted was to be seen, to take their place in history.

It seemed Aurora's only wish was to disappear.

THE BED SHOOK, waking Phillip from a dream of battle. Aurora kicked it again. "Phillip, wake up. Your fever broke two days ago, it's time you bathe." She wrinkled her nose. "You reek and the smell has permeated my home."

A low chuckle rose from him. "I reek, huh?"

"You smell like a dead animal."

He grinned, struggling to sit and noting how she didn't help him. His eyes found the basin she'd filled and the cloth and soap she set beside it. "Are you going to give me some privacy at least?"

Color tinged her cheeks. "Of course." She paused on her way out the door. "Just... don't make a mess."

"Wouldn't dream of it."

With a satisfied nod, she left him to his bath. He pushed to his feet and slipped out of his trousers and underclothes. The chill hit his skin, and he realized he'd freeze if he tried to wash himself all at once. Lowering himself clumsily to the floor beside the washbasin, he rubbed soap into the cloth and cleaned himself as best he could.

He lifted his butt to slide his underclothes back on, no longer wanting to sit bare-assed on the cold floor.

He gripped the edge of his shirt and tried to lift it. Searing pain stabbed through his stomach, stemming from his still healing wound. A cry died on his lips as he tried again.

Each time he moved his arms, his skin pulled tight across the wound, sending him tumbling into agony. With ragged breaths, he cursed.

A knock sounded on the door, and it opened before he said anything. Aurora poked her head in, eyes going wide when she saw him sitting without his trousers.

"Oh..." She bit her lip. "Um, I thought you'd be done by now. I'll give you more time."

She was about to close the door when he yelled, "Wait!"

She stopped, her eyes returning to him in question.

He sucked in a shaky breath. "I need help." Just uttering those words was a struggle.

Her mouth rounded as she understood what he was saying.

"Please." He implored with his eyes. Awkward wouldn't begin to describe it, but it was better than smelling like a dead animal as she'd claimed he did.

At the palace, his mother's maids helped her bathe, but he'd always demanded he do it himself. He'd never been gravely injured or sick and in need of help.

Now, as he sat in his most vulnerable state, he needed someone.

He saw the moment she came to the same conclusion. She stepped inside and shut the door to keep out the worst of the cold. Removing her cloak, she draped it over a chair and toed off her boots.

"What can I do?" she asked, her voice quiet.

He pushed away the embarrassment as he gestured to his shirt. "I can't get it off."

She nodded, going into the mode he'd seen once before when she'd cut into his wound to drain the infection. It was as if she forced herself into a back part of her brain and a cold shell of her took over.

He didn't want her to be that person. When she reached for his shirt, he grabbed her hand. "Thank you."

She nodded, the warmth he'd glimpsed on occasion returning to her eyes. This was the girl who'd held his hand as fever ravaged his body, who'd cried for him, a stranger, and he was a prince she claimed no allegiance to.

She slipped her hand from his and lifted his shirt, her

fingers skimming his torso. A shiver raced through him that had nothing to do with the cold. She pulled the shirt over his head and then lowered herself beside him, taking the soapy cloth from his hand to dip it in the water.

She was so close, yet also still so far away.

CHAPTER NINE

AURORA

For once, Aurora managed to keep her thoughts inside her head instead of blurting them out like the simple fool she was. At least she managed to keep her hands from shaking as she ran the soapy cloth along Phillip's strong back. His muscles pulled tight with tension, and she let her other hand wander over them, chasing the dripping water away.

When her fingers dug into his shoulder, he groaned, not seeming to notice the noise coming from his own mouth.

At the sound, Aurora pulled her hand away and turned to get more soap on the cloth.

"Don't stop," he whispered, his eyes closed. "Please. That... when you..." His eyes slid open and settled on hers. "I've been stuck in that bed for so long, sometimes it doesn't seem like my body will ever recover."

Aurora didn't know from personal experience what he meant. She'd escaped a prolonged illness or injury in her life, but she'd taken care of both her father and grandmother in their final days when they felt as if their bodies failed their minds.

And soon, she'd know what it was to be confined to a bed too. When she woke, would her neck hurt from so many years in the same position? La Dame promised she would wake, but not for one hundred years, not until everyone she may have loved was long gone.

She'd never questioned the knowledge that La Dame would live that far into the future, but what kind of world would it be?

And why did La Dame want Aurora? Part of Aurora always wondered if it was only because she never backed away from one of her curses. She didn't like to lose and saw Aurora as nothing more than a prize, a girl to call her own.

She shook her head, returning her focus to Phillip. A scar ran from just underneath his shoulder blade to the center of his back. She dabbed it, tracing the faint line with the cloth. "Why do you do it?"

"Do what?" He sat impossibly still as she continued to wash his back.

"Fight. You stand on those battlefields ready to lay down your life. Why?"

He pushed out a breath. When he finally answered her, his voice was low as if any loud noise would disturb the peace between them. "I'm the prince of Bela. I don't have a choice."

She scooted around to face him and rubbed the cloth down one arm. "There is always a choice."

"Gaule cannot be allowed to gain further access into Bela."

"And what of the Belaen incursions into Gaule? Both kingdoms are at fault, it seems."

His brow creased. "We must show them what they risk in crossing our borders."

She sighed. "And I'm guessing they feel the same way." She wiped at his cheek. "Two kingdoms who wage a war that has lasted for generations and all they win are more deaths, more ravaged lands. There will be no peace as long as each kingdom tries to cross the other."

He lifted one arm, grimacing at the pain shooting through him. Gripping Aurora's wrist, he stopped her movements. "We aren't at fault, Aurora. They're savages."

She smiled sadly. "In battle, I imagine they are. But Gaule is not uncivilized. They have towns, a government. Those men and women you claim are nothing more than savages have families who would mourn their deaths just as deeply as your family would mourn yours." She freed her wrist.

"I need to wash your hair. Can you lean back?"

"I can try." He wouldn't look her in the eye, and she suspected it was because of her defense of Gaule. Was he angry with her? Should she care? Some things needed to be said no matter the audience's opinions or emotions. Bela and Gaule had been fighting needlessly for a long time, and the people were hurting. Much of the news La Dame brought her was false, but she'd known the truth in those words about Gaule.

Phillip rested back on his elbows, a flash of pain crossing his face before he suppressed it. She'd learned early on that the prince refused to show weakness. Being taken care of didn't sit well with him. It forced a vulnerability on him she was sure he'd never felt before.

She cupped her hands and scooped water to pour over Phillip's hair, letting it trickle back into the basin. She smiled down at him, knowing he couldn't see her as she ran her hands through the dark strands, unable to help herself. He moaned low in his throat, so she did it again.

"Damn, that feels good." One side of his mouth curved up.

Aurora should have stopped, she should have just rinsed it

quickly, but her hands massaged his scalp. His body relaxed like he was clay in her palm.

"Aurora," he whispered.

She didn't respond as she scrubbed in the soap.

"Are you still in pain?" she asked, using her hands once again to pour water over his head.

"What?" The lines of stress disappeared from his face as his eyes remained closed.

"The pain. Is it still there?"

"Oh." When he opened his eyes, a guilty expression settled over his features. He hadn't been listening to her. "I'm sorry... but your hands..." He shook his head. "The pain, yeah. I still feel it when I move."

"Sit up." She moved to his front again to examine the wound. Red tinged the seam of his scar, but otherwise it looked well on the mend. She probed the skin around the wound with her fingers, leaning close to get a better look.

When she felt a hand on the back of her neck, she lifted her eyes to find Phillip watching her. Her mind couldn't quite grasp the fact that the prince of Bela was sitting in her cottage half naked and looking as if he might eat her alive.

His hand slid down her back and it was only then she realized how close they were. His other hand ran the length of her jaw before pulling on her bottom lip.

"Aurora." The way he whispered her name sent heat jolting through her. She loved it because of what it did to her. For that same reason, she hated it.

Less than two weeks. This wasn't supposed to happen. Her curse barreled toward her like a horse galloping at full speed. There was no stopping it. Yet, she couldn't help making it even worse. She wasn't supposed to have anything to leave behind.

She nodded once, and Phillip's grip on her tightened

before he pulled her onto his lap. He claimed her lips as if they'd always been his, as if he'd been waiting for them his entire life. This time, Aurora wanted this, she was ready for it.

Water ran down Phillip's chest, soaking into Aurora's dress, but she hardly noticed as her hands ran up his heated skin and into his damp hair.

Phillip pulled her tighter against him as his tongue pushed past her lips, tasting her, devouring her. Her chest heaved against his, desperate for a breath.

She pulled away for a second to suck in air, and Phillip's eyes darkened. "I've never known anyone like you." He rested his forehead against hers.

A nervous chuckle escaped her lips. "A crazy forest girl?"

"When I woke after my fever broke and you kissed me..." He grinned. "I thought surely I'd died and gone to the after. I've wanted to kiss you since the first time you argued with me."

She pursed her lips. "You're a prince, Phillip. Shouldn't you want people to always agree with whatever you say?"

He ran his thumb along her lips. "Most women I've known enjoy my company because of the crown that will one day sit on my head. But you... I think you like me less because of it."

She pulled away from him, and he didn't stop her. He'd known the pleasures of many women. It was only another reminder that their worlds didn't match. Even if she was not cursed, she could never truly have him. She pushed to her feet, staring down at the wet front of her dress.

"I'm going to need to change."

"Aurora."

She turned away from him. "You sure do enjoy saying my name, don't you?"

She heard him struggling to his feet behind her but didn't turn to help.

"Talk to me," he demanded.

"I'm sorry, your Highness. Once again, this is my fault. It never should have happened. Your wound is healing well. You should be fine to travel in another few days. Excuse me, I have work to do." She rushed out the front door before he could stop her.

Aurora found Lea grazing behind the cottage in a part of the forest where wild grasses grew. Frost covered the ground, and it was only then she realized she'd forgotten her cloak. The chill of the air permeated her wet dress, just another reminder of her idiocy from moments before.

Phillip Basile was going to have a grand life. A life of adventure... a life of love.

And that life wouldn't include her. It couldn't.

A scream exploded from her chest, and she couldn't stop it. Birds flew from the trees in surprise, and Lea jerked her head up. Aurora yelled again, releasing her fury. Her magic tingled in her fingers, and she let it flow free. Red and orange flowers sprouted from the ground, looking almost like fire. She would have sworn the earth itself rumbled.

She continued releasing her power, felling trees and twisting vines up others, until she had nothing left inside her except a broken heart.

Phillip hadn't broken it. The pieces were shattered by life itself. By circumstance.

She fell to the ground, all energy leaving her, and the last remaining parts of her escaping in tears. Her entire body shook, and she wished in that moment the curse could take her. Not two weeks from then. Now. She didn't want to wait for it any longer.

She didn't want the anticipation to crush her. She refused

to break before the curse, refused to let La Dame have that satisfaction, but she could feel the parts of her scattering on the wind.

Strong arms slid beneath her, lifting her into the air with a grunt of pain. All thought disappearing from her mind, she rested her head against the soft fabric of her rescuer's shirt.

Phillip carried her inside and kicked the door shut before setting her down. He dipped his head to gaze into her eyes, but she couldn't focus on him.

"You're freezing." He stroked his hands up and down her arms.

Aurora briefly registered the fact that he'd gotten dressed. The dirty washbasin sat in the center of the room. Phillip studied her for a moment longer before lifting her arms. She didn't protest as he lifted the dress from her frame. She didn't stop him when she saw the pain his movements caused.

All she could do was stand frozen as Phillip dug through her chest, pulling out various articles of clothing. He returned with a soft sleeping gown. He did his best to keep his eyes from drifting to her bare skin as he slipped it over her head.

"Aurora," he whispered, cupping her cheek. "What happened?"

He didn't want to know what had drained her energy. As a magic wielder himself, he knew the dangers of using too much, of letting it control you. He wiped a tear from her cheek.

"Please." His voice broke. "There's something you aren't telling me. I..." He pressed the side of his face against hers, his breath warming her skin. "You're scaring me."

Fear. The very thing she'd told La Dame she had none of. She hadn't feared leaving because there was nothing to leave behind. Everyone she'd ever loved was dead, waiting in the next life. She had few possessions, no friends.

Finally, she lifted her gaze to his. It took every bit of strength she possessed to get the words out. "You've made me afraid."

A stricken look crossed his face, and he opened his mouth to speak, but she shook her head. She hadn't known she had any tears left when they cascaded down her cheeks unchecked.

"I wasn't supposed to be afraid."

CHAPTER TEN

PHILLIP

The name Phillip Basile struck fear in the hearts of many people. He was Bela's general, their greatest warrior, and the prince who kept the savages at bay.

But now, that word sliced through his heart. Fear. How could Aurora be afraid of him? Her shoulders shook, and he couldn't take it any longer so he pulled her against his chest. After a moment of hesitation, her arms wound around his waist.

"I don't want to frighten you," he whispered into her hair. "Never."

She sniffed and tightened her hold on him, carefully avoiding his wound. Her words were muffled against his chest. "You..." She sucked in a shaky breath. "It's not you. Well, it is, but not the way you think."

"What's going on, Aurora?" There was a piece of this puzzle he didn't have.

She shook her head, still pressing her face to his chest.

"I'm not going to force you to talk about it, but I want you to know you can trust me."

"Trust the prince?"

"No." He pulled back to stare into her eyes. "Not the prince. You can trust me. Just me." He pulled her toward the bed. "Come. You should rest."

She didn't protest as he helped her into the bed he'd spent so long in. She turned on her side, her glistening eyes boring into him.

"I'll make some tea." She'd brought him a comforting cup of tea so many times during his recovery, it was his first thought now. After his recovery, it felt good to take care of someone else. She'd been so strong for him, and he could do the same for her.

When he brought the tea to her, she closed her eyes. Her tense body told him she wasn't sleeping though.

"Do you want your tea?"

She made a sound in the back of her throat. "No. I want..." Her eyelids slid open, and she sucked her bottom lip into her mouth. "Would you stay with me? Just for a while."

He nodded, setting the tea on the table nearby, before returning to her side. He sank down onto his knees next to her and brushed the hair away from her face.

Just as she'd done when he was sick, he wanted to watch her in case she needed him. He'd never experienced such a draw to anyone in his life. Something about her seemed sad, and he wished he could take away every bit of pain she'd experienced in her life. She didn't deserve to be an anonymous resident among the trees, no one ever knowing she was even there to begin with.

A tear leaked from her closed eye, and he didn't think as he pulled himself onto the bed and curled his warm body around her chilled limbs. She rolled over, so they were chest to chest and buried her face in his shirt.

As her body shook, he rubbed circles along her back,

saying nothing. He closed his eyes and rested his chin on her head. For the first time, the thought of leaving her to return to the palace seemed an impossible choice. The worries about his family searching for him or his friends assuming he'd died retreated to the back of his mind when the only thing he wanted was to make the crying girl smile again.

He tightened his hold on her, hoping one day she'd trust him enough to tell him about the weight crushing down on her shoulders.

PHILLIP WOKE ALONE with the silver light of the moon casting shadows across the cottage. He missed Aurora's warmth immediately and sat up in alarm, worried where she'd gone. He didn't have to worry long because his eyes found her sitting on the ground facing the hearth where a roaring fire blazed.

The only sound was the crackling of the flames, and he slid from the bed and approached her. Her shoulders hunched forward as she hugged her knees to her chest. She didn't look at him as he sat beside her.

Part of him wanted to pull her back into his arms where she'd felt so right, but the other part sensed it wasn't the time for that.

She stared into the flames, and when she finally spoke, there was no emotion behind her voice, only coldness.

"I'm cursed." Her entire body seemed to shudder at the word.

He said nothing as he waited for her to continue, to explain what she meant.

"When I told you I belong to La Dame, I wasn't claiming

any sort of loyalty to her or disloyalty to Bela. If I could, I'd run a sword straight through her heart."

He blanched at the coldness with which she spoke of killing the Draconian queen.

She continued. "But we both know that wouldn't kill her. Her magic allows her to heal." She shook her head. "When I was born, my mother grew very ill. My father, in the king's employ at the time, called on some of the most powerful sorcerers in Bela. They tried to save her. Yet, she only faded faster. Then a woman appeared. My father claimed he didn't know who she was at the time. He was too desperate to question anything. He loved my mother very much." She sucked in a breath.

Phillip didn't take his eyes from her.

Aurora closed her eyes. "I've heard this story so many times I remember every word. My grandmother wanted me to know why my life was not my own and why it never would be. She didn't want me to hate my father, but wanted to make sure I would never repeat his mistakes. To know La Dame is more dangerous than she appears."

"Why would you hate your father?" Phillip sat enthralled in the story but also anticipating the part that had turned Aurora into the sad girl before him.

"La Dame told him she could save my mother. At that point, my father would have done anything. When La Dame said it would come at a cost, he agreed to accept any price. He thought whatever happened would fall on him. But, that's the thing. La Dame is crueler than any of us ever imagined. She doesn't accept payment from those willing to pay. She chooses what she takes. And what she wanted was me."

"You?"

She nodded. "La Dame doesn't die. She doesn't age. She will wait for what she wants for a very long time. And she also enjoys pain. It's entertainment to her. That's why she gave my father the first eighteen years of my life, so he'd know me enough to mourn me for the rest of his life."

Phillip's hands shook as he draped them over his knees. Each word she spoke struck him straight through the heart. "Eighteen years? What happens then?"

The flames danced off her irises, and she rested her chin on her arm. "I go to sleep." She sucked in a breath. "For one hundred years, I will sleep. La Dame's plan was to make it impossible for my family to see me again, for the world to turn over. When I wake, I'm supposed to have only her." She wiped furiously at a tear on her cheek. "Want to know some irony? The illness La Dame cured my mother of came again a year later. This time, she refused any healing. My grandmother said she died of a broken heart over her good health costing her daughter."

"How old are you?" Phillip's question sent a chill through his bones. He'd heard of La Dame's curses, but never imagined they were real. He never thought the foreign queen actively preyed on his subjects.

Aurora finally turned to look at him, a cold acceptance in the dark depths of her eyes. "Seventeen years, eleven months, and twenty days."

Phillip shook his head, something cracking inside his chest. His breath caught in his throat, and he would have sworn his heart stopped beating.

"Ten days," he whispered. It made so much sense now. Why she convinced him to refuse La Dame's healing when he was sick. She saved him the agony her father must have felt every day until the day he no longer felt anything at all.

Phillip reached forward, needing to touch her, to feel that she was there with him. His eyes glistened with unshed tears as her story sank in, shredding his heart to pieces. His fingertips grazed her cheek. "I only just found you."

Her lip quivered. "I wasn't supposed to have anything to leave behind. When my grandmother died, I had no more ties holding me to this earth." She closed her eyes, leaning her face into his palm. "Why are you doing this to me?"

"I know you're scared, but Aurora, everyone should have something to leave behind." He rose onto his knees and inched closer. "Everyone should have something to lose."

Her wide eyes found his, and she shook her head. "I just wanted to go to sleep and have the world forget I was ever here."

"Who could forget you?" He leaned down, pressing his lips to hers.

She tasted of salt from her tears and longing. How long had she sat in these woods waiting for the day her life would pause? He inhaled her sadness, trying to lift it from her. Instead, it only amplified, turning into desperation as their lips remained pressed together.

"You will be remembered," he whispered against her lips. "Forever."

She whimpered and pulled him tighter against her, leaning back so he lay on top of her. He kissed a trail over her damp cheeks, replacing her tears with what he felt for her. Was it love? They hadn't known each other long, but he'd never felt like his soul was being ripped right from his body. He knew then, when he lost her to La Dame's curse, she'd take a piece of him with her.

Aurora ran her hands up under his tunic, touching every bit of skin she could find. "Phillip, I need you to make me forget, just for tonight."

He pressed a kiss to her neck. "This isn't about forgetting, my love. It's about remembering."

CHAPTER ELEVEN

AURORA

Aurora let all thought of the curse drift away as she explored Phillip's smooth skin. His muscles strained underneath her touch.

In that moment, he was no longer the prince of Bela, and she wasn't the nobody girl with an expiration date to the life she knew. They were just two people, drawn together by something neither of them could explain.

She turned him over, pressing her body down on him and trailing kisses along his chest while curling her fingers in the soft hairs. When she reached the scar, the wound that brought them together, she pressed her lips to it, thinking of how close that one place came to taking Phillip from this world altogether.

When she'd first brought him to her home, she hadn't wanted him to die out of some weird sense of guilt since he was in her care. Now, she needed to know he would be okay when she was gone, that he'd live to become a great king and an even better man.

History may never know her name, but it would tell of Phillip Basile. When a tear dripped onto his stomach, Phillip pulled her back up, wrapping his arms around her waist, he held her against him as if afraid to let go.

He finally released her, and she sat up, pulling her sleeping gown over her head. Phillip's blazing eyes widened. "Aurora," he whispered. "You don't have to..."

She pressed a finger to his lips. "It's okay." She smiled down at him. "I want this."

He only hesitated for a moment before standing and scooping her into his arms, his heated expression masking the pain she knew the act must have caused him. His lips claimed hers once again as he stumbled to the bed, dropping her onto it in his haste to remove the rest of his clothing.

She laughed when he hovered over her, crawling onto the bed like the wild animal he appeared to be. He lowered himself to hold her in a crushing hug that lasted longer than it should have. She spared a glance at his wound, thankful it hadn't opened again. When she felt hot tears on her shoulder, she pushed him back, wiping her thumbs under his eyes. She'd never seen a grown man cry. Even her father's eyes remained dry each time he talked to her of the curse.

"Hey," she whispered. "Don't cry." She'd had years to come to terms with the curse and realized he would only have days, but it twisted something inside her to see his eyes looking so lost.

"Come with me," he whispered.

"What?"

"To the palace. To my father. Maybe there's something he can do."

She sighed. "Phillip, not even the Basile power can break one of La Dame's curses."

"We have to try." His voice broke on the words.

She cupped his cheek, drawing his lips back down to hers. This kiss was slower than the others, deeper as they each poured everything they felt into it. She pulled back and pressed her lips to his forehead. "Okay. We can try."

That night, Phillip showed her everything inside of him. He opened himself completely, and she'd never been more sure about anything in her life.

Aurora was in love with the prince.

Their bodies fit together as if they were made for each other, two pieces of the same puzzle. When she was gone, would Phillip still fit into that puzzle?

The Basile power couldn't help her, but she'd let Phillip have this last bit of hope.

As the dawn came, they lay together with only a blanket for warmth, but Aurora wasn't cold. She rested her head on his chest. "Do you think I'll dream in my long slumber?" She tilted her head back to peer up at him.

He didn't answer her as his eyes locked on hers.

She reached up to run her hand through the coarse hairs along his jaw. "I hope so."

She'd wanted to get a smile out of the smiling prince, but his face remained somber. She didn't want to remember the sadness he'd had for her at the end, but the fight she'd seen in him before he knew the truth. The man who admitted to needing help bathing, yet argued with her at every chance. The one who braved a wicked storm to find where the girl he barely knew had gone.

He slid out from under her and sat on the edge of the bed. "I no longer care if I'm well enough to travel. I'd like to make for the palace today."

She scooted to sit beside him. "Okay."

He looked to her in question.

"He thought I was going to argue with him." She laughed, the words only meant for herself.

The smile she'd wanted appeared on his face. "Talking to yourself again?"

She shrugged and wrapped her arms around him. "It's time we return you to your home, your people."

"You're my people."

"For now, but they will be there long after I'm gone, and they've missed their prince for too long."

His shoulders drooped at her reminder, but she didn't regret the words. She didn't have time to live in a false reality.

If she was going to get through these last few days without breaking down, she had to do so with open eyes. No pretending.

"Hey." She pressed her lips against his shoulder. "It's okay."

He twisted to look at her and it was only then she saw the state of his wound. The area around the scar had reddened. They should have been more careful. "Yesterday you couldn't even bathe yourself." She brushed her fingers against the scar. "How much pain were you in when you lifted me up? When we—"

He took her hand and kissed her knuckles. "It was worth it."

She sighed. "Fine. We can leave today, but we travel slowly, easily. If you tire or if the pain becomes too much, we rest. Promise?"

"Yes." He pressed his face against hers. "I promise."

She touched his lips lightly before pulling herself from the bed. Embarrassment shot through her as the blanket fell away. She'd forgotten she didn't have a stitch of clothing on.

Phillip watched her as she hurried to the trunk to dig for traveling clothes for both of them.

It didn't take long to dress and ready supplies. When they stepped outside, Lea greeted them. The sun rose fully by the time they put a saddle on the mule—much to the beast's dismay.

"You need to ride." Aurora gestured to the animal as she tied their bags of supplies to her saddle.

"We can both ride her." He held out a hand.

Lea snorted.

Aurora rubbed her between the ears. "Please, my friend. One last trip for you and me."

Lea seemed to sense the seriousness of the moment because she stopped protesting, standing still for Phillip and Aurora to climb onto her back.

Aurora took a final look at the cottage she'd called home since she was a little girl. It was where her father said goodbye to her. Her grandmother breathed her last within those walls.

Until a few short weeks ago, Aurora had been alone with only her mule and herself for company. The cottage held every thought she'd had, every feeling. Yet, as her eyes scanned the stone walls, she felt nothing for them.

Possessions never meant anything to her. You can't take the things you own into a century long slumber. You also can't take the people you love. She leaned forward, squeezing Phillip from behind. Love. She rested her head against his solid back, knowing that was what had her heart thumping heavily in her chest.

She hadn't planned it. She'd fought it from the moment she laid eyes on him. Something pulled them together, forcing her to bring an injured man she'd never seen before into her home.

Above the trees, the walls of Dracon rose in the distance.

Once she fell into her sleep, La Dame would come for her. She'd take her beyond those high walls.

But until then, Aurora would bask in her final days of freedom, of light. Because for her, the future only held darkness. It always had.

CHAPTER TWELVE

PHILLIP

"Tell me about your family." Aurora's voice drifted through the darkness, curling around them and creating a sense of calm inside Phillip.

It was a three-day ride to the palace, and they would arrive tomorrow. The trip had been uneventful, save for Aurora's frequent demands to stop and let him rest. He hated to admit it, but he was relieved each time. His full strength had yet to return and spending each day in a saddle did nothing to help.

Phillip bent down to throw another pile of sticks onto their fledgling fire. They'd set up camp as soon as they found tree cover after riding through the open plains and rolling hills Bela was known for. He'd always loved his Kingdom. The beauty lay in both the people and the land. He found it hard to believe there was anything else quite like it in the Six Kingdoms.

His protection magic hung over them like an invisible cloak.

"What do you want to know?" He settled beside her, and

she set the blanket across his lap.

She blew on her chilly hands and held them toward the flames. "Tell me something no one else knows."

He thought for a moment. "You want me to reveal all the kingdom's secrets?" He quirked an eyebrow and laughed.

She bumped his shoulder with her own and leaned close to whisper. "I promise not to tell anyone. Tell you what, I'll keep my lips sealed for the next hundred years."

His smile dropped. It wasn't the first time Aurora tried to make light of her impending fate. He knew she didn't believe his father's magic could help her, but Phillip refused to give in to the curse.

Aurora was scared, but she tried not to let him see it. Sadness tinged her eyes, but she did not speak it.

He wanted to know all of her, and yet she continued to keep the deepest parts of herself from him. So, he decided she would know him at the very least. She'd know his heart, his soul. Maybe it would push her to fight harder to stay.

He wrapped an arm around her shoulders, and she leaned into him.

"My father never wanted me to go to war." He smiled at the memory. "The first time I told him I needed to lead the men, he refused. I was too young, he said. I didn't understand the horrors of battle. So, I went anyway. I stole from the palace to join the troops as they marched out to meet the hordes of Gaule. I wasn't an officer and had no men of my own except my two best friends who'd come with me. But during the battle, two of the generals were slain and Bela was losing. I found a horse and stopped the retreat to lead a charge. At first, it was just Alfred and Chandler behind me. Three men against an army. Then the others joined us."

He laughed. "My father tried to be mad at me when we returned and the story was told. In the end, he just ruffled my hair and told me he'd never wanted me to see the images he was sure would never leave my mind."

"Did they?" she asked. "Leave your mind, that is."

His grip on her tightened. "No."

"What about these friends of yours?"

"Alfred and Chandler." A smile lit his face. "They've been with me since we were boys."

"You love them."

He nodded.

She seemed to relax at that. "Good. I want you to have people in your life who make you smile, Phillip. Because you should always smile." She turned to face him and lifted a hand to touch his cheek. "I don't want you to be sad. You're going to have a grand life. We haven't known each other long. It won't be hard to forget about me, to move on and become who you're meant to be."

He clasped her wrist and held her hand against his cheek. "Stop."

She shook her head. "These are the kind of conversations that can't be avoided."

"I don't care what happens in the future." The words burst from him with every bit of energy he possessed. He dropped her hand like it burned and jumped to his feet to pace in front of the fire. "Aurora, I lo—"

"Don't." Now it was her turn to be angry. "Don't you say it, Phillip Basile. I will go into my slumber never forgiving you."

"Why? What's so wrong with having feelings? With being a real person?"

"You don't get it, do you? I agreed to come to the palace for you, not for me. There is no changing my fate. I have lived for years content that sleeping for one hundred years wouldn't take anything from me. I'd wake up and go on to live my life.

That fate... I could live with. Don't you dare fall in love with me." She turned, putting her hands on her head in exasperation. "This was a mistake. I shouldn't have come. I shouldn't have kissed you that first time."

"No." He advanced on her until she backed up against a tree. "You don't get to regret that." He towered over her, bending down to look into her face.

"I—"

"It's my turn to speak. I have lived my life for battles. Maybe that's what drew me to you. You fight me on everything. I'm a prince. My life has never been my own. People tell me where to go, who to spend time with. These past weeks I've been my own man, and I'll be damned if someone tells me what I can do with my heart—even if that someone is you."

His eyes searched hers, unsure of what he saw.

She sucked in a breath, but he wasn't finished.

He put a hand against the wide tree trunk on each side of her. "The first time you kissed me, I only knew I wanted to taste you once more. The second time, I never wanted to stop. You think I'm delusional in my hopes of breaking your curse, maybe I am. But, Aurora, I love you. And in a few days if your eyes can no longer see me, I will love you still."

He wiped a tear from his face with a curse and took a step back. "Dammit! You're an infuriating woman."

"Phillip." Aurora sniffed. "I think I love you too." Even though it would only cause her pain in the end.

"You think?"

"I don't want to."

He reached out and pulled her into his arms, resting his chin against her soft hair. "I know."

He made it a point that night to remember everything about her. The slight bowing of her legs, the faint scar behind

87

her right knee. Each dip and curve of her body cemented in his mind. Every perfect imperfection.

He'd always had everything he ever wanted in life. It was a life of luxury, but he'd never known the most important part was missing.

Someone to share it with.

And with each passing day, the impossibility of keeping Aurora with him became clearer.

THERE WAS no place like the palace of Bela. Sitting atop the white cliffs, it loomed over the churning sea. The marble walls sparkled like a diamond in the sun.

As soon as Phillip led Aurora through the bustling town, the tension he'd felt since their conversation the night before began to ease. He was home.

No one recognized him in common clothes and with an unshaven face, which let him move unimpeded. As the general for a kingdom at constant war, he spent too little time in the capitol. They saw him during the army's parades or tournaments, but he may as well have been a foreigner.

They revered him, sure, but as one revered an idol, someone unattainable. It wasn't the same love they had for his parents. While his father grew sick, his mother ran the kingdom with grace and kindness. The people adored her.

Aurora had been quiet since the castle came into view in the distance.

"Are you okay?" He pressed a hand against her lower back to keep her moving forward. With his other hand, he pulled Lea's reigns.

She chewed on a lip, a motion he'd grown familiar with. Not much got to Aurora, but when she was nervous, that lip...

He wanted to pull it out of her mouth and into his own, but the vulnerability in her eyes stopped him. He turned into an alleyway that led to the busy docks. The smell of salt and fish swirled around them, an odor that was so familiar it had Phillip grinning.

His smile dropped when he noticed Aurora's shaking frame. "Hey." He put his fingers under her chin to tilt her head up so she'd look at him. He searched her face to discern what had her so nervous. "What's wrong?"

"Do..." She sighed. "Do I bow when I meet the queen?"

His smile returned. "You're nervous about meeting my mother?"

"She isn't just your mother. She's the queen of Bela." She gestured down to her simple, travel-stained dress. "And I'm me."

"There is nothing wrong with being you, Aurora. My mother will see that. I promise. Honestly, she'll just be happy I've returned."

She seemed to steel herself, straightening her spine. "Okay."

"Okay?"

"Stop repeating me and take me to the palace." She covered her face with a hand. "Words I never thought would come out of my mouth."

His smile stretched wider than he'd thought possible, and he kissed the side of her head before leading her back out onto the road.

The path from the town to the palace took them up a hill to where a bridge allowed them to cross a small river. Guards streamed to and from the castle gates, but Phillip kept his head down. He didn't want to be recognized before setting foot inside. He wanted to see his mother's face for himself.

The gates of the castle stood open as they always did

while the sun was out. Guard towers rose on either side, pointing toward the sky. The stone beneath their feet turned to marble as they neared the courtyard.

All Belaen citizens were welcome at the castle. The guards didn't stop any from coming in. The royal family's residence was heavily guarded in the back, but the rest belonged to the people. Phillip walked the familiar direction of the stables where a face he knew well greeted him.

Garek was a young orphan who worked and lived in the stables. When Phillip was at the palace, he let the kid trail around after him.

Garek shot straight up from where he'd been sitting. "Prince Phillip?"

Aurora tensed beside him and Phillip slid his hand into hers as he turned from weary traveler to prince. "Garek."

The kid gave him a gap-toothed grin. "We thought you was dead."

Phillip patted his chest as if checking for injuries. "Nope. Not dead last time I checked. But I am dead tired." He gestured to Lea.

Garek's smile dropped, and he scrambled to take Lea's reigns. "Yes, sir. Of course, sir."

"Garek," another voice bellowed. "I need my horse saddled. I'm riding out with the scouts."

Phillip didn't turn. "Don't talk to the boy like that."

Silence hung in the air for a long moment before a hand gripped Phillip's shoulder, ripping him from Aurora. "Phil?"

Phillip stared at Chandler, a grin spreading from one side of his face to the other. "Hello, Brother."

Chandler yanked him into a crushing hug, caring little for their audience. "You're alive." He pulled back, putting a hand on the side of Phillip's head to get a good look at him. "How the hell are you alive?"

"Disappointed?"

Chandler scrubbed a hand over his face. "Incredibly disappointed." He released a breath, disbelief coating his features. "How?"

Phillip reached behind him, and Aurora slid her hand into his, joining the two men. "She saved me."

Chandler's eyes widened, and he nodded. "Good. That's good. I imagine there's a story here." He clapped Phillip on the shoulder. "You're really here?"

Phillip laughed. "I'm really here."

"Well, come on then. There are a hell of a lot more important people than me who will want to know."

"What about the scouts?" Garek called after him.

"Scouts can wait, boy. The prince has returned."

They followed Chandler inside. "The entire palace will hear now that Garek knows."

Phillip shrugged, trying to appear nonchalant as anticipation built in his gut. Inside the palace, servants and guards who'd worked closely with him recognized him despite his attire. They watched him pass with wide eyes and hushed whispers. Phillip tried to acknowledge them. He tried to smile and wave, but his body wouldn't cooperate when all he wanted to do was find his parents.

Chandler led them toward the royal residence.

"My mother isn't in the throne room?" Phillip glanced to Aurora to make sure she was okay. She stared straight ahead.

Chandler shook his head and motioned for the guards to open a door for them. "She does most of the kingdom's business by your father's bed."

"It's that bad?"

Chandler paused at the door to the queen and king's private room. "It's good you've come when you did."

A guard knocked on the door. Phillip expected to see a

servant poke her head out, but instead, the queen herself appeared. She looked to the guard in annoyance without seeing the rest of them. "The king is not to be disturbed."

"Mother." Phillip stepped forward.

His mother's eyes latched onto his, recognition lighting in them. "Phil... what... no... you're..."

"Here, Mother. I'm here."

She fell into his arms, a sob escaping her throat. The Balaen queen was raised to believe any show of emotion was a weakness. When he was a child, she taught Phillip the same. As he aged, though, he could see his father's influence take root, and his mother began to use her emotions to strengthen herself. Now, she didn't shy away from crying or screaming if she needed to. She believed a queen needed to be just like any other person.

He held her tightly for another moment before pulling back, remembering who stood beside him. "Mother, this is Aurora. She's the reason I'm alive." He gave Aurora a warm smile. "She saved me."

His mother wiped her face and turned with all the grace of a queen. "Dear." She reached out and grasped Aurora's hands in her own. "The kingdom owes you a debt."

Aurora shook her head. "I didn't do it for some reward."

The queen smiled. "You have my thanks." She lifted a hand to cup Phillip's cheek. "Thank you for bringing my boy back to me."

CHAPTER THIRTEEN

AURORA

For the first time, guilt curled in Aurora's stomach. She'd trapped Phillip in her cottage, keeping him away from the people who loved him. She'd said it was because he couldn't travel until he regained his strength, and there was some truth to that, but she still felt as if she'd hidden him away and caused the kingdom to mourn.

His mother glanced at him every chance she got, a genuine smile on her face, as she led them through the royal apartments. As magnificent as the rest of the palace was, it didn't compare to the luxury afforded to the king and queen. Lavish carpets of velvet spanned each room. Silk curtains hung in windows that overlooked the sea. Aurora ran her hand along a carved mahogany table, finer than any furniture she'd ever seen.

She tried to hide her surprise when the queen led them into her own bedchamber.

"Father." Phillip rushed to the bed and fell to his knees beside it. The king lay wrapped in furs. His chalky white skin spoke of severe illness. Gray hair stuck up in every direction, covering various bald spots.

It took a moment for him to wake and focus his eyes. When he did, a light entered them. He tried to lift his hand, but it dropped back to the bed. Phillip reached for it, clutching it as if he was afraid to let go.

"Phil." The voice was so soft, Aurora barely heard it.

"I'm here, Father." Phillip bowed his head.

"You've returned, my boy." He smiled, the action seeming to take every bit of strength he possessed. "Good. That's good. Now I can rest in peace."

"No, Father. Not yet. I'm not ready."

The king closed his eyes. "Death does not ask us if we are ready, son. Only if we are finished. I think I have done all I can."

Phillip's desperate eyes met Aurora's, and he gestured her forward. "This is Aurora. Father, you once told me if I found someone to love, to hold on with both hands. I'm trying. I'm trying so damned hard."

The king's eyes slid open once more. "Ah. My boy is in love." He turned his gaze on Aurora. "Something isn't right. I can sense it."

"The Basile power," Phillip explained to Aurora. "It is the counterbalance to La Dame's."

The king's eyes hardened. "That's what it is. You carry a piece of La Dame's magic."

"A..." Aurora cleared her throat. "A curse, your Majesty."

Phillip leaned closer to his father. "She only has a few days before she falls into a long sleep. You have to help her, Father. Please."

The queen gasped, covering her mouth with her hand. She put her free hand on Phillip's shoulder. "He doesn't have the strength to use his magic, Phillip. He has tried, and it no longer comes to him."

Aurora had never believed the Basile power could break her curse, but hearing the words still sent a dagger through her heart. That was it. Her final chance. There was no saving her from her fate. She stumbled back from Phillip, bumping into the queen in the process.

Phillip jumped to his feet, but before he could react, his mother gripped his arm. "Your father needs rest, son. And you need to recover from your travels. I'll have a room set up for Aurora."

"No." He fixed his eyes on his mother. "She'll stay with me."

Relief bloomed in her. If Aurora only had a short time remaining, she didn't want to spend any of it away from Phillip.

To the queen's credit, she accepted the demand without argument. "I'll have wash water brought to your rooms and food. Go. Rest." She touched his cheek. "The kingdom is going to need you soon."

Aurora glanced at the king once more, but he'd already fallen asleep. Phillip wrapped an arm around her waist and guided her out the door. Neither of them spoke until they entered the prince's apartments.

Where the king and queen's rooms were lavish, Phillip's were simple. A beautiful wooden bed sat atop a fur rug. At the far end, a marble hearth sat with no fire inside. Two glass doors opened onto a large balcony.

Phillip brushed past her and threw open the doors, letting in a blast of chilly air, before storming out onto the balcony. He gripped the railing and hung his head.

Aurora approached, wondering if she should give him

time to himself. She stopped moving and was about to turn back around when his pained voice reached her.

"There has to be something more we can do."

Aurora stepped forward, her eyes sweeping across the ocean. Waves crashed against the cliff face. Birds swooped down over the water as if this day was just like any other. And she wanted it to be. She wanted to stop thinking about what was going to happen and just be there with the man she loved more than she ever thought possible.

Only a short month ago, she was alone. She thought she was content, that she could just fade into her curse and wake in the future to live a new life.

Then he came. Phillip changed everything. He ruined her.

His knuckles turned white where he gripped the bronze railing. Aurora laid her hand over his, her voice low. "I came here with you to give you a last shred of hope. Even if your father was strong enough to use his power, we do not know it could break the curse." She pried his hand off the rail, but he still didn't look at her. "I need you to do something for me."

He finally turned his tortured gaze to hers. "Anything."

"Let me go."

He started to protest, but she held up a hand.

"Love me while I'm here, while I can love you back, but don't spend the rest of our time looking for a way to stop the inevitable." She ran her hand up his arm, stopping at his defined bicep. "I want to stay with you more than anything in the world, but we are fated to be apart. Don't make me feel sadness in my final days. I want to feel joy."

"Joy," he whispered, one side of his mouth ticking up. He nodded and pulled her against his chest, wrapping her in his strong arms. "I can do that."

She breathed in his familiar scent of pine and relaxed against him, wishing he could hold her for the rest of her life.

She pulled back, tipping her head to look up at him. "How is your wound today? Does it hurt?"

A grin spread from one side of his face to the other. "Are you trying to get my shirt off?"

"No," she sputtered. "I..." Two days. That was all she had left, she reminded herself. She'd take what she wanted from them. "Yes. Take it off."

"Your wish is my command." He released her and shrugged his shirt over his head, revealing the trim chest she'd spent so much time marveling at. He dropped his shirt and pulled her inside where they tumbled onto the bed.

"Wait." Aurora kissed him with a laugh. "I really do want to check how you're healing." She scooted down his body until she was eye level with the bandage on his abdomen. She removed it and poked at the raised scar. "I don't think you need a bandage anymore."

"No." He pulled her back up. "But I need you."

His kiss consumed her every thought as he invaded her mind and took over her body. She barely remembered what it was like not to feel this way, to not have someone who completed her. Before, she'd only lived for herself.

Phillip's tongue pushed into her mouth, battling with hers. Sometimes she thought they were made to battle each other, to challenge each other.

By the time a knock sounded on the door, they'd lost themselves in each other. Phillip sat up with a curse and wrapped a blanket around his waist. He opened the door to reveal a bevy of servants.

Aurora burrowed under the bedsheets as two men carried buckets of steaming water into the adjoining wash room. A woman entered carrying a tray of food followed by a man with a pitcher of drink.

They made quick work of their duties before filing out the way they came. Phillip walked to the tray and poured them each a cup of wine before popping a grape into his mouth.

Aurora crawled from the bed and took the offered wine. "I don't think I could ever get used to being served like this."

Phillip didn't respond and Aurora said nothing else as the reality hung over them. She'd never have to get used to it because she'd be gone. She wondered what would happen to her once she fell asleep. La Dame would most likely come for her, refusing to leave her in the Basile household.

She stepped around Phillip to enter the washroom. "A bath sounds glorious."

Phillip's arms wound around her from behind and he kissed her shoulder. "Come on." He led her to the large copper tub that was now half filled with water.

Aurora stepped in and reached out a hand to Phillip. He took it, joining her. They lowered themselves into the warm water facing each other.

On the opposite side of the tub sat a tray with sponges and soaps. Aurora reached for a sponge and lathered it up. She leaned forward, running it along Phillip's chest.

"This reminds me of the first time I gave you a bath." She smiled. "When you pretended to need help."

Phillip laughed. "I did not pretend. Do you know how hard it was for me not to touch you?"

She bit her lip and shook her head. "No, because I got to feel your skin under my fingers all I wanted. In the name of helping a wounded man, of course."

"Of course." He laughed.

She could have drowned in that sound, letting it surround

her until it was all she heard. She hoped he'd laugh in her dreams.

He leaned forward, catching her lips with his for a quick kiss. "Marry me," he whispered.

Her eyes snapped to his. "What?"

"I want us to have that."

She leaned away from him, needing to clear her mind. "You're the prince of Bela, Phillip."

"I'm aware."

"You can't just marry anyone. You need a wife who will give you heirs." She hated the desperation in her voice, but thinking of Phillip with anyone else sent a jolt of pain straight through her.

"I don't want anyone else." He reached forward and pulled her onto his lap. Water sloshed over the sides of the tub. "I only want you."

She relaxed against him. "I want you too."

"Is that a yes?"

She smiled and pressed a kiss to his jaw. "Yes."

Once she was gone, Phillip could remarry and have many children, but for now, he was hers.

Pounding sounded from the door in the main room, breaking them from their haze. Phillip pulled away with a curse. "Never any privacy in this place."

Aurora grazed his cheek with her fingers. "Their prince has just returned. They're excited."

The pounding on the door echoed through the suite of rooms. Phillip kissed her once more before rising. Water streamed down his magnificent frame as he reached for a bath sheet. "Finish bathing then join me out there for some food."

She nodded, unable to take her eyes from his body as he wrapped the bath sheet around his waist and stepped from the water. Wet footprints trailed him from the room.

Aurora scrubbed the remaining travel grime from her skin before dipping her head back under the water. She untangled her hair with her fingers and sat up again.

By the time she'd dried herself, she realized she only had her soiled clothing to put back on. Along the back wall sat a wardrobe. There had to be something in there. She padded across the cold marble and opened the doors. Phillip's clothing hung in an orderly fashion, probably not by him.

Bypassing his uniforms, she found a long tunic and pulled it over her head. The hem stretched down to her knees, almost like a dress. It would have to do for now.

Twisting her hair into a braid, she draped it over one shoulder and stepped from the washroom, freezing as she took in the sight before her.

The man they'd met in the stables stood talking excitedly to Phillip along with a second man. Phillip smiled—so at ease around these men—and she instantly knew they were the friends he'd told her about. They'd known each other since they were children.

She stood unnoticed, watching them, reveling in the sight of Phillip without the worry he held in his eyes each time he looked at her.

"He's going to be okay," she whispered to herself.

As if they heard her, all three men turned her way. "Aurora." Phillip rushed toward her, his eyes taking in her attire. He retrieved a robe and draped it around her. "Come." He wrapped an arm around her shoulders and pulled her toward the other men. "This is Alfred." He gestured to the man she didn't know. "And you already met Chandler."

Alfred smiled at her before turning back to Phillip and shaking his head. "I just can't believe it. We left you injured in the woods and then couldn't find you after. We assumed you were dead."

"I would be." He pulled Aurora in against his side. "But then she came."

Surprising Aurora, Alfred dropped to a knee in front of her. "We owe you a debt, miss."

She hugged her arms across her chest. Everyone at the palace continued to say how much they owed her, but she knew they'd never get a chance to repay. What was she supposed to have done? Leave a dying man alone in the woods? Wouldn't anyone have done the same? She didn't want them to raise her up on a pedestal she didn't deserve when the truth was plain. It hit her with the full force of a blast of magic. Phillip Basile would have been better off had he never met her. She should have helped him and then dropped him off in the nearest village before he woke. But she'd been selfish in her curiosity and now, here she stood in the palace. The prince deserved a life with endless possibilities. He didn't deserve to have everything he wanted taken away with the same curse she'd lived with most of her life.

Alfred was still kneeling when Phillip's words snapped her from her dark thoughts. "We're getting married."

Alfred jumped to his feet. Both he and Chandler wore matching grins. "Married?"

Phillip nodded.

Once they got over their shock, they both rushed forward and enveloped Phillip and Aurora in a crushing hug. Aurora blinked back tears at their joy. They celebrated their friend making a lifelong commitment, not realizing it would barely last a day.

Phillip chuckled, his thoughts obviously not going the same direction as hers. "Tomorrow." His voice was muffled against Chandler's shoulder. "We will marry in the morning."

Both men pulled back and exchanged a glance. "Tomorrow?" Chandler asked.

"Isn't that awful short notice to arrange a royal wedding?"
Phillip didn't miss a beat. "It won't be a royal wedding.
Just close friends and my parents."

It was then Aurora realized what a big mistake this was.
There was no way Phillip Basile could get away with
marrying a common girl, especially without the rest of the
kingdom invited.

"Phillip," she said, her voice soft. "We should talk about
this."

Alfred and Chandler exchanged a look. "We'll give you
two some privacy. Have one of your men wake us if there is to
be a wedding." Alfred gripped Phillip's shoulder. "We are
glad you're back."

They showed themselves out, and Aurora sighed as she
retreated farther into the room. Phillip waited a beat before
following her. She climbed onto the high bed and sat with her
legs dangling over. It wasn't how a lady of court would rest in
a prince's room, but she'd had no noble training. If she were
really going to be Phillip's wife, she assumed they'd make her
sit through proper lessons.

She lay back to stare at the canopy overhead, wishing it
was tree cover she saw instead. Already, she missed her forest.

Phillip stood at the table, eating cheese from the tray.
Aurora turned her head so she could watch him. He still
hadn't put clothes on and the bath sheet hung low on his hips,
making it hard for her to think. She'd never considered herself
someone who'd become so mesmerized by a man, but then
she'd never seen a man quite like Phillip before.

He chewed slowly and swallowed. Water dripped from
his hair to run in a single stream down his cheek.

"Enjoying the show?" he lifted one brow.

Aurora's cheeks flushed, but she didn't look away. "Yes."

The thing with living your last days was there was no reason to lie. By the time she woke from La Dame's slumber, everyone she'd ever met would be long in the earth.

Phillip wiped his fingers on the bath sheet and sauntered toward her with the slow gait of a predator. He leaned over the bed, tasting her lips in quick, repetitive kisses. She longed to just pull him down to join her, but her body wouldn't cooperate.

He crawled onto the bed and lay on his side. "You said we had to talk about tomorrow."

She tried to regain control of her breathing and couldn't stop the words from slipping out of her mouth. "He isn't going to like this."

Usually, when she talked to herself, he smirked or laughed in amusement. This time, a crease formed in his brow.

She stared at the ceiling again. "Now, you've gone and done it, Aurora."

"Hey." He placed a palm against her cheek and turned so her eyes met his. "Talk to me."

"Sorry. When I get nervous, I can't help it."

"I know. What I don't know is why you're nervous."

A laugh bubbled out of her. "Really? How about the fact that right now I'm in the palace of Bela? I met the king and queen today. Currently, the prince is lying beside me looking like..." she waved a hand at him. "... that. Not to mention that after tomorrow, none of this will matter anymore because I'll be gone." Her chest heaved as if she'd just run a length around the palace.

One side of Phillip's mouth tipped up. "What do I look like?"

When she swatted him, he laughed and caught her hand. "You have to ask? You're the prince. People probably fall all over you constantly."

He nodded. "They do. But with you, I'm not the prince,

okay. Stop saying that. I just want to be the man from the cottage deep in the woods."

"But that isn't reality. You want to be the man in the cottage. I want to be a girl who isn't cursed. We don't get to choose our destinies."

"I love you. I do get to choose that."

She placed a hand above his heart, feeling his heated skin. "Some would say love isn't a choice."

She scooted closer and pressed the side of her face to his chest, needing to hear his heart beat solidly. The steady rhythm calmed her as his words took root in her mind. She thought over her own words. Love wasn't a choice. If it were, she wouldn't have chosen it. She'd have given herself over to the curse easily, instead of trying to fight it at every turn.

Phillip's arms wound around her back as she drifted off, still lying sideways across the bed.

CHAPTER FOURTEEN

PHILLIP

As soon as Aurora fell asleep the night before, Phillip tucked her in beneath the covers and went to find Alfred and Chandler. He wanted to lie with her the entire night, but there was too much to do.

His friends gathered a few trusted servants and together they worked through the night. Growing up, the palace had been like a family. People worked their entire lives for the royal family, bringing their children and grandchildren to work there as well.

And they all loved their prince.

Phillip went about his tasks, finding more and more to do to keep from remembering what tomorrow held. This was about today.

He should have been tired after not sleeping all night, but he felt more energized than ever.

Taking in the room before him, Phillip smiled. It was perfect. He'd wanted to have the wedding in his mother's garden to allow Aurora to feel at home, but Chandler convinced him it was too cold. The old chapel would do. It hadn't been in use since his parents' wedding, but they'd kept it in working order to honor their own marriage.

White lilies littered the floor, Aurora's favorite. She'd kept a garden of them at her cottage. Pale pink silk draped across the chairs and silver balls hung from it. Green garland stretched across the ceiling to give the space an outdoorsy feel.

Chandler stepped up beside Phillip, rubbing his eyes. He yawned. "You really love this girl, don't you?"

Phillip turned to clap his friend on the back. "More than you could ever know."

"Then why did we rush to do a wedding in a day?"

"It means a lot to have your help with this."

Chandler crossed his arms. "That's not an answer."

Phillip met his friend's eyes, knowing his mistake immediately. His joy evaporated, leaving behind only an emptiness as though the curse stripped everything from him. He opened his mouth to speak, but no words came.

"Shit, Phil." Chandler gripped his shoulder and steered him from the bustling chapel to the unused chaplain's office. "Tell me what's going on."

Phillip sat on the corner of the desk and clasped his hands together, hoping his friend couldn't see them shaking. He'd always told Chandler everything. Ever since they were boys, they'd confided in each other. He sucked in a breath and began the story.

He told him of meeting La Dame and learning about Aurora's curse.

When he was finished, Chandler released a series of curses. "Why hasn't someone dealt with La Dame by now?"

Phillip shook his head. "We don't know if even the Basile power is a match for hers. It could mean an end of Bela if either she or the Basile heir is destroyed. It's a risk we have not been willing to take." He wiped a hand across his face, thankful his friend acted as if he didn't notice his tears.

With Aurora, Phillip had to remain strong. He had to joke and make plans and act like everything was normal between them, like he wasn't terrified of each passing moment.

"I'm sorry, Phil." Chandler hung his head. "I wish there was a way we could help."

"I thought if I brought her here, the Basile power could do something. At least, that's what I told myself. I think I just wanted her here when it happens. When she falls asleep for the last time. I won't let La Dame have her."

Chandler pressed his lips together. "One hundred years, Phillip. You'll be long gone. You can't keep her in the palace that long. What happens after you're gone?"

"I don't have to figure out everything today," he barked.

Chandler held up his hands in front of his chest, but before he could respond, the queen poked her head into the room.

She smiled when her eyes rested on her son. "Phillip. I was just informed of the wedding my staff spent all night preparing for."

He hadn't wanted to wake his parents until it was time for the ceremony. Part of him had been afraid they'd try to stop him. He waited for her chastisement, but it never came. Instead, she gestured him into the hall.

Two maids stood carrying a long white dress with intricate beading and lace spanning the surface.

"Mother." He glanced from the dress to her in question.

"I only hope it fits her."

Phillip pulled his mother into a hug. She let out a grunt of surprise. "Thank you."

"I want you to be happy, son. Even if it's just for a day."

They all kept saying that as if the marriage would no

longer matter once Aurora was no longer with them. They didn't understand. She would be his wife until he took his last breath. But he didn't tell them that, and he didn't dare voice it to Aurora. She wanted him to move on, but there was no moving on from her. She was a part of him now, deep in his soul. He couldn't imagine a life with anyone else by his side.

Just the thought of it brought tears to his eyes. He'd never let go of the hope he could one day break her curse.

He took the dress from his mother and left to go wake his sleeping beauty.

Aurora was still fast asleep when he entered the room. Her wild blond hair lay draped over the pillow, and the blanket tangled in her legs. Noble ladies even took classes on how to sleep properly to avoid snoring or improper sprawl.

He'd never been more glad Aurora was no noble. She snored softly and even that was adorable. He didn't think there was anything she could do that would make him think less of her. He stood there watching her until finally draping the dress over a chair and approaching the bed.

Sitting on the edge, he brushed the hair from her face. "Aurora." He bent so his lips grazed her cheek as he spoke. "Wake up, love."

She grumbled something unintelligible, and her leg kicked out instinctively as if trying to knock him from the bed. She rolled away from him.

He grinned as he lowered himself beside her, her back to his front, and wrapped an arm over her waist. Pushing her hair aside, he kissed the back of her neck.

She hummed low in her throat. "Do that again."

He kissed her just below her ear.

If their fates were different, he'd have enjoyed waking her up every morning for the rest of their lives.

She turned in his arms, still not opening her eyes. "Where did you go last night?"

"That is a secret." He kissed her nose. "Come on. We have to get you ready."

Someone knocked on the door. Right on time. Phillip rolled off the bed to go let in the two maids who'd help Aurora prepare.

Aurora sat up in a daze. "What's going on?"

One of the maids dipped into a curtsy. "We're here to prepare you for your wedding, miss."

As if she'd forgotten what the day held, Aurora's eyes widened. She looked to Phillip, pleading for help, but he only winked and sauntered from the room.

In only a short time, he'd be married to the love of his life. Phillip grinned as he rejoined Alfred and Chandler.

They both gave him sad looks, and he put a hand on each of their backs. "Don't do that. Please. I need today to be about everything I've gained, not everything I'm about to lose."

To their credit, both men instantly wiped the sadness from their faces.

Phillip laughed. "That's more like it. Let's get ready. I'm getting married today."

CHAPTER FIFTEEN

AURORA

Aurora didn't ask for the maids' names. She didn't want to get to know anyone else she would have to leave behind. They forced her from the bed, and it was only then she realized how tired she truly was.

Her limbs were heavy, making her movements sluggish. No. She shook her head. She wasn't supposed to feel the curse for one more day yet. Rage ripped through her at the thought. Why her? Why did she have to disappear?

As quickly as the rage came, so did the nausea. She didn't even make it to the chamber pot before the contents of her stomach erupted onto the floor.

She dropped to her knees as her stomach heaved, trying to empty the last few drops. Tears stung her eyes. What was happening to her?

The maids stood frozen, staring at the vomit now covering the floor as she struggled to her feet.

"Um, I'll find someone to clean that." The younger of the two darted into the hall, her red hair flying out behind her.

The second maid was an older woman with a bonnet

covering her gray hair. She stepped to the table and poured a cup of water before approaching Aurora. "Here you are, dear."

Aurora accepted gratefully and drank quickly, trying to erase the taste from her mouth.

The older woman put her hands on her hips. "Are you feeling ill? We can't have you sick at your wedding. From what I hear, it's a small affair. I can tell the prince you need to postpone."

"No." The word burst out of Aurora. There was no postponing this. She lowered her voice. "I'm not sick."

"Well, are you pregnant? That would explain the quick wedding."

Aurora put a hand on her stomach. "I don't think so, but how would I know?"

"Vomiting, for one."

Aurora shook her head. It was probably just the nerves.

The maid tsked. "It's too early for morning sickness, anyway, I'd assume. You haven't known the prince long. Probably just the nerves." She didn't ask more questions as she led Aurora to the washroom. Aurora cleaned herself up while someone arrived to clean her mess in the bedroom.

Before she knew it, the maids set her hair in an intricate weaving atop her head. She peered into the looking glass, not recognizing the woman who stared back at her. What would her father think of her now? Her grandmother would have liked Phillip. She had enjoyed any man who was a bit challenging.

The older maid walked in carrying the most beautiful dress Aurora had ever seen.

"Is that... for me?"

The maid nodded. "From the queen."

Aurora reached out to feel the silky fabric and scratch of

the lace. She closed her eyes, letting the circumstances sink in. The queen had sent her a dress so she could marry the prince. What kind of world had she entered?

Only a month ago, she'd spent her days among the trees, content with her loneliness.

She slid out of the robe she'd been wearing and let the maids slip the dress on over her head, careful not to mess her hair or rouge. The fit wasn't exactly perfect, but it would work.

Soft fabric hugged her curves tighter than she'd have liked, impeding her walking even more. A silk train streamed out behind her. She ran her hands over the collared bodice and short sleeves that left the rest of her arms bare.

She almost asked about that before the younger maid held up a pair of long ivory gloves. Aurora slipped them on, feeling like she belonged in the palace for the first time.

She could walk among them, endure their stares. She could do anything if it meant meeting Phillip at the end of the aisle.

Someone knocked on the door before letting themselves in. Chandler appeared, a smile softening his handsome features. His dark hair was slicked back from his face, and he wore a pressed soldier's uniform.

"I'm here to escort you." He offered her his hand.

She placed her palm against his and rose. "Thank you."

The palace passed by in a blur as Chandler led Aurora through the corridors. Early morning sunlight cast a glow upon the walls. Eyes followed her as she walked. The people of the palace must have known something was happening that day, but they didn't stop her.

Chandler glanced sideways repeatedly as if unsure what to say as they walked. Aurora sighed. "He told you."

Chandler nodded. "I'm sorry. I wish there were better words to offer you."

They stopped outside a closed door and Aurora turned to him. "Take care of him. After I'm gone. Just... promise me you'll be there for him."

Chandler met her gaze unflinchingly. "I will always be there for him."

She could see the truth in his eyes, and it eased some of the weight on her heart. She released a tired breath, refusing to let her exhaustion ruin this day.

Chandler pulled open the doors, and Aurora gasped.

A chapel spread before her, covered in white lilies and pink silk. A few servants and guards sat near the back. The queen sat in the front row, and the king had even left his bed for this.

At the front a priest stood next to the most beautiful sight Aurora had ever seen. Phillip's uniform was impressive, but she barely noticed it as she caught his eyes. Emotion swirled in their depths, a mixture of joy and sadness that left her gasping for breath.

How could a single day be both the happiest and hardest day of her life?

Phillip's lips curved up as a single violin played a sweet melody.

Alfred, standing next to him, elbowed him and spoke softly in his ear. Phillip's smile widened.

"Are you ready?" Chandler asked.

That simple question could have so many meanings. Was she ready to marry Phillip? More than anything. Was she ready to leave him? Never.

Instead of voicing any of that, she only nodded and let Chandler lead her into the aisle. The queen turned in her seat, tears springing to her eyes as she gazed at Aurora.

"Do not cry, Aurora," she whispered to herself. "You are a badass forest woman. You don't cry at weddings."

"Did you say something?" Chandler asked, humor in his eyes.

"No. You must be hearing things."

His laughter told her he heard the pep talk she'd given herself. She'd have died of embarrassment if she wasn't going to be as good as dead the next day, anyway. She sighed to herself. Apparently, now she was joking about her impending fate. At least she hadn't voiced that out loud.

She didn't realize she'd reached Phillip as the internal conversation waged in her head. He cleared his throat and took her hand from Chandler's.

"Sorry," she whispered.

He only grinned.

She barely heard a word the priest said as she lost herself in Phillip's gaze. She must have said her part in the ceremony at some point, but she didn't take it all in until the priest announced her as "Princess Aurora Rose Brynhild Basile."

Princess.

Her.

Aurora Brynhild.

Phillip pulled her against him and kissed her as if it was the very last time, and he never wanted to let go.

"I love you," he whispered against her lips. "I will always love you."

A tear slipped from her eye as she grazed his cheek with her fingers. "One hundred years won't make me stop loving you."

He kissed her again, but they broke apart when commotion surrounded them.

The queen's wail reached their ears, and by the time they rushed to her side, the king had collapsed.

"Get a healer," Phillip yelled.

His mother shook her head. "It's no use." Tears streamed down her face. "We knew the danger of him leaving his bed, but he wanted to be here."

"Mother," Phillip pleaded. "We have to do something."

She lifted glassy eyes to him. "I promised I'd let him go when it was time."

Two guards appeared ready to take the king wherever he needed to go. The queen held up a hand to stop them. "This was his favorite place in the palace."

Aurora slid her arm through Phillip's. One moment, they'd been celebrating and the next... She couldn't take the thought of Phillip losing so much in one day.

The king's chest rose one final time before going still. His wife sobbed, and his son stumbled away from everyone.

"He's gone." Phillip ran a hand through his hair, pulling on the ends. Chandler tried to put a hand on his arm, but he shook him off.

As if struck, Phillip cried out in pain. His legs buckled beneath him, and as his knees hit the stone, he gripped his head.

Aurora wanted to run to him, but the still crying queen held her back. "It's okay. This has to happen."

He collapsed onto his side and writhed on the floor for what seemed like hours before going still.

The queen gestured to the guards. "Take the prince back to his room." She turned to Aurora. "My dear, I wish this day was different. I wish my husband could have lived and that you could remain with us. Go, be with your husband. He'll be okay in an hour or so. I don't think I'll see you again."

Aurora wished she could have said something clever or at least hugged the queen, but all she managed to do was turn and follow the guards carrying Phillip.

They carried him to his rooms where they laid him on the bed and he curled in on himself. Aurora pulled a chair to the bedside and took his hand in hers.

"Phillip, please be okay."

She didn't know how long she sat rubbing circles on the back of his hand before his voice wrapped around her. "Aurora."

Her head jerked up. "You're okay?"

He groaned as he stretched to his full length. "I feel... different." A smile curved his lips, but then dropped as if he remembered the events of the day. "My father is dead."

She nodded. "You remember?"

"I can feel it." He pushed himself up. "The Basile power. It's inside me now and that can only happen if the person who carried it is gone."

"I'm sorry, Phillip."

He lowered his gaze. "We've known this was coming for months."

"Knowing something is coming doesn't make it any easier." She gave him a pointed look.

"No. I don't suppose it does." He swung his legs over the side of the bed and rested forward with his elbows on his knees. "I'm going to mourn him for a long time. My father was a great man, the best father I could have had, but I can't start today. Not when I'm looking at you knowing I am going to lose you too."

She stood and crawled onto the bed beside him, leaning against his side. "Try it."

"Try what?"

"You have the Basile power now. I still don't know if I believe it can break the curse, but we have to try, right?"

"Aurora." Phillip's eyes widened. "I don't think you understand. The Basile power... it's like a thunderstorm, uncontrollable. At least at first. I can feel it inside me, ripping through my limbs. It's all I can do to hold it in. Each new heir has to train before they can use it. It's too dangerous otherwise. I could kill you."

"I don't care."

He froze. "Aurora—"

"No, listen to me." She forced him to turn his body toward her. "If there is even the smallest chance we can stay together..." She clenched her jaw. "I would rather die trying than give up."

He ran a finger over her features as if memorizing them for a lifetime of only memories. He closed his eyes, his hand stilling against her cheek.

Finally, he blew out a breath, and his shoulders sagged. Aurora knew she'd won.

She stifled a yawn and forced a smile instead.

Phillip kissed her forehead and pulled himself from the bed. "Lay down."

Aurora obeyed without hesitation.

Phillip leaned over her, pressing his hands against her skin as he closed his eyes.

"What are you doing?" she asked.

His voice was quiet when he spoke. "Looking for the threads of her magic. My father taught me how to do this to better target my own shield power." After a while, he blew out. "Okay, I've got her."

Aurora's own magic tingled in her fingertips as if calling out to his.

Phillip's face strained in concentration as his magic flooded her. Her skin grew scorching hot, burning from the inside out.

She bit back a cry of pain and blinked away tears, not wanting Phillip to stop.

"I've found traces of the curse," he whispered, his energy waning. "Only a few moments longer. I just need to use my power to sever the connection." He bit his lip.

As if shocked, he yanked his hands away and scrambled from the bed. "I think I did it. I almost lost control and hurt you, but the curse is gone. I felt it break." His chest heaved as he tried to catch his breath, disbelief in his eyes.

Aurora lifted her head, still weighed down by exhaustion. She was too tired to share in his elation, but his next words sent a jolt to her system.

"That's not all." He jumped back onto the bed, grinning. "Aurora, you're pregnant. I felt it. My magic called to another Basile heir, feeling its presence in a rush of power through my veins."

Pregnant?

Before she could process the word, Phillip tackled her in a hug. His tears dampened her shoulder. "I'm not going to lose you."

She wrapped her arms around him, not quite believing his words. The curse had been a part of her for so long, and she knew it still was. It had to be.

But a baby?

For one final night, she wanted to pretend they were a normal couple who were about to become a family. She wanted that reality more than anything. If she fell into La Dame's slumber at midnight, what would happen to the child?

She wiped away her tears and hid her despair behind a smile as she pulled back to look at Phillip, wishing she could feel his joy.

CHAPTER SIXTEEN

PHILLIP

Phillip had prepared much more than a ceremony for his new wife. He'd begged the palace chefs to stay up with him throughout the night. They made a feast. All he wanted as he issued the orders was for Aurora to know how much he loved her, for her to feel safe before closing her eyes.

He hadn't admitted to himself that he'd needed to feel safe as well. He'd needed his family around him. And now Aurora would be his always, yet his father was gone.

He'd missed the final month of his father's life, yet he didn't want to regret any of his time with Aurora. Phillip had always believed in reasons. Everything had one. Every action. Every word. Every event.

Maybe his father dying in that moment had a purpose. He'd been fading away for so long and finally took his last breath when Phillip needed the Basile power most.

Phillip lay in bed beside Aurora who dozed after their big morning. He no longer feared when she fell asleep because he knew she'd wake again to smile at him.

He lifted a hand and curled his fingers. Like everyone in

Bela, he'd been born with magic in his blood. His protection wards were his birth power, but the Basile power was his inheritance. He'd seen the magnificent things his father could do with it before he grew too weak. He'd been training and preparing for the magic. Birth power was a part of the wielder, just an extension of themselves. But Basile power—it was a living thing with a mind of its own. The kings of Bela used it to protect the kingdom, but it used them as well. He'd seen his father change when releasing his magic, his face twisted in anger.

Even now, as he lay in bed beside his new wife, ire curled in Phillip's gut. His father always told him the secret was to be able to decipher which feelings were his own and which belonged to the power.

A knock came from the door and Phillip rose, pulling his tunic off the bedpost. He shrugged it on and opened the door.

Alfred and Chandler grinned at him. A host of servants carrying trays of food waited behind them.

Phillip crossed his arms and raised a brow.

Chandler tried to push past him into the room, but Phillip blocked him.

Alfred laughed. "We expected you two in the hall for lunch. When you didn't show, we realized we couldn't let this feast go to waste."

Phillip peered around him, realizing the trays held the dishes he'd ordered the cooks to prepare for the wedding celebration.

Chandler shrugged. "We tried to convince the queen to join us."

Phillip shook his head, knowing exactly what his mother's response would have been. She needed time alone as they prepared the king's body for the ceremony that would take place in the coming days. It was why he hadn't yet gone to her. His mother was a loving woman, but there was a part of herself she didn't share with her son. His father had given Phillip every bit of himself.

A pang of loss ripped through Phillip, but he knew it was nothing compared to the grief his mother experienced. Yet, if her son came to her, she'd only turn him away. And he couldn't handle that, so he saved them both the pain.

He sucked in a breath, trying to push the overwhelming sadness from his mind. "Fine, you can come in. Just give me a moment first." He shut the door and walked back toward the bed.

Aurora talked to herself in her sleep just as she did when she was awake. It was one of the many things he loved about her. He smiled and bent down to brush his lips against hers. "Wake up, my sleeping beauty."

Her eyelids fluttered open, and it took a moment before recognition set in. He knew the look she gave him—as if she was surprised every time she woke. He supposed it would take her a while to get used to the notion that a deep slumber was no longer her fate.

"We have guests," he whispered, kissing her again.

She freed her arms from the blanket to pull his face down to hers again. This kiss wasn't light like the others. She inhaled him. He growled as she pulled him onto the bed.

Someone pounded on the door. "Phillip, open this door." Alfred.

"Tell them to go away." She barely broke away enough to speak.

He grinned against her lips, but before he could respond, someone pounded again.

This time, Chandler's voice carried through the heavy wood. "Stop whatever you're doing. The food is getting cold."

Phillip groaned and rolled off her.

"Food?" she asked.

"Yes. Get dressed. It seems we have company." He leaned back toward her once more. "It's a good thing I get to do this for the rest of my life." He pecked her lips and turned away from her.

She scrambled to pull a dress on over her head and tied the laces.

Phillip opened the door just as she was running her fingers through her hair in an effort to tame it. She didn't realize how much he liked it wild.

A flurry of activity ensued in which a bevy of servants carried trays to the table in the center of the room. The rich aroma of carved meat filled the air and Phillip watched as Aurora's eyes widened. A grin formed on her lips, but it dropped just as quickly. Their future together was not something that could be celebrated when the pallor of death hung over them, cloaking them in sadness.

Alfred and Chandler each took their turns hugging her as if they'd known her their entire lives. It warmed Phillip's heart to see the men he considered brothers accept her so completely. He only wished his father had gotten the chance to know her as well.

When the servants left, and it was just the four of them, Aurora stepped up to the table to study the offerings. She was practically drooling.

He suppressed a laugh. "Go ahead, wife, eat whatever you'd like."

She turned to him.

"What?" he asked. "Are you really that excited for dinner?"

She shook her head, but didn't stop staring.

He couldn't help the smile curving his lips. "Why are you staring?"

"You called me wife."

He scratched the back of his neck. "Well, yeah. That's what you are in case you forgot. There was a ceremony. I said some things. You said some things."

She smiled, joy warring with sadness on her face.

"Stop."

"What?"

"You're still staring."

She laughed. "Am I making you uncomfortable?"

"You're making me uncomfortable," Chandler spoke up.

Heat rose in Phillip's cheeks, and he tried to hold it back. He didn't ever blush. He was a prince. Confident. Sure. Yet, the way she looked at him laid him bare. She saw everything, each vulnerable part.

Alfred made a gagging sound. "Just kiss her so we can move on with our lives."

Phillip raised one eyebrow, a challenge, daring Aurora to make the first move in front of his friends. It was one thing when it was just the two of them locked away in her isolated cottage. But here in the palace, among the people he'd known his entire life, he wanted her to claim him.

She stepped forward, and just when he thought she was going to kiss him, she reached back to the table, grabbed a roll, and stuffed it in her mouth.

Alfred and Chandler laughed. For a moment, it was as if they could all forget the events of the day.

Phillip shook his head and turned to them. "We have an announcement."

Aurora tried to say something, but her mouth was still full so it came out as a whimper in her throat. He took advantage of her momentary inability to stop him.

"Aurora's curse is broken."

The words hung in the air, no one wanting to breathe for

fear they might be taken back. After a beat of silence, Alfred and Chandler jumped up, engulfing both Phillip and Aurora in a hug. They asked questions, and Phillip answered as best he could. The Basile power allowed him to find La Dame's magic inside Aurora and snap the thread. He'd felt it the moment it broke.

They all sat around the table and piled their plates high with food.

As they finished eating, Phillip spoke up again. "La Dame's magic wasn't the only thing the Basile power felt in Aurora." He reached beside him to take Aurora's hand. "We're going to have a child."

His friends wore matching grins as they congratulated him. Contentment sank into Phillip as he looked around the table. It was a contentment he didn't want on the day his father died, the day he knew his mother would sink into grief.

Soon, he'd become king, much sooner than he'd have liked.

Chandler raised a cup, and they all fell silent. "To the old man." He meant Phillip's father. He'd always called him that, even though the man was a king. "He was the best of Bela. May we remember his lessons and strive to do as he did."

Phillip nodded, tears springing to his eyes. "He loved this kingdom. He loved all of us."

They knocked their glasses together and took long drinks, letting the somber tone hang over them like a cloak, taking away the joy from only moments before.

Alfred leaned back in his chair. "Now that the Basile power once again rests in someone who can wield it, Gaule will be kept at bay. Will we push into Gaule?"

The word 'savages' was on the tip of Phillip's tongue, but he glanced at Aurora, remembering their discussion in the cottage. They were people just like his own subjects. "No. I think it's time for a bit of peace, don't you?"

Aurora graced him with a breathtaking smile.

Alfred cursed.

Phillip fixed his stare on him. "What?"

"Do you know how bored I'll get in a time of peace? I might have to find a hobby—like knitting."

A laugh burst free of Chandler. "You couldn't knit to save your life."

Phillip rubbed his thumb against the back of Aurora's hand. "I already miss my father." He released a shaky breath and looked to Aurora. Her eyes calmed the agony within him. "But I think we're all going to be okay."

Her eyes watered, and he reached out to catch a tear, not understanding where they came from. "Don't cry," he whispered, leaning toward. "Please, don't cry."

"I love you," she whispered.

He pressed his lips to hers, speaking to her without words, infusing his strength into her until she found her own. Because she would. Aurora Rose Brynhild was going to be his queen, and Bela was a lucky kingdom.

"That's our cue to leave." Chandler stood and pulled Alfred with him. "We'll see you two in the morning."

Phillip pulled away. "No, you probably won't. Tomorrow I'll need to deal with what happened today. My mother won't be in any shape to make arrangements for my father. She won't let me be there for her, but I can at least do that."

Chandler put a hand on his shoulder, squeezing lightly. "We're here for whatever you need."

They left, and Phillip returned his attention to Aurora. Moonlight streamed through the window, casting her pale skin in a silver glow. He reached out, needing to touch her, needing to feel her. This night was supposed to be their last. He closed his eyes, holding her face close to hers.

"Phillip," she whispered, gripping his chin. "Open your eyes."

When he met her gaze, he knew she was reading everything inside him. He held nothing back.

She shivered, but not from the cold. "I'm here." Her words were like the promise he needed to force his limbs to move.

She yelped when he scooped her up and carried her to the bed.

"Forever," he whispered as he bent to taste her lips. "Starts now."

CHAPTER SEVENTEEN

AURORA

Aurora couldn't sleep. Ironic, considering. She lay on her side, watching Phillip's chest rise and fall in a steady rhythm. His ruffled hair hung forward into his eyes, and she brushed it away to memorize every inch of him.

She ran a hand down his firm chest, curling her fingers in the soft hairs. She wasn't trying to wake him. One thing she'd learned about Phillip Basile was he was a heavy sleeper. It would take her hand traveling a lot lower for him to rouse.

Exhaustion weighed down on her, making it hard to breathe. It wasn't the usual nighttime sleepiness. No, this was La Dame's magic, the magic Phillip thought he'd freed Aurora from. She hadn't had the heart to tell him she still felt the ties binding her life.

Slipping from the bed, Aurora walked to the window, lifting her face to the full moon. How close to midnight was it? She rested a hand on her stomach, wishing she could feel the life growing inside her. All she felt was tonight's dinner rising up in her throat. She swallowed back bile and forced out a breath.

"I don't know what will happen to you." This time, she didn't speak to herself, but the child she'd never know. "I'm so sorry I can't protect you."

In that moment, she understood her parents in a way she'd never imagined. La Dame placed the curse on Aurora in exchange for her mother's life, but they hadn't known it at the time. For years, until his death, her father only looked at her with guilt in his eyes. He hadn't been able to protect his daughter. He'd gone to his grave blaming himself.

Aurora didn't blame her parents. La Dame did this to her. Would the sorceress come for her? Most likely. She wouldn't let Aurora slumber in peace.

Aurora walked to the balcony doors and opened them. A gust of cold air bit into her skin, but she wanted to feel it, needed to feel it.

She hugged her arms across her chest and stepped out, hoping no one on the palace grounds would look up and see her in only her underclothes. Only the night patrol would be out at this hour.

She walked to the hanging plants in the corner and let her magic flow out. White lilies sprouted forth. It was the wrong time of year for them, but Phillip had hung the plants, anyway. For her.

The growth calmed her as she sank into her power, forgetting the rest of the world existed. She longed for the greenery of her woods. Would they be covered in snow by now? Things had seemed so simple when it was just her and Lea and the trees.

Chandler had told her Lea was enjoying the luxury of the palace stables, and she didn't doubt that. It would be a good life for the mule.

Strong arms wound around her waist, and she leaned back

into Phillip. She wouldn't tell him she could barely stand on her own at the moment, that leaning on him allowed her to remain upright. She'd spend too much time in the near future lying down.

Phillip kissed her neck. "What are you doing out here? It's freezing."

She ignored his question to ask one of her own. "What time is it?"

He rested his chin on her shoulder. "Probably close to midnight."

Midnight. She closed her eyes, a single tear escaping. She couldn't let Phillip see the sadness in her, so she blinked any remaining tears away.

He turned her in his arms and pulled her against his naked chest. "I woke up and found you gone. I didn't like the feeling."

Unable to form words without letting a sob escape, she reached up on her toes to press her lips to his.

When she pulled back, he seemed to sense something was wrong. He gripped her chin, tilting her face, so she'd look at him. He waited with a patience she didn't deserve.

"Phillip." She froze, sensing the moment her magic disappeared. The lilies she'd created only moments before withered and died. Aurora shook her head. "No. I'm not ready."

Concern flashed across Phillip's face. "Not ready for what?"

Tears blurred her vision until she could barely see him standing before her. Her heart slowed in her chest.

She wiped the back of her hand across her eyes. "Phillip, there's not much time, and I need you to listen to me." She gripped his waist for support. "You need to let me go."

His brow furrowed. "Let you... what?"

"I don't want you spending your entire life trying to figure out a way to get me back. You deserve more than that. You deserve the best kind of life. Full of love and... and family. Promise me." Tears streamed down her cheeks.

Phillip gripped her tighter. "Aurora, tell me right now what's going on?"

"The curse."

He shook his head. "We beat it. You and me. We broke the curse." He looked to her with such fear it nearly ripped her heart right from her chest.

How was she supposed to wake up in one hundred years to a world where this man didn't exist? To him, a lifetime will have passed. To her, a single night.

She stumbled sideways, but he caught her.

"Aurora." If she'd thought the fear was enough to crack her heart, the tears on his face broke it in two.

She collapsed against him, her legs no longer able to hold her up. He lowered her to the ground, and the cold tiles soothed her burning skin. Ice wound through her, snaking up her veins and into her heart, slowing it further.

She never once took her eyes from Phillip's face. He breathed heavily, his breaths turning to steam in front of his face. *He's too cold,* she thought. *He should have stayed in bed.*

She hadn't wanted him to see it. She didn't think she could stand his pleading eyes and choked voice. This slumber was supposed to be her torment, not his. It was why she'd isolated herself for so long. Carrying someone else's pain was its own kind of torture.

He bent over her. "I love you. I will always love you."

"You have to let go." Her voice was so weak she wasn't sure he heard it.

He bent forward, claiming her lips one last time before pulling her onto his lap and rocking back and forth.

Aurora's eyes slid closed as she gave into the blessed peace. All fear and pain disappeared as the curse welcomed her into its blessed darkness.

CHAPTER EIGHTEEN

PHILLIP

A loud keening sounded in Phillip's ears, and it took him a while to realize it was him. The sound ripped from his throat, and he couldn't pull it back.

Just like he couldn't bring Aurora back to him. He couldn't make her lips tip up into one of her heartbreaking smiles. He no longer had the ability to make her groan low in her throat as he kissed her.

Emptiness. That was all he felt as he sat on the cold tile of the balcony with the frigid wind battering against his unfeeling skin.

Phillip cradled Aurora's lifeless form, tears cascading down his cheeks. He pressed his face into the soft blond hair he'd loved so much and inhaled everything that was Aurora. "I broke the curse." Her hair muffled his words. "I saved you."

Only he hadn't. Whatever he'd felt with the Basile magic obviously wasn't what he thought. Aurora saved him all those weeks ago. She kept him from the edge of nothingness. He'd thought he could do the same for her.

"I failed you," he whispered.

Her skin shone almost translucent in the starlight. He smoothed his hands over her arms. Her hair stood on end. Not dead. She wasn't dead. He bent forward to lay his head against her chest, needing to hear her beating heart.

The door to his room burst open and guards flooded in. Phillip barely took notice of them until Chandler's "shit" reached his ears.

He lifted his tear-stained face to the two men who knew him better than anyone, wanting them to tell him none of it was real.

"Is she..." Alfred clenched his fists at his side.

"The curse." Phillip's entire body shook.

Four arms came around him as Chandler and Alfred knelt on either side. They held him as he held Aurora. Other guards stepped onto the balcony.

Phillip's muddled mind couldn't come up with their names.

"Do we need the healer?" one of them asked, his panicked eyes flicking from Aurora to Phillip.

It was only then Phillip realized how bare Aurora's body was. He lunged away from Chandler and Alfred, covering Aurora with his large frame. "She's cold," he yelled. "Someone get me a damn blanket."

A blanket appeared and Alfred took it from the guard. He put a hand on Phillip's shoulder to pry him away. Instead, Phillip ripped the blanket from Alfred and draped it over Aurora before standing and lifting her into his arms.

He carried her past the guards and servants lingering in his room and set her gently upon the bed, looking as if she'd only gone to sleep for the night. He crawled in next to her and curled his body around hers.

When darkness came for him, he only wished he could stay in it with her.

WHEN PHILLIP WOKE, he had one blissful moment where the world lay open before him. One moment where he rolled toward Aurora, planning to kiss her awake.

When his warm lips pressed into her still ones, the truth slammed into him, and the world shut down until all he saw was a dark tunnel of a future.

A sob worked its way up his throat, but he had no more tears to cry. The magic underneath his skin tried to turn his grief to anger, but the former was too strong, too fresh.

A cough let him know he wasn't alone, and he turned his head to find his mother sitting beside the bed.

She had the courtesy not to give him a smile neither of them felt. There was no pity in her eyes, only understanding. In the space of a day, they'd both lost the loves of their lives.

He'd let her grieve on her own the day before as he knew she'd want, but she knew better than to do the same for him. A silent tear tracked down her reddened cheek, and she leaned forward.

"Alfred and Chandler stayed most of the night, but I sent them to get some rest." She reached forward to brush her thumb over his cheek.

The events of the night before returned to him at that. "There were guards and servants and..." He shook his head. He didn't understand. How had they known?

She tilted her head. "You were quite loud, Son. A few of the guards heard your cry from the balcony. They worried something had happened to you. Luckily, one had the good sense to wake Alfred and Chandler. When they arrived, they found you outside in the cold with a sleeping Aurora. None of them understood what had happened to her, but your friends assured them she was okay. Still, a guard woke me a few hours ago to tell me what happened."

Phillip tried to process her words, but they barely registered in the fog of his mind. Only one thought blocked out all others, he bolted upright. The baby.

He turned to Aurora, taking in her pink cheeks. He touched her lips, feeling a puff of air release, before taking hold of a strand of magic and reaching out. He didn't know how to search for the child specifically, but he let his power buzz over her skin.

His mother watched in confusion.

And there it was. A tiny flicker from the Basile power. His magic curled through her womb, warming at the thought of another Basile heir.

He pulled it back slowly until he was no longer connected to Aurora. He missed the connection immediately.

"She's pregnant," he whispered to his mother. The moment seemed to call for hushed words.

She covered her mouth with her hand, and fresh tears sprang to her eyes. The queen stood and moved to sit on the edge of the bed. She reached out and pulled Phillip to her.

"Son, I could say I'm sorry, but I know how pointless that word is. A mother never wants to see her child's heart break so completely. If your father were here, he'd have something very wise to say about the time you spent in love with her being worth a lifetime of grief."

"That sounds like him." He sniffed and rested his chin on her shoulder. "We have to bury father today."

She nodded. "And lay Aurora to rest."

He pulled back to look down at the woman who was supposed to be his forever. "We don't know if the baby will be born alive, but we do know La Dame wants her." He turned burning eyes back to his mother. "I won't let her have Aurora. Not any more than she already does."

"We'll figure this out, Phillip." She patted his cheek and climbed from the bed. "I love you, Son. You're going to make a wonderful king. You're going to make both your father and Aurora proud. When she wakes in one hundred years, she will hear great tales of King Phillip Basile."

He finally offered her a weak smile at that thought.

She left and was true to her word. The next few days were a flurry of activity. His father was buried in the hall of kings with all the ceremony he deserved.

In the days that followed, the kingdom crowned Phillip. He went through the motions, feeling neither aggrieved nor elated at the prospect of taking on such responsibility. It didn't matter to him. None of it did.

The queen set up a beautiful room for Aurora. Large windows let sunlight filter in, turning the yellow walls golden in their glow. A marble hearth sat a one end and Phillip vowed to never let the fire go out.

Aurora was dressed in a pale pink gown, beautiful in its simplicity. They tucked her into the sheets of silk and the best furs they could find.

She looked like a doll, ready to come back to life at any moment. But Phillip knew he wouldn't get to live to see her wake.

Her belly grew and in time, hope entered Phillip's life again. Hope that some part of Aurora could remain with him.

When the baby was born, Aurora groaned and cried out in her sleep, yet did not wake. Phillip held her hand and kissed her lips. He would have given anything to have her squeeze his hand. Just once.

The prince came as the summer doused the palace in heat. A tiny baby who knew nothing of the cruelty in the world. He didn't yet know he'd grow up without his mother to hold him or tell him she loved him.

It wasn't fair. No child should have to live without a mother.

The first time the child opened his eyes, Phillip stopped breathing. It was as if Aurora stared back at him with all the understanding in the world. That was the power he got from his mother. Whatever magic he ended up having, this little boy would be the only person who could reach Phillip. It wasn't until that moment, Phillip realized he'd practically died all those months ago when Aurora left him. He'd gone through the motions of his life.

But just as his mother had, the boy could bring him back to life if Phillip let him. He rested his forehead against the baby's. "It's just you and me, Wulfric."

The queen stepped up beside him. "Wulfric?"

Phillip nodded. The word meant inherited power, and he knew Wulfric would have every bit of Aurora inside of him. He was a part of her.

Phillip walked away from his mother, his son still cradled against his chest. "We don't have her, buddy, but we will always have each other." She would have wanted that.

He wiped away a tear and stared into the blue orbs that looked so much like Aurora's. The baby held his gaze as if reading his mind and agreeing to his words.

He walked back to the others, lifting his voice. "Meet Prince Wulfric Brynhild Basile." He let his eyes fall on Aurora once more. She lay in a clean gown with fresh sheets, looking just as she had each day of her slumber.

He sent out a thought, imagining she could hear it.

I couldn't protect you, but I will protect him. I promise.

He probably imagined her smiling in her sleep, but he liked to think it had been real.

PART II

CHAPTER NINETEEN

LA DAME

Fog curled around the spires of the Draconian palace as La Dame dismounted her horse. Her trip into Gaule went well and preparations for their invasion of Bela were under way. The sudden urge to bathe, scalding the stink of Gaule from her skin came over her.

She shook off the thought and walked through the massive double doors that seemed to lead right into the mountain. The entryway was deserted save for a guard awaiting her return.

"Your Majesty." He quickened his steps to match pace with her. "There is a problem."

She sighed. There was always a problem when she was home. Rapunzel, eighteen now, caused... issues with her constant need of freedom.

She didn't understand that her mother was protecting her from the evils of the world. She loved her more than anything else in this life. Her fondness for Rapunzel even eclipsed her old obsession with Aurora Brynhild.

She'd never retrieved Aurora once the curse set in because

Rapunzel filled the hole in her heart she'd once thought would never be whole. A need for family. For someone to care about.

Now, La Dame had different plans for Aurora. For eighteen years, she'd searched out every person who'd studied magical ability in Dracon, bringing the brightest minds into her confidence. Once they were no more use to her, she made sure they couldn't share their knowledge with anyone else.

Because they'd come up with a theory about the Basile magic that kept Bela safe.

A theory La Dame was willing to lose Aurora over.

The guard followed her to Rapunzel's room before leaving La Dame to deal with her daughter. With a weary sigh, she pushed open the girl's room.

Rapunzel sat on the corner of her bed, her back hunched as tears rolled down her face. Blood trickled from her lip.

La Dame crossed her arms over her chest. "You tried to protect the boy again."

Rapunzel met her mother's gaze without fear. "He doesn't deserve what your guards do to him."

"He is not one of us, dear. He deserves what I say he deserves."

Her shoulders shook, and La Dame crossed the room. She put a hand under Rapunzel's chin and forced her head back. "You should heal yourself."

"And let everyone forget that one of your people attacked me?"

"There are rules in this palace, daughter. Between your constant attempts to leave and your stupidity when it comes to the prisoner, I don't know what to do with you."

A mother's greatest burden was punishing her child. As a young girl, La Dame suffered at the hands of both her parents. It was their duty to make her stronger.

One day, Rapunzel would thank her for hardening her.

It hurt La Dame to do it, but she grabbed Rapunzel's shirt and hauled her to her feet.

"Mother!" Rapunzel cried.

Tears gathered in La Dame's eyes. She didn't want to do it, but there was no other way to teach obedience.

Letting her magic trickle out through her fingertips, she used it to bind Rapunzel's arms to her side and force her from the room. As Rapunzel tried to cry out, La Dame stole her voice.

Straightening her spine, La Dame yanked on her magic like the end of a rope, tugging her daughter along past loitering guards and servants and into the lower levels of the palace. The cavernous stone room stretched between her and her destination like a sea she had to cross.

Emotional exhaustion battled with her magic, wanting to overcome it and make her pity her daughter. Instead, she pictured her father's face and heard his words.

This will do you good, daughter. You'll see. One day you'll see cruelty is the only way.

She'd seen it sooner than he'd imagined.

As La Dame pushed Rapunzel into a bare room with a dirt floor, she shut the door. Peering through the metal bars, she knew one day Rapunzel would see it too.

Her mother loved her. And she'd do anything to make her strong.

CHAPTER TWENTY

RIC

Wulfric Brynhild Basile, prince of Bela, was never one to follow the rules. At just over seventeen years old, he craved adventure more than the stuffy life inside the palace he called home.

He'd ridden two days to get to the wall that separated Bela from Dracon. His father, King Phillip, thought he'd left to join the patrol unit stationed on the Gaulean border. It was a prince's duty to be involved in all things.

But his dreams had led him here. Yes, dreams. While he was surrounded by people with powerful magic who could do incredible things, he had images in his mind. He couldn't even control them. As a young boy, other kids at the palace teased him mercilessly. His only true friend had been the old mule, Lea, until she died many years ago.

Now, a kid who had no business following him joined him by the wall.

"Ric, wait up." Travis panted as he caught up. Their horses had grown restless as they neared the wall, so they'd left them behind.

"You shouldn't be here, Travis." Ric used his hand to shield his eyes from the sun as he gazed up at the large stone structure.

"So you've said a million times since we left the palace." Travis crossed his arms over his chest.

When Ric glanced back at him, he almost laughed. At thirteen years old, Travis always tried to act like an adult. "Uncle Chandler is going to kill me."

Travis twisted his face into a scowl. "My father still thinks I'm a child."

Ric held in a laugh, knowing the kid wouldn't appreciate it. He was still a child. He was a product of Uncle Chandler's stupidity. Chandler slept with another man's wife. When that man showed up at the palace with a scrawny looking four-year-old and left him, Chandler hadn't known what to do. Luckily, Uncle Alfred was there to help him raise the child. They acted like good friends, but Ric wasn't born yesterday.

He'd grown up with almost exclusively men for company —other than his grandmother. His mother lived in the palace too, but that was another story.

"What did you see in your dream?" Travis asked, his posture relaxing as curiosity got the best of his irritation.

Ric pressed his palm to the wall, sliding it over the rough surface. Memories assaulted him, but he couldn't pick one out from the other. All he knew was they didn't belong to him. "A house." The image froze in his mind until it was all he saw.

"A house?" Skepticism rang in Travis' tone.

Ric only nodded. "But not here. Go get the horses. We're close."

He didn't know why this dream was different. It wasn't the first and wouldn't be the last, but as soon as he woke up, he knew he had to find out what it meant. There was something his magic wanted to tell him.

He may not be able to use his power to protect the kingdom like his father, but he sure as hell could do something useful. He had to. He was so damn tired of being the useless prince, the one with no offensive magic, only dreams he couldn't control. His father didn't have any other children, and the people of Bela saw him as a disappointment.

Travis led the horses back to him, and the two boys mounted up. Ric knew the way like he'd been there a thousand times. His magic laid out the path forward.

They rode through dense forest, stopping when they reached the most beautiful sight Ric had ever seen. White lilies stretched as far as he could see, the same flower his father brought his mother whenever he had the chance.

The king never offered up stories of his queen. No one knew why that flower mattered. Ric barely knew anything of his mother. He'd tried asking anyone who was around when his mother arrived at the palace, but he got the distinct impression none of them had known her well. Uncle Alfred and Uncle Chandler only told him she'd had eyes that could see into a man's soul.

Ric hadn't ever seen her eyes, but he'd imagined them, longing for her to look at him just once.

They rode through the clearing of flowers slowly, reverently, as if it was a special place. When they crashed through the trees on the other side, Ric pulled up on the reins. There, among the lonely forest, was a house.

House was probably generous. The cottage was small and looked like it had been abandoned for a long time. Vines wound up the stones, wrapping around the structure in an unnatural way. It was as if the forest itself attempted to keep people away from its hidden gem.

"Do you think anyone lives here?" Travis asked. Ric didn't miss the fear in his tone.

He slid down from his horse and led him forward to tie him to a nearby tree. "No, Travis." He didn't know how he knew it with such certainty. "I don't think anyone has lived here in a long time."

He rounded the corner of the cottage. A broken feeder sat out front. Whoever lived here had owned a horse. It wasn't much of a clue, but it was better than nothing.

He touched one of the vines as if it would attack him. "Vines don't grow like this. Someone used magic to seal up the cottage."

His own magic curled inside of him, a warmth in his belly. It wanted to show him its dreams, but he pushed it down, needing to stay in the present.

"Who would live this close to the wall?" he whispered to himself, pulling a knife from his belt.

"Um, Ric." Travis hung back. "If someone is trying to keep people out, don't you think there's a reason? Maybe we shouldn't—" His words cut off as Ric sliced through the vines without another thought.

"I have to see it," he whispered.

The door wasn't locked. Why would it be with vines holding it closed? As soon as Ric was through the final vine, he kicked open the door and stepped inside. A musty scent assaulted him.

Inside, it looked like a moment of someone's life had frozen in time. A bed sat off to the side, its sheets still rumpled from use. The floorboard creaked underneath his feet as he crossed to the stone hearth. Whoever had lived here enjoyed a simple life. What had made them leave? Ric felt a kinship with the unknown occupant. They must have seen the world in a different way than most.

Travis had a different thought. "What a lonely life."

Ric shook his head and brushed shaggy honey-blond hair

away from his eyes. "Just because someone is alone doesn't make them lonely." Defensiveness entered his tone as his eyes scanned the small washroom and kitchen. A rusted teapot sat on the counter waiting to be hung over a fire. Beside the hearth was a pile of firewood. "We'll stay here tonight."

"Here?" Travis swallowed. "Wouldn't we be more comfortable making camp in the woods?"

"No." Ric sat on the edge of the bed, feeling the energy drain from his body. His magic exhausted him whenever it wanted him to sleep so he could see the dreams. It had something to tell him. "Start a fire, Travis. I need to rest my eyes."

Travis lifted a brow. "It's mid-day."

"I'm the prince. Just do as I say, for once." Realizing how harsh that sounded, he sighed. "Please."

He didn't know if Travis started the fire because he joined his magic as soon as he lay down in the stranger's bed, falling asleep like an anchor pulled him beneath the surface of his uncontrollable dreams.

No images accompanied the dream that came to him. Only words.

In his dream state, he didn't recognize the voices at first.

"I only just found you."

A woman spoke. "I wasn't supposed to have anything to leave behind. When my grandmother died, I had no more ties holding me to this earth." She paused. "Why are you doing this to me?"

"I know you're scared, but Aurora, everyone should have something to leave behind. Everyone should have something to lose."

Aurora. It was then he realized what he was hearing. His parents.

His mother spoke again. "I just wanted to go to sleep and have the world forget I was ever here."

"Who could forget you?" He'd never heard his father sound so sincere. *"You will be remembered,"* he whispered. *"Forever."*

Ric tried to wake, but he was no longer in his own dream. His magic took him into the mind of someone else, someone who remembered every detail of that moment. As he sank into the moment, energy zipping along his skin, the images became clear. He saw his father as he was when he was younger, before the ghosts entered his eyes.

Ric loved his father. They'd always had a close relationship, but he always felt his father held on to him too tightly as if his birth had somehow brought his mother back. Sometimes, he'd catch his father staring at him with glassy eyes.

Phillip Basile was a great man, a great king. Gaule no longer threatened the border as they once had. Prosperity reigned in Bela. But out of the public eye, he was broken. Ric used to think it was his job to hold his father together, but he'd learned that was an impossible task.

He pulled himself from the dream, and his magic snapped back into him. He bolted up in bed.

Night had fallen, and Travis' soft snores drifted over from his spot in front of the fire. The orange glow cast the cottage in a new light. As Ric let his eyes scan the room, he realized where he was. He'd seen it in his mother's dream. This was hers. His magic led him here, gave him a piece of her as he'd always wanted.

His lips stretched into a smile as he pulled himself from the bed and went to shake Travis awake.

The boy groaned and rolled over to stare up at Ric.

"We have to go."

Travis sighed and sat up. "It's the middle of the night."

"I know, but I need to get home. I need to see them."

"Who?" Travis pulled his long brown hair into a tail and tied it back before rubbing his tired eyes.

"My parents." He gave no more explanation as he doused the fire and gathered the few belongings he'd brought. His eyes adjusted to the darkness quickly. He'd spent enough time sneaking around the palace grounds in the middle of the night that he was used to it.

Travis stumbled, crashing into the small table before righting himself.

He couldn't explain the sudden urge to get home, but that was the first time he visited one of his mother's dreams, and he needed to look into her face.

And his father... he finally understood everything he'd lost. In that dream, he'd felt the emotions between them. The love. The fear. The heartbreaking realizations that they couldn't fight the inevitable.

They mounted up, leaving his mother's cottage behind, knowing it could tell her story to someone else. By the time the sun rose, they were well on their way to the palace.

CHAPTER TWENTY-ONE

PHILLIP

Phillip Basile walked through his mother's garden with a purpose. She'd planted the back half with white lilies without telling him many years before. Gardening had been her way of coping with the grief of losing her husband.

Phillip chose a different path, a more violent one. He'd left only days after Aurora fell into her slumber, accompanying a unit of his army. Once the Basile power rested with a man who could wield it, they couldn't let Gaule go unpunished for ravaging the Belaen border when the old king was dying and unable to hold them back.

Aurora would have been ashamed of him and how he treated the Gauleans. There was blood, lots and lots of blood. He hadn't been able to stop the magic from latching on to his desperation and turning it to anger.

It was only when he returned and looked into the serene face of the woman he loved that he realized what he'd done. She'd once mentioned Gauleans too had families and villages. During that time, Gaule had a lot of warriors to mourn, but at least they would no longer push into Bela.

And his mother gardened.

He almost laughed at the thought of their different approaches to grief. They'd kept it to themselves, rather than sharing it with each other. At least at first. Then he'd found the flowers she planted, and he knew she understood.

Since that time, not a day had gone by when Phillip didn't bring Aurora a lily. Even when they didn't grow due to the time of the year, he kept some preserved with his magic. She wouldn't have cared if they were living or not.

He bent to pick the day's flower and held it to his nose, inhaling the familiar scent. She'd have liked that one.

His mother watched him from the other side of the garden, and when he approached, she kissed his cheek.

"What was that for?" he asked.

"Just softening you up before I deliver some news." Her expression turned serious.

"What did he do now?" He knew whatever she said had to be about Wulfric. His mother wanted little to do with the running of the kingdom anymore, but she'd thrown herself into the raising of her grandson wholeheartedly.

"I don't want you getting too angry, Phillip. You know that boy. I'm sure he's fine."

Phillip crossed his arms, careful not the crush the flower, and started walking. His mother fell in step beside him.

"Just tell me," he ordered.

She sighed. "I ran into Alfred this morning. He didn't want to tell you this and face your anger."

"I don't have anger."

She raised an eyebrow but pushed on. "It seems Travis has left as well. He wouldn't tell his father where he was going, but he told Alfred. Apparently, the prince had a mission."

Phillip shook his head. "He was supposed to accompany

the unit I sent to the border. He begged and begged for me to send him. He even claimed to want to be a general like I was."

She smiled. "That boy doesn't have a single fighting bone in his body. He'd rather go off and create his own adventures."

Phillip knew that better than anyone. He'd raised the boy, but Ric was every bit his mother's son. He knew it wasn't appropriate for a prince to be such a loner and to evade his guards at every chance, but he'd never had the heart to force him to change. Ric knew full well his father would let him get away with anything.

Phillip's mother patted his arm. "Go easy on the lad."

"Don't I always?"

Her brow creased. "No. Sometimes you expect too much of him. He isn't Aurora, and he won't bring her back to you. Maybe it's time you let your son have a bit more independence."

He sighed. His mother was right. She usually was.

He entered the palace, and she told him she had a tea to get to. He barely noticed her leaving as he walked the familiar hall to the room that held his heart. Nodding to the guards stationed there, he pushed open the door.

Seeing Aurora in that bed would never fail to take his breath away. She looked just as she had the last time she'd stared at him. He'd aged in their time apart, but she hadn't. Her skin still held the glow of youth. Her blond hair was combed to perfection.

Two maids were assigned to Aurora. They kept the fire in her room going as if it provided some kind of life for her. They also bathed her regularly. One of the maids looked up from where she was smoothing the blanket over Aurora. She dipped into a small curtsy, her gray head bobbing. "Your Majesty."

"Thank you, Cora. May I have some time with my wife?"

"Of course, sire." She flashed him a sweet smile and hurried from the room.

Phillip walked toward the bed, reaching for the withered flower in the vase on the table next to it. He replaced it with one that was full of life and set the dead one aside before leaning down to brush his lips over Aurora's forehead.

"Good morning, love." He sat in the chair that never left her bedside. The maids knew better than to move it. Phillip wasn't the only one to use it. His mother visited on occasion.

One time, he'd found Ric just sitting there staring at his mother. Phillip knew the boy wanted to feel connected to her more than anything and struggled to find that connection. He rarely visited her anymore because it only frustrated him. He wanted to know her.

Phillip wished he could tell his son everything he knew. He wished he could share every bit of the woman she was. But the words never came and eventually, Ric stopped asking.

It was probably out of some misguided attempt to make it easier on his father. Ric constantly put his own desires aside to protect Phillip. Phillip let out a pathetic laugh at the thought. A teenage boy shouldn't have to take care of a grown man, but who was he kidding? Ric had been doing it long before he was a teenager.

"I miss you, Aurora." He sighed and leaned forward to take her warm hand in his. "Wulfric has run off on some adventure again. He evaded his guards and even took Travis with him. But I can't stop him. I can't take the curiosity from him. He wants to know the world, and he wants to do it on his own terms. He doesn't like to have to depend on other people. Sometimes he's so much like you it hurts."

"Then don't stop me." Ric's voice came from the doorway.

Phillip turned to face his son, surprise coating his features. Ric leaned against the doorframe like he hadn't a care in the world. "Your Majesty." He dipped his head, but Phillip didn't miss the teasing tone in his voice.

"Get over here, Son." He stood. When Ric sauntered toward him, he wrapped him in a firm hug. "How are you here? I only heard you hadn't gone with the army this morning."

Ric chuckled. "If you let me breathe, I'll tell you my master plan."

Phillip hadn't realized how tightly he'd been holding his son. He released his grip on the lanky teen and returned to his seat by the bed.

Ric brushed his hands down his arms as if releasing wrinkles caused by his father. Smart ass. One corner of his mouth tilted up in a wry smile that only lasted a moment before he grew serious and approached his mother. He didn't touch her. He never did. But his eyes didn't leave her face. "How's Mother today?" It was a silly question, and they both knew it. She never changed even though the rest of the world continued to turn around her. He was almost to the age she'd frozen in, and it should have freaked him out. Instead, he felt connected to her, like she wasn't so different from him.

Phillip pushed a hand through his dark hair as he studied his son. He'd been prepared to yell the next time he saw him, to punish him in some way. But now, as he saw the boy standing next to Aurora, he didn't have the heart.

He'd always tried to find himself in Wulfric's features, but he was all Aurora.

"She'd have loved you," he whispered.

Ric closed his eyes and inhaled a breath. "Well, at least my children may get to meet her before they die. If she's still here, that is."

It had always been hard to fathom how even his son would be long gone by the time Aurora woke. He'd waited for the day La Dame came for her, ready to protect her with every bit of magic he possessed, but she never arrived.

He'd seen no signs of the Draconian queen in Bela since Aurora fell into her slumber, but Phillip knew she was watching. It was her source of entertainment to have the palace under a constant cloud of grief. Aurora had told Phillip to move on, to be happy, but he'd never even considered it.

He reached forward to tug Ric's hand. "Are you okay, Son?"

Ric's entire posture changed. His shoulders dropped, and he turned away, probably not wanting his father to see whatever emotion clouded his eyes. Phillip squeezed his hand tighter. "What is it? Did something happen while you were away?" He hadn't bothered to ask where his son had gone. Ric would tell him in time. It was the kind of relationship they had. They trusted each other.

When Ric finally spoke, his voice shook. "I was there."

"Where?"

"There! The wall. The—"

"Cottage," Phillip finished for him as realization dawned. "You went to the cottage?" He rubbed the back of his neck. "I'd ask how you found it, but I already know." He tapped the side of his head. Wulfric had always considered his magic a weakness. He'd wanted a power that let him go to battle and prove himself. But Phillip knew it for what it was. The dreams allowed Ric to see much more than anyone else. He understood things no teenager should. They'd led him on many adventures as he tried to understand the images he saw.

But still, Phillip hadn't expected this.

Ric stepped up to the table and touched the flower petals. "It was hers. All of it. The cottage. The flowers."

Phillip's eyes snapped to his son. "The flowers are still there?"

Ric nodded. "I felt her presence there more than I ever have in this room, but..."

Phillip stood and gripped Ric's shoulders to stop his constant moving. He dipped his head to meet his gaze. "What else?"

"Father." Tears pooled in his eyes. "My dreams... they turned into hers." A tear rolled down his cheek, but he didn't brush it away. Ric had always been a sensitive boy, not afraid of his own emotions.

Phillip stumbled away from him, crashing into the bed, jostling Aurora. A moan left her lips, and the sound struck him straight through the heart. It wasn't a new sound. In the beginning, he'd run to her every time she'd so much as twitched, hoping against hope she was awake. Each time brought more disappointment than the one before. Eventually, he realized there was no hope at all.

He gripped the edge of the bed to steady himself, but was unable to look at his son. "Explain. Please."

Ric huffed out a shaky breath and dropped into the chair his father had vacated. "I was dreaming like normal and suddenly I heard you and Mother."

"How did you know it was her?"

"I knew, okay." Blond strands of hair fell into his face as he bent forward and rested his elbows on his knees.

Phillip nodded. He'd never questioned the things Ric saw in his dreams. He could feel the dreamer alongside him and knew the things they felt. It was a special gift that allowed him to bond with those he visited in their minds.

"She told you she was afraid."

Phillip closed his eyes. He remembered that day so clearly. He'd never forgotten anything she'd said to him. She was so mad at him for giving her something to lose.

He was so cocky back then. It hadn't truly hit him what

her curse meant until she collapsed into his arms on that cold balcony. Over eighteen years had passed since that night, but the pain was still fresh.

"The dream wasn't much." Ric seemed disappointed at his own words. "But it made me want to come home and see her."

"Your Uncle Chandler is going to scalp Travis for joining you."

Ric lifted his head, a grin breaking through. "Uncle Alfred will protect him. He knew where we were. He can't say no to Trav."

Phillip laughed and ruffled Ric's hair. "Seems to be a running theme in this palace."

"Are you saying I have you wrapped around my finger?"

"I'm saying I should confine you to your rooms for at least a week for this stunt."

"But you won't." Ric flashed his teeth and stood.

Phillip shook his head without a word. There was nothing he could say to contradict the truth. He swung an arm around his son's shoulders and squeezed him to his side. "Just promise me you'll be safe always. I couldn't stand losing you too."

Ric wrapped an arm around Phillip's back as they stood beside the bed. "You're always saying we didn't lose her, Father. She's right here."

Sometimes, he needed the reminder. But maybe it was the reason he hadn't been able to move on. Some part of him still hoped she'd wake up and smile at him. Just once.

Ric shrugged off Phillip's arm and leaned forward to kiss Aurora's cheek. "Bye, Mother. I'll see you in your dreams."

Was it wrong to be jealous of a teenager? Phillip would trade every bit of Basile power running through his veins for a chance to walk into her dreams. It was selfish since the Basile power kept Bela safe, but sometimes he couldn't bring himself to care.

Ric squeezed Phillip's shoulder as he passed by on his way to the door. "I'll be sure to tell you before I escape my guards next time," he called back.

Phillip watched him go with a laugh. "I wish you could know our son, Aurora. He's going to be a great man. Thank you for him, for leaving a part of yourself."

He leaned down to kiss her lips once more before leaving her behind. He had a kingdom to run, people to protect. She'd told him he'd be a great king, and he was determined to make her proud.

CHAPTER TWENTY-TWO

RIC

Ric marched through the palace courtyard, aware of his two guards tailing him. They hadn't been happy when he ditched them to leave the palace. Usually, even as the prince, Ric didn't need a constant guard presence in his own home. If his father had known about the abuse he took from the other palace children when he was younger, that would have been different. They made a sport of testing their magic on him. He remembered certain instances so clearly. One of the boys lifted him into the air with a flick of his finger and tossed him onto one of the high parapets. An older girl used her magic to move stones to help him down.

But now he was no longer the boy prince, instead taking on a role in the running of the kingdom, and they chose to ignore him instead.

He didn't mind. It suited him to go through his studies alone. Instead of practicing with kids his age, he learned swordplay from the army units stationed at the palace. They treated him as one of their own despite his lack of offensive magic.

He shook his head in annoyance but ignored his guards. His father sometimes regaled him with stories of being guarded by his two best friends. Ric didn't have friends. He had... Travis.

Travis ran toward him and skidded to a halt at his side. "What did the king say?"

He'd been home for over a week, but hadn't yet seen Travis. Ric's father said Chandler was not as forgiving as the king, and Travis had been restricted to his own home all week.

Ric shrugged. "He was glad to have me home. It helps that I've attended all his meetings this week like he's always trying to get me to do."

Travis shook his head in disbelief. "I wish my father was like yours."

Ric laughed at that. "There is no one quite like Phillip Basile."

"You've got that right."

Travis had always worshipped Ric's father as some kind of hero. He didn't see the cracks behind the king's façade of strength.

"Where are you going?" Travis asked.

"My rooms. I'm bushed."

"Aww come on. I was thinking we could spar."

Ric wanted to remind Travis that every time he tried to fight the prince, he ended up flat on his ass. He refused to use his magic against Ric, claiming it wouldn't be fair. He had the ability to speed up his movements. It was a huge benefit to a scrawny kid like him.

"Another time." Ric kept walking. He'd felt his magic draining him all morning, the first time since he'd entered his mother's dreams. He hoped he'd get to see her again when he closed his eyes.

Travis finally got the hint and let Ric enter the palace

without further impediment. He lumbered toward his room, shadows playing at the edge of his vision as the dreams crept in. He stumbled, slamming his shoulder into the doorframe and he rushed into his room and dropped his sword to the floor. Sunlight lit the room, but he barely noticed. All he saw was his plush bed. He shut the door in his guards' faces and walked toward the bed, collapsing face first.

He was out before his head hit the pillow.

It took a moment for the image to become clear, but when it did, he was sucked into it as a scene played out before him. An unknown force dragged a girl across the floor, and all Ric could do was watch.

The voice that spoke to her was deep as a second figure entered the image, standing off to the side. "I've told you before not to disobey my commands."

"Please," the girl whimpered. She came to a stop and rubbed her bare knees where they'd scraped against the stone floor. They were in some kind of cavern with arched ceilings.

"Do not beg, girl. It is beneath you."

A whimper escaped the girl's throat, and she lifted her face. Long golden hair fell down her back. Kind eyes clouded by tears stared at the second woman. "I'm not begging." There was an unexpected strength in her voice.

The dark-haired woman smiled, but there was no joy behind it. "Then what is it you're doing?"

The girl stretched out her bloody legs in front of her. "Buying time." She pressed her palms against her skin and the wounds stitched themselves back together. She wiped the blood with her skirt and lifted her chin. "You can commence punishment now." Her eyes shown with defiance and courage. Ric had never seen anyone so beautiful as the dirt-covered girl with fire in her eyes.

A scream ripped through the air as she flew backwards

and slammed into the wall, the force pinning her in place. At the collision, Ric's eyes snapped open, as his magic ripped him from the scene. His chest heaved, and sweat coated his brow.

What was that? He wanted to go back. He had to. Squeezing his eyes shut, he tried to enter her dream again, needing to see her face. Her defiance washed over him. Something horrible was happening, yet she remained whole, unbroken by her circumstances. He could see that even after just a short glimpse into her mind.

He had to know who that girl was because the strength in her eyes wasn't something he'd ever forget.

His breathing calmed and his exhausted body relaxed back into sleep. This time, his dreams were not of the magical nature. This time, all he saw was her face.

When he woke, it was evening, and all he knew was he had to save her.

CHAPTER TWENTY-THREE

PHILLIP

Phillip tipped his mug of ale against his lips and eyed his two best friends. They thought he didn't know what stood between them, that he hadn't known for years. They'd never felt the need to explain themselves to anyone else though, and he respected that.

Alfred shot Chandler the kind of look that made Phillip hide his grin behind his cup. He'd had a long day of meetings and that was before he'd had to hold court in the throne room, listening to the problems of his people.

To say he was exhausted would be an understatement. Yet, as usual, he hadn't wanted to go back to his empty apartment within the royal wing. Wulfric wasn't at dinner, and Phillip knew he wouldn't want to spend just another night sitting with his father by the fire. The kid needed room to come into his own without his father suffocating him with his own loneliness.

He'd seen the same loneliness in Ric, but he hoped he'd grow out of it. Kids were cruel and not even being the king's son protected Ric from their taunts.

Phillip lifted his eyes to find both Alfred and Chandler staring at him, assessing him.

"What?" He took another sip of ale and let his eyes skim the simple furnishings of their home. They lived in a small house in the village just across the river from the palace. A stone fireplace sat cold this time of year. Wooden chairs made a semi-circle around a table. Alfred and Chandler were gone much of the time on missions for the crown. They no longer guarded Phillip. He'd promoted them and given them their own men to command.

When they were gone, Travis stayed at the palace. These men were Phillip and Ric's family, and they protected them as such.

Chandler chewed his lip as if biting back words sitting on his tongue. Alfred didn't have the ability to hold back. "We think you need a queen."

Phillip choked on his ale, letting it dribble down his chin as he coughed and pounded his chest. "Excuse me?" he rasped when he'd finally caught his breath.

Chandler sighed, turning his gaze to Alfred. "I told him you wouldn't like the idea."

"What idea is that exactly?" Phillip couldn't fathom what they meant. He tried to believe they weren't saying what it sounded like.

Alfred didn't stop. He set his ale on the table and leaned forward. "Bela needs a queen."

"Bullshit." Phillip tried to tamp down on the anger rising to the surface, but his magic always made that difficult, and he found himself clenching his teeth. "Bela is in good hands. It has been for the last eighteen years."

"We're not saying it hasn't." Chandler scratched his jaw. "But you, Phillip... you can't keep living like this."

"And how am I living?"

"Like she's coming back." Alfred's words sent ice down Phillip's spine. "You've spent the last eighteen years of your life trying to find something that doesn't exist."

Chandler put a hand on Alfred's arm to stop him and turned sympathetic eyes on Phillip. "What he meant is you're living in the past. There is no way to break the curse."

Alfred shook off his hand. "No, that's not what I meant, or not completely, anyway. You visit her every day. You sit by her bedside and talk to her as if she can hear you. I've even caught Ric doing the same thing. Do you think that's healthy? For the two of you to hold on so tight to a woman who may as well be dead?"

Chandler had the decency to wince at Alfred's words.

Phillip stood and kicked back his chair. He drained the rest of his ale and slammed the mug on the table before leaning forward, both palms pressed against the wood. "And you think I'm going to just what? Move on? Forget? She's my wife."

Alfred's eyes blazed as he stood to face Phillip. "She hasn't been your wife in many years."

Phillip rounded the table before he knew what he was doing and gripped Alfred's shirt. Alfred didn't protest as his king slammed him down against the table.

Phillip's magic begged for release, to be unleashed on any man who spoke about Aurora in such a way. "She will be my wife until the day that I die."

Chandler tensed, ready to step in, but Alfred held up a hand, stopping him.

The fire receded from Alfred's eyes, but the look that replaced it cut deeper. Pity. He looked at Phillip as the rest of the kingdom did. The poor king with all the power in the world. The one who'd been unable to save the woman he loved.

Phillip released Alfred and stepped back, hanging his head. "I don't need your pity, and I don't need a wife."

Alfred rubbed his chest and righted himself. "Think about Ric."

Phillip flipped his palm open, sending his magic toward the door. It burst open, revealing the king's guard standing in the night. He stepped toward them, knowing he had to leave his friends before he said something he couldn't take back. He stopped at the door, not looking back. "I think about my son every damn day of my life."

He'd wanted to say something else, but Travis came running up the path to the house. He stopped in front of Phillip. He bent over to catch his breath, but Phillip didn't mistake it for a bow. He'd always said family didn't bow, and however he felt at the moment about the two men he'd left inside, it didn't change who they were.

"Sire." Travis breathed heavily. "I... the palace... you..."

"Spit it out, boy."

"They're looking for you everywhere at the palace." He tilted his head back to peer up at Phillip. "Something is wrong with the queen. The... uh... sleeping one."

Travis said something else, but Phillip didn't hear him as he charged forward, ordering his horse to be brought to him. Once he mounted up, he thundered across the bridge toward the palace with his guards at his back.

He pulled the horse to a stop inside the gates and jumped down, leaving the others to tend to his horse. He didn't remember running through the palace halls or entering the room, but when he saw Aurora, his heart stopped. Three people crowded around her bed. One of her maids, Phillip's mother, and the palace healer. What was a healer doing here?

He steadied his breathing and walked forward. His

mother was the first to see him. "You're here. Thank the magic."

She reached out to grip his arm and pulled him forward.

"What's going on?" His eyes flicked from the healer to Aurora. He hadn't had a chance to see her that day. A thick sheen of sweat coated every inch of skin, dampening her hair.

She moaned, and Phillip jumped forward to grip her clammy hand.

The healer continued examining her. "I can't seem to find the cause of the sickness, your Majesty."

"Sickness?" He swallowed.

The healer, a short balding man with a round stomach, nodded. "Her skin is hot to the touch, and her heart is beating faster than it should. I have some herbs that may help, but I'm afraid there isn't much I can do. Her body will need to fight this off."

Fear surged through him. Aurora was sick, and they didn't know why.

The door burst open again and Ric appeared, looking as if he hadn't slept in days. Dark circles hung under his red-rimmed eyes, and his wild blond hair lay skewed across his forehead. He walked forward with a slow gait and stopped beside his father. As he looked at Aurora, Phillip saw his own worry mirrored in his son's eyes.

"I just heard." He shook his head. "I was sleeping."

Phillip studied his son. "You don't look like you've slept at all."

"It's the dreams. They're not exactly restful."

Hope stirred in Phillip. "Do you think you could enter your mother's dreams again? Maybe you can find some answers."

"I'm sorry, Father." Something deflated inside Phillip.

"You know I can't control them. Lately, I'm only dreaming of one girl."

Phillip clasped his son's shoulder for a moment before sitting on the edge of the bed.

The healer finished his examination and rubbed sweet-smelling herbs on Aurora's skin.

He left and the maid and Phillip's mother went with him after promising they'd check in on Aurora soon.

Ric dropped into the chair by the bed and leaned his head back.

"You should go back to bed, Son. You look as if you might drop. I'm not leaving your mother and will let you know any changes."

Ric fixed his father with a stubborn stare he'd perfected over his teenage years. "I'm not leaving her either."

Relief flooded through Phillip. He hadn't admitted to himself just how much he needed his son. Alfred and Chandler were wrong. He wasn't alone, and he didn't need to move on. He only needed his family.

Phillip didn't know if Aurora could sense what was happening to her in her slumber, but he imagined she was afraid. He pulled the covers from her heated skin and lay down beside her, pulling her soft body into his arms.

He fixed his eyes on his son who'd already fallen asleep beside the bed and spoke softly into Aurora's ear. "We're here. Don't be afraid. You're going to be okay."

As he fell asleep, he imagined he was back at the cottage with her. She'd wake in the morning to give him a face-splitting grin, sending his heart hammering. Then she'd argue with him about something—usually because she was right. They'd talk and make love. And at the end of the day, he'd know she'd still be with him come tomorrow.

He couldn't shake Alfred or Chandler's words. Aurora

would never be dead to him. Not when she was right there. Not when some small part of his heart still hoped he'd see her beautiful eyes again. But maybe his friends were right about that too. He'd searched for eighteen years, consulting every book, every powerful magic wielder in Bela. Maybe there was no way to save her.

And if not, all he could do was make sure she had a good life to wake up to. He'd be long gone, but he'd make sure she was taken care of as long as he could.

CHAPTER TWENTY-FOUR

PHILLIP

Aurora didn't get better. Each day she drifted further and further from the people who loved her. The skin on her bones turned ashen. Her face lost its roundness. And still, they had no answers.

The healer looked up from where he was bent over the girl who no longer looked like she was in a serene slumber. Instead, pain coated her features.

"There's a fever going through the village." He sighed. "Many have died. I don't know what to do for Aurora. I'm very sorry to say she won't last much longer."

Phillip could barely process the words the healer said and didn't notice when the man left. Dying. Aurora was dying. No. She was supposed to live a full life when she finally woke. She was supposed to get to experience the wonders of the world and maybe meet her grandchildren and great grandchildren.

Phillip sank to his knees beside the bed, his legs unable to support him any longer. He stared into Aurora's pale face, knowing he'd failed her once more.

A sob lodged in his throat and no tears fell. He'd given everything to her and there was nothing left. No piece of his heart remained to be broken further.

He didn't know how long he stayed there. Hours? A day? Four strong hands gripped his arms and hauled him to his feet before Alfred and Chandler wrapped their arms around him. They were there, despite the fact that he hadn't spoken to them since their conversation at their home.

Their embrace was so like the first night he'd lost Aurora, he found himself pushing away from them.

Alfred rubbed the back of his neck. "We just heard."

Chandler tried to reach for Phillip again, but Phillip stepped back. "We're so sorry, Phil."

If they'd heard... Wulfric. Phillip stumbled to the door, not wanting his son to hear the prognosis from anyone but him.

He'd been selfish, grieving when he should have been thinking of his son. He was keenly aware of Alfred and Chandler following him. When he got to Ric's rooms, they stayed in the hall, something he was grateful for.

He didn't know what he'd expected. Maybe to find Ric crying, worried about his mother. Instead, as he pushed through the door, he came to a stop, seeing Ric rushing around the room shoving clothes and other essentials into a sack. He only gave Phillip a quick glance before continuing what he was doing.

Phillip crossed his arms. "Where do you think you're going?"

"Don't worry about it."

Phillip caught the back of Ric's shirt and pulled him to a stop. "Don't worry about it? Do you know what is happening in this palace right now? It isn't the time for one of your adventures."

Ric pulled his shirt free. "Of course I know. That's why I'm going."

"You're the prince of Bela. I've let this go on long enough. You can't just run off."

When Ric finally turned his eyes on his father, they swam with unsaid emotions. "Mother is dying. Travis heard it from the healer's son. Are you going to tell me it isn't true?"

Phillip blew out a breath, barely able to control the sadness swirling inside him. "She's very sick." As he said the words, his shoulders fell. He walked farther into the room and sat on the corner of Ric's bed. "I'm so sorry."

"Why?" Ric came to a stop in front of Phillip, forcing him to look up. "Why are you sorry? Did you make her sick? This isn't your fault. Stop blaming yourself and just let me go."

"I can't do that."

"Father—"

"No." Phillip hardened his tone and his magic buzzed along his skin. He released it to latch the door. "You're not leaving this room."

"Please, you don't understand."

"I do understand. You want to run away, to be alone to deal with your grief. Your grandmother and I are cut from the same cloth as you, kid. I've seen it all before. Hell, I've felt it all before. But being alone doesn't solve anything. We're going to lose her. No amount of running will change that."

"But, Father, I can save her."

Phillip's eyes snapped to his son's, and he swore his heart stopped beating entirely. "What are you on about, boy?"

Ric dropped onto the bed beside him and put his head in his hands. "It's these dreams. Sometimes they're trying to tell me things, other times they're useless. I can't usually tell the difference, but this time..." He shook his head. "It doesn't matter. You'll never believe me. Everyone in Bela just thinks their prince sees pretty pictures in his head. Sometimes, I think that's all my magic is too."

Phillip placed two fingers under Ric's chin and tilted his head up so their gazes locked. "Tell me and I promise I'll believe you."

Ric's body shook as a sob escaped his throat. Relief washed over his face for an instant before it was gone. "There's a girl. You wondered why I look like I never sleep, and it's because I see her every time I close my eyes. The things that are happening to her. I know I need to save her."

"I don't understand how you think this can save Aurora."

Ric breathed in deeply. "I was getting to that. In the very first dream I had of her, she was hurt. I watched her heal herself, Father."

"There has never been a Belaen with healing magic. It isn't possible."

Ric's eyes darkened. "She isn't Belaen. She lives in the palace of Dracon."

A tremor shot through Phillip. Dracon. La Dame's kingdom. He'd only met La Dame once before, but everyone knew the stories. She was powerful enough to curse Aurora to one hundred years of slumber.

Realization slapped Phillip in the face. "You were going there? To Dracon." If La Dame got her hands on the prince of Bela, who knew what she'd do to him.

Ric wrung his hands in his lap. "I thought you'd stop me, and I need to do this. I can't explain it, but it's like my magic is directing me to go. If she can help Mother, isn't it worth the risk?"

There was a time he'd have said yes. Aurora was worth any risk. He'd give up his life to save her, but his son?

"I know what you're thinking." Ric stood and faced him. "You don't want to put me in danger, but don't I have a right to decide for myself? I'm almost eighteen, Father. A man. And my mother is dying. You'd do anything for her. Don't I get to do the same?"

Phillip wanted to say no. He wanted to keep Ric in that room, bound by magic, while he went in search of this healer himself. But his son was right. He knew his own mind, and he had to do this.

Phillip assessed his son and crossed his arms. "I assume Travis is preparing the horses?"

A guilty look flashed across Ric's face. "I wouldn't have let him enter Dracon with me. I swear."

"Tell him we need three extra horses."

Ric's brow shot up in surprise.

"I'm coming with you." Phillip got to his feet. "We're going to save your mother." He gripped his son's shoulder, and it sagged in relief.

"You really believe me?" His eyes glassed over.

"Of course I do. You're my son."

Ric nodded, releasing a shuddering breath before jerking his eyes to Phillip's. "Three horses?"

Phillip walked to the door. "There are two men probably pressing their ears against this door right now who won't let us get far without them." He pulled open the door and both Alfred and Chandler stumbled in.

Phillip only raised a brow. "Gather whatever you need. We're going to Dracon." He glanced back at Ric. "My son is going to lead us to the woman who can help Aurora."

IN PHILLIP BASILE'S thirty-eight years, he'd only ever stood at the base of the Draconian walls once before. It was a two-day ride from the palace, but that wasn't why he'd stayed away. A large swath of land on the Belaen side sat wild and untouched. His people hadn't settled there with the foreboding air hanging over the place.

Phillip's father rarely spoke of Bela's neighbor except to issue short warnings about La Dame. Bela's focus for many decades had been on keeping the armies of Gaule from overwhelming Bela.

There was a major difference between Gaule and Dracon, though. Dracon had magic. It was less densely populated than Bela, but beyond that, they knew little of the people who resided there. No one knew how their magic functioned or why they blindly followed the ancient sorceress.

Phillip's gaze wandered up the stone structure that seemed to reach all the way to the sky. There was only one person who could manage to get people across that threshold without an invitation. There would be no walking through the gates for them. La Dame would welcome them only as prisoners.

Memories assaulted Phillip. La Dame appearing at Aurora's cottage. Aurora's pleas with him not to accept her healing. He'd never imagined she wasn't the only one in her kingdom with the ability to heal.

A chill crept into his bones despite the blazing heat of the afternoon sun. It was one thing to say he believed his son's magic had shown him the girl, but now he also had to trust that Ric's power had led them to this very spot.

"I want to be over that wall and hidden within Dracon by the time we lose the light." Phillip turned to his small band of friends. Two middle-aged guards. Despite the chill still existing between them, it calmed Phillip to know they were there.

The two boys, however... neither of them should be in

such danger. He'd been surprised when Chandler allowed Travis to come, but maybe he'd come to the same conclusion as Phillip. They couldn't control the destinies of their sons.

Chandler slid from his horse to join Phillip and lifted his eyes. The sun prevented them from seeing the top of the wall. "Do you think there are guards up there?"

Phillip rubbed his jaw, considering the question. He thought of La Dame and the power emanating from her. "No. She doesn't believe anyone will try to cross her."

"We have to get in there now." Ric's hiss wrapped around them.

"Why?" Phillip asked. He sensed his son's rush wasn't just about his mother's illness.

Ric gripped his head, shaking it from side to side as if in pain. "I don't know," he groaned. "My magic... it senses something."

"That's not much to go on, boy," Alfred groused.

Ric lowered his hands and curled them into fists as his magic got hold of him. Phillip recognized the signs. He was no longer under his own control.

"Ric." He held a hand out, approaching cautiously. "Come back to us. Don't let the magic control you."

Ric's eyes snapped to his. "I can't... it's the only way." His eyes rolled back in his head for a brief moment before the irises were visible again. "The magic is the only way to get to her." He walked to the wall, setting his palms upon it.

Phillip shared a look with Alfred and Chandler and they all watched Ric carefully as he closed his eyes.

"Use the Basile power," Ric whispered, still not returning to them. "To get us over the wall."

Phillip shook his head. "La Dame will know something is wrong."

Ric yanked his hands back from the wall. "She isn't here. I

can feel it. My magic is reaching for her and finding her far across the Gaule border." His entire body sagged with relief. "La Dame is helping them prepare to attack Bela."

Alarm shot through Phillip. Gaule was going to attack, and he'd left. He barely had to look at Chandler before his friend pulled himself into the saddle. "I'll alert the army." He took off without a single command from his king.

If La Dame aided them, Gaule might actually stand a chance. Phillip shook his head. He had a mission to complete. He trusted his generals. With any luck, he'd be able to join them in a few days' time.

This was for Aurora.

"Put your hands on the wall," Ric said, still not sounding like himself.

Phillip didn't question the order. He just obeyed.

"Use your magic to pull the stones." Phillip gained the Basile power when his father died. He'd spent years training with it, molding it, testing it. But what Ric told him to do—or more accurately, what Ric's power told him to do—went against everything he knew of his power. If he pulled the stones, the entire section of wall could rain down upon them.

Ric dropped his voice and Phillip sensed his son coming through. "Father, trust me." Then Ric was gone, and the deep voice of his magic returned. "Pull the stones at the same time you push them back."

So, he did. Phillip focused all his concentration on shifting the stones until they moved and a row of them jutted out, winding up to the top of the wall.

Ric didn't hesitate before starting to climb. He didn't seem to notice the narrow steps or the height.

Phillip went next, hugging the wall and doing his best not to tumble to the ground. Alfred sent Travis before himself.

All Phillip could hear was the wind rushing in his ears

until a scream ripped through the silence. Travis. Phillip whipped his head around in time to see Travis lose his footing and try to grab for the step, his fingers only inches away.

"Travis," Alfred screamed, reaching for him.

Phillip pulled his magic forth, calling on the winds to help him. Travis' body lifted in the air before being slammed back into the wall. Phillip didn't release his magic until he was sure the boy had a stable foothold.

He caught Alfred's wild eyes. Alfred gave him a nod of thanks, and Phillip continued up the steps. Ric hadn't slowed when Travis fell, but Phillip had to remember Ric wasn't the one making the decisions in his mind right now.

They finally made it to the top. Phillip looked at how far they'd come and swallowed. On the other side, the mountains of Dracon stretched before them, snowcapped even in summer. A single road led through the pass without a house in sight. Most of the people of Dracon lived either deep within the mountains or in the central town near the palace. His knowledge of Dracon was basic at best. Phillip learned very little about the kingdom in his studies as a boy and never imagined he'd set foot in the place.

"Come on." Ric led them down the other side of the wall without incident. As soon as they were down, he waved to his father.

Phillip touched the stones to return them to their usual smooth wall face.

He hiked his bag higher on his shoulder, wishing they could have brought the horses. They'd left them roaming on the other side. Belaen beasts knew the land as well as anyone. There was plenty to eat and streams crisscrossed Bela, winding through the woods. They knew how to survive better than humans did in the woods.

And when their king returned, they wouldn't be difficult

to find. They were trained to wait for their riders and wouldn't wander too far.

"Come on." Phillip started down the road, trying not to think of the fact that they now stood within Dracon. "We need to find a place to spend the night." Gray clouds had started rolling in, and he didn't want to get caught in a storm.

They ventured into the wilds of Dracon. Evergreen trees spread up over rolling hills, climbing the side of the nearest mountain. Despite the looming landmass hanging over them, it looked little different from Bela.

CHAPTER TWENTY-FIVE

RIC

Golden hair flowed down the woman's bare back over criss-crossing scars marring her pale skin. Was she a prisoner? She had to be. Ric's eyes twitched beneath closed lids. They'd been inside Dracon for three days now, and the dreams had grown more intense. He couldn't explain it. It was as if the closer he got, the more he could *feel* her rather than only see the images playing in his mind.

His magic wanted to reach out and wrap her in its power. He got the feeling, whoever she was, she wouldn't only save his mother, she'd save all of them. Him. His father. She'd erase the half-life they'd been living and replace it with something... more. Just more.

He had to find her.

A lock rattled, and the girl's head snapped up, her eyes wide but not with fear. There was something else in them. Defiance? Strength? She shifted her naked body back into the shadows and curled in on herself, waiting.

The door open and her body relaxed. A man entered

slowly, cautiously, as if approaching a wild animal. In his hand, he held a bundle of fabric. He extended it to her.

She shook her head, and for the first time, Ric's dream of her included more than images. For the first time, he heard her voice. "I can't take that. La Dame is punishing me for my disobedience. She will clothe me when she returns."

"Rapunzel." The man sighed.

Rapunzel. Rapunzel. Rapunzel.

Her name bounced around Ric's skull until he couldn't hear anything else. He'd wanted to know her name, needed to know it.

They finished their conversation, and Rapunzel finally took the clothes, sliding a woolen dress over her small frame. She jerked her head up, her gaze going past the kind man, and landing on... him?

Ric sat up, panting. For a moment, it had felt like Rapunzel could see him, sense his presence. But that wasn't possible.

He swiped his hand through his damp hair and shrugged off the blanket his father had put on him when he fell asleep beside the fire the night before. He got to his feet, scanning the sleeping forms of the King of Bela, Alfred, and Travis. Three people who shouldn't have followed him and his magic into Dracon. If something happened to them...

So far, their mission had gone without any problems. Most of Dracon was little different than Bela with farm fields and hills rolling up toward the base of the mountains. The population was concentrated in the center, near the massive gates and ominous palace. Ric's magic had led them on an indirect path, taking longer than it should have. They all knew it was to avoid the Draconian patrols, but it was frustrating nonetheless. For the first time, he felt the power he'd been born with had some use, making him more than just a prince who would one day have his father's power.

But, today would be different. Today, they'd venture down the path to the palace of the dark sorceress. Whether she was present or not, it would hold many dangers.

Ric walked far enough from camp to relieve himself in peace. When he returned, his father was awake and busy stirring up the long-dead fire.

Ric sat down beside him with a heavy sigh.

As he prepared breakfast, his father glanced sideways, giving him a long look. "Did you sleep at all last night, Wulfric?"

Ric shrugged and leaned forward against his knees. "Some."

"These dreams..." His father shook his head. "When your magic first became apparent, I didn't understand it. I wanted to, but... dreams like yours aren't even a part of the Basile powers. All I knew was how relieved I was."

"Relieved?" Ric had always assumed his father was disappointed in his power. Phillip Basile was a great general before he ever became king. He'd led Bela's forces and made a name for himself. Wouldn't he want the same for his son? For the prince to be a man Bela could count on?

His father sighed. "I wasn't proud of it. I didn't want you to grow up the way I had. I spent my youth practicing with swords and learning battle tactics. I was fourteen the first time I rode into battle. The things I've seen... I never wanted that for you. It never leaves, like a constant shadow hanging over your life." He paused for a long moment. "And a part of me was relieved I'd never face the same fear as my parents did every time I left home with the army. They never knew if I'd return. I couldn't..." His words cut off.

"Father—"

"No, I need to say this, because I know what you think of your power. I know the trouble you've faced from your peers for having magic with less obvious uses. I didn't want to lose you, Ric. Not like I lost your mother. Not only because you were all I had left of her, but because you were you. My son. The best of me. And now... this magic I thought was so safe has led us to the most dangerous place in the world. I always wanted to keep you safe, and I still do, but I'm also so damn proud of you. You never question your power. You just do whatever you have to."

Ric's eyes shone with unshed tears. His father had never told him he was proud before. Ric knew he was loved, but being loved wasn't enough. He wanted to be the kind of man his father was. He wiped the back of his hand across his eyes. "I love her too, father. I've never seen the color of her eyes. I've never heard her voice or felt her arms around me. But she's my mother. I may never get to meet her, but I won't stop until we're sure she gets her chance at a life—even if it's long after we're gone."

His father put an arm around his shoulders. "I have to believe she knows you. Somehow, you're in her heart too."

He willed his oncoming tears away as Alfred and Travis roused themselves to join them. They ate a breakfast of stale bread and oatmeal. It didn't matter what Ric put in his mouth, he didn't taste any of it. Not with the anticipation of the coming day sending adrenaline racing through his veins. It latched onto his magic until his skin buzzed with energy.

They'd already been gone too long. They needed to return to Bela, to his mother. And today, they would find the woman who could help her.

AN ANGRY BOOM rumbled through the sky as dark clouds kept the sun from lighting the world. As they packed up their camp and made their way into the center of Dracon, heavy rain pelted them, warning them away.

In the early morning storm, shopkeepers struggled to open their stores. People scrambled to get in out of the rain, including the town guards who ducked into taverns for protection.

Only Ric and his companions braved the torrential weather, doing their best to appear as if they belonged.

Ric stayed alert. On either side of him, his father and Alfred walked, their postures tense, ready for an attack that never came. They were worried when Ric's magic wanted to lead them straight through the center of town, but it had known what it was doing.

Outside the market square, the Draconian roads jutted out like spokes on a wheel, meandering into different parts of the kingdom. Ric stood still for a moment, waiting for his magic to tell him which one led to the palace.

It didn't take long before the familiar pull had him turning to one of the roads on the right, like a compass needle leading him to their destination. "Ready for this?" he shouted over the thunderous storm. Rapunzel's kind eyes flashed in his mind and whatever his father said, he didn't hear. He took the first step, having an odd sense they were running out of time.

He picked up the pace, only slowing when a structure came into view. "The palace," he breathed. The home of the dark sorceress was carved right into the side of a mountain, its onyx stones standing stark against the snow-tipped backdrop. Two spires stretched up toward the sky, looming over the road below.

Ric's heart hammered against his ribs as he tried to regain the breath the sight stole from him.

"Shit." Alfred's one word wrapped around them, encompassing everything they felt.

Travis whistled, fear sparking in his eyes. Ric hadn't asked him if he regretted coming, but the boy had barely spoken since almost falling from the wall. Maybe it was the general aura of Dracon keeping him quiet. Ric didn't know. All he knew was it was unlike his friend.

Ric's father was a silent presence at his side, because he understood. This place deserved no words.

Ric started forward at the urging of his magic. Common sense told him to wait, to search for guard locations, to scout for the best entry, but his magic knew the way.

His father shot out a hand to hold him back. "What are you doing, son? We need a plan. I can probably get us into one of the upper windows if I do the same trick with the stones as I did on the wall."

He closed his eyes, picturing Rapunzel's face. Shaking his head, he pulled his arm out of his father's grip. "Father, do you trust me?"

"Always."

"Then I need to do this alone."

"Don't be absurd, Wulfric." Alfred clenched his jaw. "I didn't come all this way just to abandon my prince when he needed it the most."

Ric didn't know why a strain still existed between his father and Alfred, but the words from the latter had his father staring at his friend in gratitude. Ric didn't have time to dwell on their problems. He only knew he needed to get into that palace.

"Please." He set pleading eyes on his father. "I have to do this."

"The girl," his father started. "The one who can save your

mother... she's in there? This is about her? What if La Dame finds you?"

Ric shook his head. "La Dame isn't here. Remember? She's busy stirring up trouble in Gaule. I don't know what's going to happen, Father, but my magic hasn't led us wrong yet."

Alfred scrubbed his jaw. "Magic isn't supposed to lead." He was right. Belaens spent their lives learning to control their power, to keep it from controlling them. It was a living thing, but it was still owned, chained to the user. Ric's magic somehow managed to become him rather than only a part of him. Maybe he was weak to let it, but he didn't think so. It took strength and courage to follow where it led.

His father released a groan. "I can't believe I'm sending my son into that place alone."

"I won't be alone, Father." Because she would be there.

After a thick beat of silence, his father issued a single nod and gestured for Alfred and Travis to fall back into the trees lining the road, concealing them from any passersby.

Finally, Ric stood alone.

He could do this. No subterfuge. No stealing into the palace. His magic pulled him up the path until he stood within sight of the guards.

They lurched forward at the sight of him. "Who goes there?"

Ric swallowed back the words on the tip of his tongue, giving in to the power of his magic. It swelled up in him, taking control. "I am here to rescue a girl."

With matching growls, the guards reached for him. It took everything in him not to struggle as they gripped his arms. He clamped his lips shut to keep from crying out as an armor-clad knee connected to his stomach.

He doubled over as a jeweled hilt flashed before his face, smashing into the side of his head and sending him tumbling into the dark abyss.

CHAPTER TWENTY-SIX

PHILLIP

It took everything in Phillip not to run after his son when he saw the guards grab him. He wanted to fight off anyone who dreamed of hurting his boy.

But Ric asked for his trust. He saw the way he refused to fight back as if he'd known getting into the palace would require that sacrifice from him.

Phillip paced back and forth among the trees, cursing under his breath. He clenched his fists as his magic tried to rise, latching onto his anger. Pushing it back down, he sat with his back against the wide base of an ancient oak tree.

Were some of these trees as old as La Dame? He didn't know her true age or how long she'd ruled Dracon, only that she'd stolen the power from her own father and never relinquished it. She was an unbeatable force. All he'd ever been able to do was try his best to protect Bela from her.

But Bela didn't seem to be in her sights. It never had been. So, why was she currently convincing Gaule to attack? She had to know Gaule stood no chance in a fight against Bela.

Not unless La Dame herself joined the fight, and that wasn't her style.

He tipped his head back against the tree, letting the rain wash down his face. It slowed to no more than a drizzle, but the coolness felt good on his burning skin. His body barely noticed his soaking clothes. When they camped that night, they'd have no dry blankets. Even their food could be ruined, but he didn't open his sack to check. He couldn't seem to care about anything other than what was possibly happening to Wulfric.

Alfred's muddy boots stopped at Phillip's side. "I can't believe you'd let your son go in there alone."

Phillip peered up at his friend, the one who'd barely said two words to him in days. Yet, he was still here. He'd still come to face the dangers at Phillip's side.

"Ric wanted this."

Alfred dropped down beside him. "So? He's just a boy for magic's sake. I don't care if he's a prince or some bastard Gaulean, he shouldn't have been allowed to venture into that place on his own."

Phillip couldn't respond to that because he didn't disagree. Ric shouldn't have been allowed to go. Yet, he'd let him, anyway. He'd looked into his son's face, so sure, so confident, and been unable to deny him. Ric gave him hope they'd cure Aurora of whatever illness threatened her life, so Phillip hadn't argued.

He sighed. "Alfred, I know you don't agree with any of my decisions these days, but keep in mind that I am your king."

"I've never forgotten who you are, Phillip. I just always thought you were my friend before my ruler."

"That's not what I meant and you know it." He rubbed his tired eyes. "We've been through a lot together over the years and yet, one argument changes us."

Alfred rested his forearms on his bent knees. "Because I'm an idiot. I know you still love her. Sometimes I think it would be easier if she were truly gone. Then you could let go." He put up a hand to cut off Phillip's words of protest. "That doesn't mean I wish it were so."

"I don't want to let go."

"I know. It's just hard for us to see both you and Ric keeping parts of yourself back from the rest of the kingdom because you think they belong to her."

"They do. We both belong to her. Every bit of us."

"But you also belong to us, Phil. To Bela and also to the people who care about you."

Phillip shifted his eyes away. "I know. Sometimes I wish I was with her in slumber; that I'd wake in the future when she did, and we could live our lives together. But then, I look at my son, and the guilt nearly kills me. I know I can't keep living for a future I'll never see. I just don't know how to move forward."

"You'll figure it out when you're ready."

His shoulders dropped. "I think I am. Or, I need to be. You're right, my kingdom deserves all of me. I need to find the man I was." His voice grew quiet. "Maybe Bela does deserve a queen. Maybe the Basile power deserves more heirs."

The words physically hurt to say, but it didn't make them untrue.

Alfred grew quiet, and Phillip's mind drifted to his son as he tried not to imagine what was being done to him. They'd give it until nightfall, and if Ric didn't return, he'd storm the palace, using his magic to tear it apart stone by stone.

Alfred's panicked voice broke through his thoughts. "Where's Travis?" It was only then Phillip noticed the boy was gone.

He didn't need to answer Alfred's question because they both knew Travis too well.

He'd gone after Wulfric.

CHAPTER TWENTY-SEVEN

RIC

Pounding pain throbbed through Ric's skull and his eyelids held a weight that made them nearly impossible to open. He groaned low in his throat and rolled over, expecting to find himself lying on hard stone. Instead, a plush bed surrounded him.

He pried his eyes open to see the lavish surroundings. A red velvet canopy hung over the bed. An orange glow from the flickering flames in the hearth lit the room. Where was he? As he struggled to sit and swing his legs over the edge, his entire body ached.

The events of his welcome into the palace of Dracon came back to him. Heavy booted guards. Pleading with his father to go alone. Why had he done that?

Was he a prisoner?

Bela certainly didn't keep their prisoners in such luxury.

The door opened, and he fought the urge to hide under the blankets and pretend to still be sleeping. He needed answers.

A young man, probably only a few years older than Ric

himself, entered cautiously. A ripped tunic hung off his thin frame. Dark stubble coated his dirty cheeks. He carried a tray in and set it on a table across the room from Ric.

He arranged the teapot and cups on the tray and stepped back before facing Ric, his eyes wary. "I've been ordered to prepare you, Basile." He said the last name like it was a curse. Was the ruling family of Bela as hated in Dracon as they were in Gaule?

"Prepare me for what?" Ric's legs shook under him as he got to his feet.

"To meet her."

"Who?" He had to know.

A sly smile spread across the man's face. "La Dame's daughter." He walked toward the door.

"Wait," Ric called. "Who are you?"

The man stopped, his back to Ric. "My name is Renauld Durand." He left without another word.

Ric wanted to call him back, to get answers. He'd said he had to prepare him and just left. Renauld Durand? He'd said it so plainly, no trace of duplicity in his voice. But it wasn't possible. Was it?

Renauld Durand was the prince of Gaule who died in battle. Ric had heard the stories many times. He was the eldest of the Durand princess; the heir to the throne.

That man couldn't be him. Ric rubbed his face. He'd said Basile with all the contempt a Durand would feel. They were enemies of the most vicious kind.

For the first time since realizing he needed to enter the palace alone, he wished his father was there. He'd know what to do. Would he have to fight his way out?

La Dame wasn't here... but her daughter? Was she just as cruel, just as powerful?

Ric pushed down the fear trying to rise and instead,

closed his eyes and sank into the power of his magic. He didn't know when he'd lain back down or how he'd fallen asleep, but Rapunzel's image wouldn't go away. He had to get away from La Dame's daughter somehow and find her.

The dream faded and this time, when he woke, the headache was gone. He took stock of every ache, every pain, grateful for them because it was how he knew he still lived. He'd made it into the palace of the dark sorceress alive.

For now.

When he opened his eyes, he sucked in a breath. Maybe he wasn't awake after all, because standing before him, was the girl he hadn't been able to get off his mind.

Rapunzel wore an elaborate purple gown that flared out at the hips. Her long golden hair wound around the crown of her head.

As she looked at him, her kind eyes widened, and her small mouth fell open. "You," she breathed.

Ric shook his head. "I'm still dreaming. I have to be."

She shook her head and continued to stare.

Uncomfortable under the heat of her gaze, Ric pushed himself from the bed and stood. He lost complete control of his actions, but it wasn't the magic this time, only his heart. He crossed the space between them in three paces and pulled her into his arms, claiming her lips in a searing kiss.

A squeak escaped from her, but her surprise morphed into contentment as she responded to his touch. She flattened her palms against his chest as if needing to just feel him.

Ric's magic hummed in approval. His mind worked furiously, trying to convince him he couldn't just kiss a woman he didn't know. But he didn't care. She was the one he saw every time he closed his eyes. He'd watched her be punished by La Dame and been unable to help. He'd seen her scared and imprisoned.

And now, she stood before him, a symbol of everything he needed. Maybe the knowledge was from his magic or maybe something else, but he knew she was going to change the course of his life.

Finally, she pulled away, putting a sliver of distance between them.

Ric's mind caught up with him. "I'm sorry." He stepped back and ran a hand over the top of his head. "I shouldn't have done that."

She touched her lips. "No." Shaking her head, she moved around him to the tray Renauld had brought. "Would you like some tea?"

Not talking about it. Okay. He could do that. He breathed in deeply and turned to see how her hands shook as she held out a cup toward him.

A thought struck him. "We can't. That was brought for La Dame's daughter."

Rapunzel let her eyes fall to the ground, shame coating her features. "I am La Dame's daughter."

The knowledge struck Ric like a bludgeon. No. She couldn't be. How could the kind healer he'd been dreaming of share blood with the dark sorceress? "But... I saw you. She dragged you across a cavern. She threw you naked in a cell."

Rapunzel's shoulders dropped. "Mother..." She sighed. "I disobey her sometimes."

Disobey? Hell, when he disobeyed his father, he was only confined to his luxurious rooms. He fell into a chair, not saying a word and unable to look at her again.

Rapunzel seemed to understand he wasn't going to take the tea. She set the cup down and lowered herself gracefully into another high-backed chair. She sat regally, as atop a throne.

Because she's royal, he reminded himself. *Just like you.*

But she wasn't just like him. He already knew that.

Silence stretched between them for a long moment before she spoke. "Don't worry about your friend. We're keeping him in comfort as well."

"My friend?" Alarm shot through him.

She nodded. "The young one."

Travis. His heart dropped. The boy had followed him like he had so many times before. But this wasn't like before. This time, the danger was too real. Ric leaned forward, his voice lowering to dangerous levels. "If you harm him..."

Defiance entered her gaze. "You'll what? Call in your father to use his Basile magic against us? You wouldn't be able to get to him in time. No, Wulfric Basile, you are very much at my mercy."

"What are you going to do with me?"

Her words were so at odds with what he thought he'd known of her.

She reached for her tea, but he got the impression it was only to have something to do with her hands. After taking a sip, she set it aside again. "I saw you." Her voice was so quiet he almost missed it.

"What?"

She kept her eyes trained on the table. "Watching me." Her hands shook in her lap as her voice quaked.

All the irritation he'd felt drained out of him, and he couldn't help but go to her, kneeling in front of her. He dipped his head to meet her downturned gaze and set his hands on her knees.

She should have pulled away from his familiarity. Most women would have. They didn't know each other. Not really. But his magic tingled along his skin, alighting at her nearness. He pushed the power away, not wanting it to cloud his true feelings. From the moment he'd first seen her, he'd been drawn to Dracon. Whether his mother had fallen ill or not, he knew he'd have come.

"Rapunzel." His voice was soft. "Are you a prisoner here?"

She sniffed. "When my mother is here, I have... restrictions. But when she isn't, I run the house. The people obey me. That is the only reason you're alive. The guards are trained to deal with intruders efficiently."

"You saved me?" He didn't know what to think of this woman. "But you're the dark sorceress' daughter."

She nodded. "I love my mother, but the darkness doesn't call to me, Wulfric. You do."

Her words struck him straight in the heart. His eyes darted to her lips, watching her tongue dart out to wet them. He wanted to kiss her again, but he couldn't. He refused to forget where he was or why he was there. He gave her leg a squeeze and rose to return to his chair. "Can you do me a favor?"

She nodded.

"Call me Ric."

One corner of her mouth tipped up. "Only if you do something for me, Ric."

"Anything." The word slipped out on a breath before he could call it back.

"Tell me why you're really here."

CHAPTER TWENTY-EIGHT

RIC

Before Ric could give Rapunzel an answer, Renauld appeared, a tray of sweet meats and cheeses in his hands.

Rapunzel's expression softened when she saw him. "Thank you."

Renauld only nodded before setting the tray down and leaving the way he'd come.

Ric watched him until he shut the door, blocking himself from view. "Is that really the supposedly dead Gaulean prince?"

Rapunzel sighed. "My mother found him on the battlefield, healed him, and brought him here. Like me, he cannot leave."

Ric didn't understand. "Why can't you leave?"

"Have you ever heard the stories of La Dame's curses?"

Ric's blood froze in his veins. La Dame's curses. Like the one keeping his mother from being a part of his life. He opened his mouth to speak, but no words came, so he only nodded.

Rapunzel sighed as if the mention of the curses was only

an annoyance. She blew out a breath. "Both Renauld and I have my mother's magic tying us to this palace. If we were to attempt leaving, we'd end up right back here, but with a considerable amount of pain." Her eyes shuttered as if she was trying to keep her emotions in check.

Ric didn't know how a mother could keep her own daughter chained. He'd seen the cruelty of the curses with his own eyes. Hell, he lived that cruelty every time he watched his mother in her slumber. The only thing he'd ever wanted in life was for her to open her eyes.

He swallowed thickly, knowing the next question could change everything. "Is there... a way to break the curse?"

Rapunzel didn't look at him as she rose from her chair. "You have not answered my initial question about your reason for coming to a place that very well could have been your end, but it does not matter. You will be leaving before nightfall. I don't need Phillip Basile trying to destroy my home." She paused, her hand hovering over the door handle. "I'll see you in your dreams, Prince Wulfric."

Before he got another word in, she was gone.

RIC WAITED for Rapunzel to return. He ate more of the cheese and meat than he probably should have. Not out of any sense of hunger, only nervousness.

The silence hung over the room, only punctuated by the soft crackle of the fire. He padded across the stone floor to stand before the flames, desperately needing warmth to thaw his chilled bones. He didn't know if the palace was cold, or if the ice he felt was due to the dark aura surrounding the place.

The luxuries didn't fool him. The Draconian palace was

not a place of comfort and peace. When its mistress walked the halls, he wondered at the fear that must choke the air.

Closing his eyes, he once again pictured the desperate girl, staring at her mother with tear-filled eyes as the woman who was supposed to love her turned her magic on her; as she punished her for some perceived slight. What kind of life was that? To live under constant threat?

The Rapunzel he'd seen in his dreams had more fire in her than the one who'd stood in this very room. Where was that girl? He touched his lips, not quite believing they'd ever touched hers. For the first time in his life, he'd felt the emptiness inside him begin to fill.

And now, she wanted to turn him away.

It was probably a good thing. If he didn't return soon, his father would do something he couldn't take back. The name Phillip Basile was feared throughout the six kingdoms, his power revered. But where La Dame's immense power held a darkness, Phillip Basile's was only light.

The door opened, and he turned from the fire to find Travis in the company of Renauld Durand. Ignoring the Gaulean prince, Ric rushed to Travis and gripped his shoulders. "Idiot." He checked him over for wounds. "Are you okay? Did they hurt you?"

Renauld bristled at that. "You think Rapunzel would allow a boy to be harmed while her mother was away?"

The prince of Gaule disappeared many years ago. How long had he been in Dracon? How well did he know Rapunzel?

Jealousy clouded Ric's vision as his magic begged for anger. He advanced on Renauld. "I don't know what happens in this place." He stopped moving and grit his teeth. "All I know is an evil lurks within these walls. You are a supposedly dead prince who is now dressed in rags. I saw you... when

Rapunzel sat in her cell. You clothed her, yet I don't know why she was in there. I don't understand any of this."

Renauld crossed his arms over his chest. "Rapunzel and I... we look after each other."

There was that jealousy again. He'd spent so much time dreaming of her, but Rapunzel would never be his. He didn't know if he could save the girl his magic begged him to save.

Did she want to be free?

Ric put an arm around Travis' shoulder, in part to comfort him and in part because sleep closed in on Ric, his magic wanting to dream. His knees buckled, but before they hit stone, strong hands gripped him, guiding him to the bed.

He didn't hear Renauld's panicked words as he drifted into his dreams.

This time, he didn't see Rapunzel as she was now. The image morphed into that of a young girl following at the heels of the sorceress, pulled along by her magic.

La Dame reached behind her and gripped her arm, yanking her to the ground.

The girl didn't cry out. She didn't weep. Instead, she lifted her eyes to her mother, mouthing the words 'I'm sorry.'

La Dame's voice boomed out. "You will never run away again, child. My magic will keep you here until the end of your days."

Still, the young girl didn't cry. "Yes, Mother." She lowered her gaze.

Ric wanted to go to her, to hold her and erase the resigned expression on her face. Had that been how his mother felt when she first learned of her fate? He'd never considered what life must have been like for Aurora Rose Brynhild, destined to fall into slumber. He'd only thought about what it did to his father, to him. Phillip Basile lost her. Ric never had her. But their loss was sudden. Aurora's loss stretched on for her entire life as she prepared herself for the curse.

Ric couldn't leave Dracon without Rapunzel, and it no longer had anything to do with saving the dream girl. No, he couldn't let his mother down. She'd lived a sad life because of Rapunzel's mother.

When he woke from his dream, night had fallen. He bolted up in bed. Too late. His father would come.

Travis sat dozing in a chair by the fire. To Ric's surprise, Rapunzel had returned. She stared into the flames as if they held every answer she desperately needed.

She must have sensed him awake because she began to speak in a soft voice. "You were supposed to have left by now. Yet, here you are."

"I was dreaming of you."

Her shoulder's tensed. "Your dream is going to bring the Basile power down on my home."

"Home or prison?"

She sighed. "I don't know."

"My mother is sick." The words hurt to say, but something in him needed to tell her. "You asked me why I'm here. She's going to die."

"Aurora Brynhild." Rapunzel said the name with a reverence that surprised Ric.

"You know of her?"

"She carries one of my mother's favorite curses."

"I've never heard of any other people who bore my mother's sleeping curse."

Rapunzel rubbed the back of her neck. "I didn't say she'd used it again. Aurora is the only one. One day, many years from now, my mother dreams of having Aurora at her side."

"My mother would never stand by La Dame."

Rapunzel finally turned to look at him. "One hundred

years of slumber changes a person. Everyone she knew before will be long gone when she wakes. It will be enough to drive a person insane. You think the slumber was the worst part of the curse, but you cannot imagine what the waking will be like for her. Maybe death would be a better alternative."

Ric averted his eyes unable to look at her. He'd thought he knew her. They'd never spoken in his dreams, yet some part of him felt a connection, one he thought gave an insight into who this girl was.

But he'd just been a stupid boy infatuated with a dream of saving his mother. "My mother deserves better than a death she doesn't even know has arrived."

Rapunzel leaned forward, seeking the warmth of the flames. "You don't even know your mother."

Ric growled, advancing toward her. Renauld stepped into his path as if afraid Ric would try to hurt Rapunzel. Ric didn't know what he'd been about to do, but never that. She hadn't been wrong. He loved his mother with everything he had, but he didn't know her.

At that thought, he retreated and sank onto the corner of the bed. Travis roused himself and joined him, lowering his voice. "I'm sorry I followed you when you wanted to come alone."

Ric only nodded. As much as he wished Travis was safe outside the walls, he was glad to have an ally beside him now. His gaze fell on Renauld Durand who hovered protectively over Rapunzel. What had the two of them been through together? He was a prisoner as well, yet he seemed to trust her.

Ric rubbed his eyes. "Please." His voice broke. "Just... tell me what I need to do to convince you to help me. Anything. I'll do anything." He settled his eyes on Rapunzel who'd turned to watch him. "Death may be a mercy, you're right.

But I can't let her go. It's going to destroy us. My father... he won't survive."

Rapunzel shared a glance with Renauld. "And what makes you think that isn't what we want? Phillip Basile is the enemy of Dracon and Gaule. We should want him to fall apart."

Ric released a shaky breath as he met her eyes. "Do you know me, Rapunzel? Because I dreamed of you every night. I saw you at your worst. I saw your strength. They were only dreams, but—"

"They were real," she finished. "Very real." Her crystal eyes shone. "Living in this place, I don't always know what's good, what's right. But you, Wulfric Basile, I never questioned." She met Renauld's eyes again. "We say it time and again, but we are not our parents."

Renauld Durand was the eldest son of the cruel king of Gaule. The king who sent his people to the slaughter each time he challenged the magic wielders of Bela, knowing they'd never truly win. He was known to torture his prisoners and enjoy doing it.

And Rapunzel's mother... well, there was no explanation needed for La Dame. She was just evil.

Renauld sighed. "I can't believe I'm going to help a Belaen prince."

Rapunzel smiled at that, but it fell almost as quickly. "We lied to you, Wulfric. There's a way to break the curse my mother has laid upon us."

Renauld gripped her shoulder in support, and she put her hand over his.

Ric jumped to his feet. "Then let's do it quickly before my father comes in search of us."

She didn't respond immediately as she weighed her words. Finally, she straightened her spine and locked her gaze on Ric. "The only way to break our curses is…" She stopped, closing her eyes. "We have to die."

DIE? Ric couldn't breathe. No, the golden-haired girl he'd dreamed of couldn't die. He needed her.

Rapunzel swallowed thickly. "Our hearts must stop beating in order to loosen the magic tied to us."

"But…" Ric shook his head. "If you die—"

"We can come back." Rapunzel stood and crossed the room, stopping in front of him again.

He wanted to kiss her. More than anything. Even if it was just to stop these insane words from leaving her mouth. No one could come back from the dead.

Travis didn't seem to have the same trouble speaking as Ric did. "If you could do this, then why didn't you before? You both could have been free."

Renauld was the one who answered. "There's no guarantee it will work. It's only a theory. If we try this, we may very well never open our eyes again."

Ric didn't understand. "And yet you're willing to try? Just so you can travel to Bela and save my mother?"

Rapunzel reached out with both hands and gripped Ric's shoulders with strong fingers. "We have requirements."

"Requirements?"

"She means demands." Renauld crossed his arms.

Rapunzel ran a hand up the curve of Ric's neck until it grazed across his cheek. "I knew you'd come, yet didn't want to hope. When you first arrived early this morning, I wouldn't have considered breaking our curses. It's dangerous, but that isn't the reason. Renauld and I… we have nowhere to go that will be safe from La Dame. But, then you told me about your mother, and I realized a deal could be made."

"A deal." Ric's brow creased.

She ran her thumb over his lip before pulling it back. "I will cure your mother. You will guarantee our safety. Not only mine. You must promise the protection of the Basile magic for a Durand prince."

Ric took a step away from her, shaking his head to try to clear it. It went against everything he'd ever known to consider a Durand anything but his enemy. "Why can't he return to his father?"

Renauld's jaw clenched. "You think the Basile's are my father's greatest enemy, but you're wrong. On the day that I supposedly died, I'd gathered part of the army to abandon the fight. I only wanted to return them to their families. The idea wasn't mine though. I'd broken ranks at the suggestion of La Dame. My father was the one who shot me full of arrows before La Dame found me. Before you make this promise, you must understand. If my father learns I am alive, he will come for me. He won't stop until I am truly dead."

Rapunzel placed her hands on her hips and directed her voice to Ric. "I will come. I will help you. But you must protect Renauld even if it brings the hordes of Gaule down on Bela. Are you prepared for that?"

Ric thought of Chandler and the message he carried with him to Bela. Gaule was already coming for them. But Bela was strong. It could withstand anything. He stuck out a hand toward Renauld. "Okay."

Renauld hesitated only a moment before clasping his hand and nodding. "Okay."

Travis bounced nervously on the balls of his feet. "Now what?"

Rapunzel met his gaze. "Now we break the curse." She

walked toward the bed. "Renauld will be first because I will need to bring him back."

"Can you really bring someone back to life?" Ric asked. Not even the Basile power could do that.

"Well, no." Rapunzel smoothed the blanket on the bed. "I only need his heart to stop for a moment. He won't truly die if I act quickly enough. That's the danger. If I'm too late, I won't be able to heal him." She pulled a vile out of the bosom of her dress.

Ric's eyes widened. "You planned this. When you came back to this room. You didn't need me to convince you at all."

She only shrugged. "Renauld, lay on the bed."

He did as she asked, his pulse visibly pounding in his neck.

Ric wiped sweaty palms on his trousers as nerves set in. What were they doing?

"Oleander oil," Rapunzel explained to Renauld as she uncapped the vial and held it against his lips. "The effects will be instant. Your heart will slow. There will be pain in your stomach. I'm sorry about that. As soon as my magic feels the last beat in your chest, I will use it to begin repairing the damage. You will be back with us soon."

He gripped her hand to prevent her from tipping the vial yet. "In case I don't wake... thank you, Rapunzel. For watching out for me these many years. For being a friend when I had nothing left in this world."

She smiled softly as the first drops of oil touched his lips. He only took a small amount before a cry escaped his mouth and his hands clutched his stomach.

Rapunzel recapped the vial and returned it to where she'd kept it before taking Renauld's hand in her own. "Shhhh. It's okay. I'm here."

Ric and Travis both held their breath as Renauld's entire

body relaxed. Silence choked the room. Rapunzel leaned forward, her hand pressed to Renauld's chest above his heart.

She closed his eyes. After a few more beats of quiet, she hummed to herself.

Renauld's fingers twitched. His eyelids shifted. After what felt like hours, he roused as if he'd only been sleeping. A groan echoed around the room.

"That," he breathed. "Was not fun."

A sob shook Rapunzel, and she fell forward, covering her body with his. "I did it. You're alive."

It was only then Ric realized Rapunzel had been just as unsure of her plan as the rest of them. He sucked in air, his breath short. Bending at the waist, he put his hands on his knees. He'd been nervous, scared that this Durand prince would die.

Something was seriously wrong with this situation.

Rapunzel climbed onto the bed beside Renauld and leaned back.

Ric jumped forward before she could drink the Oleander oil herself. "Wait. How are you going to heal yourself if you're not conscious?"

She closed her eyes. "I just have to trust my magic. I don't know what will happen, but I cannot live with this curse any longer. Freedom is worth any price." Before anyone could stop her, she drank the rest of the vial.

The door crashed open just as her body relaxed and consciousness left her.

CHAPTER TWENTY-NINE

PHILLIP

Phillip crouched along the side of the Draconian palace, the darkness of the night hiding his movements.

He'd seen her arrive. La Dame. Black hair sweeping behind her, she'd ridden up the road, her horse's hooves thundering by. She had no guards with her, but she had no need of them with the strength of her power at her fingertips.

Phillip's own magic leaped with the need to explode out of him as soon as he saw her. He'd held it back, choosing instead to run the short distance to the palace. La Dame entered her home moments before Phillip arrived, leaving her horse with the guards.

Alfred followed Phillip, and the king wanted to tell his old friend to go back, that he would be no match for La Dame. Alfred was only putting himself in danger.

But Phillip only had one thing on his mind. Wulfric was in trouble.

He lifted a palm, and the guards at the front doors collapsed, unconscious. He stepped over their sprawled bodies and used his power to rip open the doors.

Somewhere in the labyrinth of halls was his son. He paused, sending his magic out in waves to bring all sounds back toward him. He followed the trail of footsteps echoing against the stone. A roar tore through the air and by the time Phillip caught up, La Dame had thrown herself onto a bed where a lifeless girl lay.

A boy he didn't recognize scrambled away, his movements sluggish. And there, in the corner was Ric and Travis. They shrank back against the wall. Ric grit his teeth as if trying to move and unable to.

Anger rose in Phillip. La Dame was using magic on his son.

He crashed into the room.

"Father!" Ric yelled, relief evident in his voice.

Alfred went to the boys as Phillip advanced on La Dame. She paid him no attention as she muttered to herself.

"Not my girl. Not Rapunzel." Tears streaked the dark sorceress' face. "Wake up, darling." She cradled the girl's body against her chest, rocking back and forth.

Phillip hesitated, feeling something other than pure hatred for the sorceress who took the life he'd wanted with Aurora.

It had been many years since he met La Dame, yet she hadn't changed at all. Hooded eyes lifted as if noticing him for the first time.

"Basile." The word was more a sigh on her lips than a curse. She let her gaze fall to her daughter once more.

Was the girl dead?

As if answering his question, her eyelids twitched.

Ric continued struggling against the magic keeping him pinned to the wall. Phillip waved a hand, sending his own power to cut the cord of control La Dame had.

Ric and Travis both fell forward. As soon as he righted

himself, Ric ran to his father's side. "We need her, Father. Rapunzel is our only chance of saving mother."

To his son's credit, there was only a tinge of fear in his voice.

La Dame's low voice settled over them. "Leave now Phillip Basile and I will let you leave with your life."

Rapunzel stirred to life, her eyes blinking rapidly.

"Not without Rapunzel." Ric stepped forward, but Phillip held him back. His son was brave, but bravery often led to stupidity.

But if that girl could save Aurora, he'd do what he needed to. His magic tingled as he rubbed his fingers together, letting it pool beneath his skin, ready.

La Dame didn't loosen her grip on the girl. "You almost killed my daughter."

Ric ground his teeth together. "You mean like you do every time she faces punishment? You're supposed to love her. You can't keep her here with magic."

La Dame growled. "You're walking on dangerous ground, boy." She settled her gaze on Phillip. "I suggest you take your son home, Phillip. You know what I'm capable of."

"Aurora is dying." He didn't know why he felt the need to tell her except maybe to see if she'd care. She had plans for Aurora that went beyond one hundred years of slumber.

Sadness flashed across her face, but it was gone so quickly he wondered if he'd imagined it. "That's a shame." Her shoulders tensed, and she rose from the bed. "Come then. Let's return to Bela."

Phillip's entire body shook at the thought of La Dame setting foot in his palace; the idea that she'd be near Aurora once more. His magic seeped out of his fingers, curling in the air around him, living and breathing and leaving his control altogether. His power slammed into La Dame, sending her tumbling from the bed.

She cursed and rolled to her feet, ready for a fight. Phillip advanced, preparing to strike. Every bit of magic he sent her way met an invisible wall, protecting her from his power.

He knew the trick well. Before he'd gained his ancestral power, shields had been the only thing he could create. And he knew exactly how to break them.

Distraction.

"Ric," he yelled.

As if reading his mind, Ric ran toward the bed. Alfred tossed a knife into the air, and Ric caught it mid-stride before he jumped onto the bed and holding the blade to the girl's neck. She barely lifted her head. Practically dying must have weakened her. She didn't fight off Ric as he dug the blade into her skin, drawing blood.

A whimper left her mouth.

The unknown boy in the room tried to get to her, but Alfred held him back.

La Dame flicked her eyes to her daughter, her concentration snapping. In that moment, Phillip threw everything he had at her. The full force of his power hit her chest like a battering ram, determined to break through her will.

She screamed and fell back, clutching at her chest. Phillip didn't let up until what felt like a knife twisted in his gut. He looked down but hadn't been stabbed. La Dame twisted her magic further. Agony radiated through his body.

He clenched his teeth, determined not to let his power falter.

"Stop," Ric screamed. He held the knife over Rapunzel's heart, the tip making an indent in her skin. Blood ran down onto her dress. Still, she didn't move.

She gazed up at Ric, something in her eyes that surprised

Phillip. Trust? Acceptance? Was La Dame's daughter giving Ric permission?

La Dame froze, baring her teeth. She lifted a palm.

Phillip crafted a shield with his power and extended it to envelop his son. La Dame would be able to break through it, but not before Ric did what he had to do.

And the knowledge of that sparked in La Dame's eyes.

Phillip had to do something and quickly. Back when it was just him and Aurora in the woods, she'd explained La Dame's curses to him. The sorceress was ancient, and she enjoyed controlling the lives of others, molding them to her will. Deals with her were dangerous because she couldn't resist dire consequences, ones no one saw coming. You couldn't predict her actions or the implications of her curses.

"Fine. Save her!" The words were out of him before he could call them back. "Please."

The only way they were getting out of here was if La Dame herself accompanied them as she wanted to. They were taking her back to Bela.

CHAPTER THIRTY

PHILLIP

Not a moment passed when Phillip didn't question his actions as king of Bela—when he didn't want to turn back and force La Dame to stay in her own kingdom of Dracon. She seemed to revel in his indecision, taking joy from his struggle.

It took less time to travel the distance from the walls of Dracon to the palace of Bela because they didn't have to climb over the wall. Instead, they rode through the massive gates as if they belonged there.

Not only did the dark sorceress ride with them, but the missing prince of Gaule accompanied them as well. Phillip rubbed his eyes as he stared up at the palace, relief flooding through him at the thought of returning home.

He nudged his horse forward into the courtyard where the chaos of battle preparation surprised him. Soldiers ran back and forth, loading wagons and mounting horses. Forgetting about his companions for a moment, Phillip jumped down and sprinted up the steps, bursting through the door, Alfred and Ric hot on his heels.

The three men marched to Phillip's office, stopping when

they found a circle of men bent over a map of the Gaulean border.

Chandler lifted his head. "Thank magic." He crossed to Phillip, scanning him as if looking for injury. His eyes shifted to Alfred, and he pulled him into a hug. "You're all okay," he breathed. Alfred nodded against him before pulling back. "Travis?"

"Here, father." Travis rushed in, winded from running to catch up to them. His father crushed him against his chest. "Can't. Breathe," Travis wheezed.

Phillip eyed the other men at the table, a few generals and others he didn't know by name. "What's happening on the border?"

Chandler rubbed the back of his neck, his lips tugging down. "Gaule attacked just as we knew they would. They were prepared for our magic, wearing our army down to the point we had nothing left other than our swords." He sighed. "They overwhelmed us, breaking through our ranks." He met Phillip's gaze.

"What did they take?"

"The fortress near the northern lands."

Phillip pushed out a breath. That fortress had changed hands many times. The first had been over eighteen years ago when he was only the prince. He would have died from the wounds suffered in that battle if it wasn't for Aurora. Phillip shook the thoughts from his mind. "What's your strategy?"

"We wait."

"Wait?"

Chandler nodded. "We're sending reinforcements to the garrison near there. They lost a lot of warriors. But we've decided to let Gaule settle in and get comfortable. We can recover the fortress and surrounding lands just as we've done many times before."

Phillip knew exactly what he meant. He wanted the king to use the Basile power against Gaule. It was the only way. He nodded and clasped Chandler on the shoulder.

Chandler lowered his voice. "Phil, someone has been filling Gaulean minds with knowledge of how our power works. That's the only way they beat us. They knew to drain our fighters, force them to use magic quickly."

"We both know who has been aiding them."

A low voice came from the doorway. "Are you speaking of me, your Majesty?"

Every person in the room froze as La Dame swept in, her black dress billowing around her legs. She smiled in greeting, meeting each eye turned her way. "Oh," she pouted. "Don't tell me I interrupted something important. Do go on. I'll speak with my new ally when he chooses to visit his dear wife." She left the way she'd come, with dramatic flair, leaving jaws open in her wake.

Phillip clenched his hands. "There are recent events to explain."

Chandler's jaw twitched. "Explain?" Angry chatter erupted from the men behind him, but Phillip only focused on his friend. "Did you bring her here?"

"We didn't have a choice if we wanted to make it out of Dracon." Ric was the one who answered, stepping in front of his father as if to shield him. "She's going to save my mother."

"Right." Chandler took a step back. "Who cares if we allow the dark sorceress herself into the palace if it saves the precious Aurora."

"Chandler." Alfred reached for him. "It was the right thing to do."

"You agree with this?" He dropped his voice so others in the room wouldn't hear. "That woman has the power to destroy Bela. I won't stop whatever you're going to do, but you will regret this. I know you, Phil. You aren't selfish. You wouldn't make a deal with the devil. Don't make us wrong about you."

Phillip nodded once and walked from the room. He'd expected Alfred to stay behind, but the big man matched his stride. "Alfred, I need you to keep me abreast of developments with Gaule. We will wait three days before leaving to take care of the problem."

Alfred patted his arm. "We trust you, your Majesty." With that, he turned on his heel and rejoined the strategy meeting. Travis had stayed behind with his father, but Ric stepped in line with Phillip.

His son was the only person who understood his need to believe La Dame would help. He was the only person with as much desperation in his heart.

When they got to Aurora's room, Phillip's mother stood outside the door, her arms crossed. "You're playing with fire, son." She relaxed her stance. "But if I could have cured your father, I would have done whatever was necessary." She reached up to touch his face. "The crown takes everything from you, leaving little of yourself behind. Aurora may never wake, but keeping her alive is your purpose. It's the noblest thing you do. La Dame does nothing out of the goodness of her heart, so all we can do is hope protecting her future life is worth the consequences."

She squeezed Ric's shoulder and walked by them, not staying to see what those consequences would be.

Phillip sucked in a breath and entered the room. La Dame sat in the chair usually only occupied by Phillip or Ric. She'd propped her feet on the bed. Rapunzel and Renauld stood along the wall as if scared to get too close.

Phillip couldn't hold his temper back as he stormed into

the room and knocked La Dame's feet from the bed. "Show some damn respect," he growled.

One side of La Dame's red lips tilted up. "Aurora isn't yours, king. I made her. I shaped her, and her future is mine. When she opens her eyes, you will be long gone from this world. Now, onto the business at hand."

Phillip moved around to the opposite side of the bed and bent over the face he knew so well. He'd memorized every curve from the point of her chin to the bridge of her nose to the angle of her cheeks. He saw her every time he closed his eyes.

A thick sheen of sweat coated her skin, but her chest continued to rise and fall. He didn't know how much longer she'd have if she wasn't healed.

He fought the urge to throw La Dame across the room when she set her long fingers against the hollow of Aurora's throat. The rattle of Aurora's breath slowed until he couldn't hear it any more as her chest cleared.

Color returned to her pale cheeks. Her lips parted to release a puff of air, and something inside Phillip snapped. He crumpled forward, resting his head on her stomach as tears fought to break free.

"She will live."

La Dame's words bounced around his mind as his heart squeezed. Aurora would live, but he never would. Because without her, there was nothing living inside of him.

Hot tears wet his face. A hand came down on his back and Phillip straightened, turning to sink into his son's embrace.

They forgot about their audience as they both broke down, wishing for a life that had never been theirs.

CHAPTER THIRTY-ONE

RIC

La Dame decided to stay in Bela for a few days... for some reason. Ric didn't really know or care why. He only wanted her gone. But when she left, would he ever see Rapunzel again?

His mother was alive for now, but many in Bela were dead. The battles with Gaule took a toll on the kingdom. Hopefully, his father would put a stop to them for good.

Exhaustion weighed his every movement as he changed out of his filthy traveling clothes. He pulled a tunic over his head, not bothering with trousers. It reached to his knees, leaving the rest of him bare.

In the privacy of his own rooms, no one would care. His servants had seen him in less.

He lay back on his soft bed, realizing how much he'd missed it. He hadn't felt his magic since returning home. Would he dream when he closed his eyes?

He tried to close his mind off from the events of the day, but they rolled through his thoughts like moving paintings. The palace healer had been pleased to announce Aurora was no longer in danger of dying, but they'd known that as soon as La Dame laid hands on her.

Ric burrowed into the warmth of his blankets as a knock sounded on his door. Assuming it was a few of the servants coming to prepare his room for the night—stoke up the fire, extinguish candles, clear the tray of tea he'd requested—he yelled for them to enter.

His body had no more energy as he lay there waiting for the bustle to happen around him. But it didn't come. Instead, a single person entered the room, shutting the door quietly behind her.

Ric jerked his head up, his eyes meeting Rapunzel's. She was dressed for bed in a long woolen sleeping gown. Her hair hung in waves down her back.

It took every bit of strength he had remaining to swing his tired legs over the side of the bed and push the blankets off. At her blush, he realized his pantsless state.

With a shrug, he stood anyway, adjusting his tunic over his rear.

"Can I help you?" He hated the coldness in his voice, but Rapunzel had barely spoken to him on their journey from Dracon. In fact, she'd said few words in the presence of her mother.

She twisted a golden strand of hair around a finger and chewed her lip as Ric walked to the wardrobe and found a pair of trousers. He stepped into them, pulling them up before turning to face her. He raised a brow. "If you're going to continue this silence, please do it in your own room. I'm exhausted."

She stepped toward him. "I'm... sorry."

He studied her, taking some small pleasure in her discomfort. Mixed with the constant thoughts of his mother had been the memory of her lips on his. Nothing had ever felt more right. For a moment, he'd thought his magic led him to her for a reason.

He sighed and scratched the side of his head. "What are you sorry for, Rapunzel?"

She turned away from him and paced the length of the room. "I knew my mother was due to return." She faced him again and walked back, her hands wringing together.

Ric collapsed onto the corner of his bed. "That's why you did it." He shook his head. "You could only break your own curse if someone else was going to be there to heal you."

She nodded. "My mother was already in the palace at that point. The watch told me the moment she'd return to Dracon." She pulled her hair over one shoulder, working her hands through it as if it was some nervous tic. "I tried to make you leave before then."

"The first time I saw you." He finally understood. "When you were cold and refused to help."

She shrugged one shoulder. "I knew as soon as my mother learned of Aurora's illness, she'd leave for Bela. Sometimes, I think she loves Aurora more than me."

"Love," Ric scoffed. "The woman imprisoned you, punished you. She put my mother to sleep, allowing her to wake only once everyone she'd ever loved was gone."

"It's complicated."

"No, it's really not. Your mother is an evil bitch who causes pain as some sort of game."

Tears sprang to Rapunzel's eyes. "I can't go back with her."

"What?" Ric snapped his eyes to hers.

"My life... I need to escape the clutches of my own mother. Please don't make me explain. You've seen what my life is like." He'd seen it in his dreams.

He stood, closing the distance between them until she was

close enough to touch. But he kept his hands to himself. "You want me to protect you? After you failed to tell me your mother was due back soon? You practically handed me over to her. I figured the deal you'd asked for was nothing more than a ruse."

A tear slipped down her cheek. "I know." She squeezed her eyes shut. "Wulfric."

Her tears did something to him, and he couldn't take them any longer. He pulled her into his arms and let her bury her face against his neck. Her lavender scent clung to his nose, and he inhaled deeper. His magic hummed in content at the feel of her.

Had his dreams only been telling him he needed to save her, or was there something more to it?

Her breath blew hot against his skin. "There's a way to break your mother's curse."

Ric pulled back, his eyes wide. "Why didn't you tell me before?"

Tears welled in her eyes once more. "It's not without cost, Ric. My mother's curses are dangerous, but none more so than her sleeping curse. There is only one way to wake Aurora. You may gain your mother, but you could lose everything else."

Ric pulled her against him again, this time out of his own need for comfort. He needed a few minutes of feeling her in his arms before he could face whatever it was she had to say because he knew he wasn't going to like it.

He dipped his head, brushing his lips against her hair. As if working of their own accord, they trailed down her cheek. Her only reaction was a soft intake of breath, but she didn't stop him. He kissed the corner of her mouth and she sighed, relaxing against him.

"Am I safe with you, Wulfric?" she breathed.

"Always."

"I've never been safe before." All hesitation left her, and she turned into his kiss, pressing her lips to his. All tension left her shoulders as she ran her hands up his arms, winding them around his neck.

Ric had to end it, but he savored the taste of her for a moment longer. He had to face the words she'd said. There was a way he could have his mother back, but he knew how dangerous La Dame's consequences were. He'd heard the story. His mother's curse was one such consequence, the result of a deal with the sorceress.

He rested his forehead against Rapunzel's, not sure how he was supposed to ever let her go. She asked him to save her but not in those words exactly. Yet, how was he supposed to prevent La Dame from taking her? His only power was his dreams, not exactly the kind of threat that would scare anyone.

But that was a problem for later. Right now, he had to know the truth. "How?" he asked. "How do we wake my mother?"

Her lips drew down into a frown, and she slipped out of his arms, closing her eyes. When she spoke again, her tone held no emotion, and it was as if she was reciting someone else's words. "True Love's kiss." She snapped her eyes open, pinning him with a pained stare.

Ric's brow creased. It sounded easy enough. His father was his mother's true love. But, he'd kissed her many times before. It couldn't be as simple as that. "Tell me everything."

CHAPTER THIRTY-TWO

PHILLIP

The palace garden was the one place that seemed to see no passage of time. Phillip knew that was strange. Trees grew with each year, towering over them. Flowers bloomed and folded in on themselves with the seasons. Winter came, covering the ground in a dusting of snow, only to melt into the ground at the awakening of spring. The heat of summer brought a lack of rain that shriveled the greenery and made the grass crunch beneath his feet, followed quickly by fall and the leafy coverings that accompanied it.

Time moved on, and yet Phillip remained locked in a state of suspension, never pushing forward, never moving on. The lines in his face deepened. A few of the hairs surrounding his face turned gray.

But in his mind, he was always the boy who fell in love with a beauty fated to leave him. He didn't regret it, not for one moment. In the month he'd with had her, he'd lived a thousand lives, experiencing all the joy he was due in his one life. How many people got to say they'd loved like that?

He sat on a stone bench watching the lilies awaken to the

rising sun. For as long as he could remember, he woke in the early hours of the morning. He enjoyed the silence of a sleeping palace. It gave him space to think before a thousand little things needed doing. As king, everyone wanted something from him. But here, in this place, he was only beholden to his memories.

Footsteps sounded against the stone pathway, and he lifted his eyes to find his mother approaching. She too was one of the things time was taking from him. She'd aged much since his father died, but the kindness in her eyes was something she'd gained with his passing. She saw each day as a gift, seeing firsthand how none of this was promised. He'd sometimes wondered if she pitied him, but then decided he didn't care. He needed her as she was now, not as the cold queen of his childhood.

She smiled when she reached him. "Phillip." She said his name with an affection that reminded him he wasn't alone. He had his mother and his son.

"Good morning." He offered her a smile he only found himself able to procure in the gardens when his mind was still.

Her eyes drifted to the flowers. "How are Aurora's beauties doing this morning?"

His smile fell. "I'm not the gardener she was."

"No." To his surprise, she laughed. "And neither am I. But Aurora had the magic of growth to help her."

"And I have the Basile power. It's multi-faceted, yet even after all these years, I can't seem to master every part of it. I know I should be able to grow things as she did, but it doesn't turn out quite so well." He shrugged.

She shook her head. "Son, your father had that power most of his life and even he did not understand it. Most of the things he found he could do were an accident at first."

He enjoyed hearing her speak of his father. She didn't do it often.

"Don't worry," she continued. "You have many years to learn. Now, that son of yours is inside pacing a hole in the palace floor."

Phillip folded his lips into a flat line. He'd never known Ric to wake early. Normally, if he wanted his son to attend any of his meetings, he had to send a servant to rouse him. The boy's dreams made his sleep far from restful.

Phillip stood. If Wulfric was just inside, he was waiting for him. He knew not to disturb his father in the gardens, but if it was important, he did it anyway.

Phillip's mother patted his arm as he moved past her, picking a flower on the way.

He stepped inside and shut the door behind him.

Wulfric froze. "Father."

"You're up early." He walked past him, letting Ric fall into step beside him as he walked toward Aurora's room. He always visited her after the gardens each morning.

Ric's eyes fell to the flower and flicked back to his father's face. A shuddering breath left him.

Phillip stopped walking outside Aurora's room and turned to his son. "What is it? You seem as if something is bothering you."

"I need to tell you something, but I don't want to tell you." Tears pooled in his eyes and he blinked them away before continuing. "You deserve to know, but I'm scared."

Phillip hadn't known his son to fear many things. He guided Ric into Aurora's room where he placed the flower in the vase beside her bed before turning to the boy. "There is nothing to fear from me, Wulfric. Whatever it is, I promise not to be mad."

Ric shook his head with a humorless laugh. "You think I'm

scared of you? No, I'm scared for you." He scrubbed a hand across his face. "I don't want to lose you."

He placed a hand on each of Ric's shoulders and peered into his eyes. "Wulfric Basile, you will never lose me. You're stuck with me, kid, until I'm old and gray."

Ric laughed, despite his eyes glassing over again. "You're already old and gray, Father."

"You take that back. Your father has many years left in these bones." He tried to laugh, but the truth was, aging scared him more than most. The older he got, the further he grew from Aurora's perpetually young state. He wasn't so old now that it was strange to continue to call her his wife, but one day he would be.

Ric put a hand over one of Phillip's wrists. "What if I told you there was a way to wake her?" His eyes drifted to his mother and Phillip followed the gaze, his heart jumping into his throat.

"Wh-what are you talking about?" He released Ric and looked to the door as if La Dame would enter at any moment. Had she offered Ric a deal? Phillip wouldn't take any deal with her because of the risk it posed to his son. He'd seen what Aurora's father did to her in trying to save her mother.

History would not repeat itself. He loved Aurora with everything he had, but Wulfric was his son, their son. He'd never let him suffer the consequences of Phillip's selfishness.

Wulfric was speaking but Phillip didn't hear any of the words until he uttered "True Love's kiss."

"True love's kiss?" Phillip asked, his voice dropping. He'd kissed Aurora many times. Was he not her true love? "What does that mean?"

Wulfric met his father's eyes once more. "Sacrifice."

"You're not making any sense. How can I wake your mother with a kiss? And what sacrifice is required?"

Fear entered Ric's gaze. "I don't want to tell you because I know what your decision will be."

Phillip pulled his son into a hug. Sometimes, Ric's maturity and independence made Phillip forget just how young he was. His lack of offensive magic made him a sensitive boy. His dreams let him into other people's lives, letting him experience emotions that were not his own.

Ric gripped Phillip as if afraid he'd disappear. When he spoke, his voice was muffled by Phillip's shoulder. "The curse has a way out, but like everything La Dame does, it's cruel. The only way to wake her is to sacrifice yourself. True love's kiss is a trade. You for her." He pulled back and walked to the chair beside the bed, dropping into it. He leaned forward, staring at the mother he'd never known. "I want her too, Father. But not at this cost."

Phillip put a hand on Ric's shoulder. "Please." His voice cracked. "Tell me everything."

Ric buried his face in his hands. "Rapunzel explained it to me. Her mother's greatest joy is watching families tear themselves apart. She could end the curse herself with a wave of her hand, yet would never do it. Aurora is her prize. She never imagined the sleeping curse would be broken because she didn't see you coming. But you'll do it. I know you will. I can't..." A sob shook his body.

Phillip tightened his grip, his magic trying to latch on to his swirling emotions. He didn't let it. He needed a clear mind to hear the rest. "Wulfric."

Ric shook his head. "You have to give her everything. Push all of your magic from your body into hers. Every last bit until there's nothing left."

Phillip stumbled back, but Ric wasn't finished. "Only someone who loved her more than himself would do this. That's why it's called 'True love's kiss'."

Phillip knew now why his son hadn't wanted to tell him. The first lesson of magic every child in Bela learned was to hold back. If you drained yourself of power before it could build back up, you'd die. If he did this...

A slow clap came from the doorway, and a chill raced down Phillip's spine. He didn't turn to her, but La Dame's presence sent waves of darkness through the room.

She shoved Rapunzel through the door before stepping through. "It seems you've figured it out. Well done, daughter."

Ric's eyes shifted, and he glared at Rapunzel as if she'd betrayed him. "She made you tell me?"

Rapunzel shook her head, tears cascading down her face. "No. I swear it. Everything I told you was of my own will. I didn't lie to you."

La Dame sighed. "She's telling the truth, of course. My daughter's heart is too soft." Disapproval flashed across her face. "Phillip Basile, it seems you now know how to break the curse. The day I first met you, I knew it was a possibility. But I also know people. They don't just sacrifice themselves self-lessly. So, your Majesty, what will you do with this knowledge?"

Phillip couldn't think. He almost tripped over his feet as he crossed to the door, turning his back on his son, on the woman he loved. He fell into the hall, slamming his shoulder against the wall. Pain radiated up his arm, but he barely felt it as his magic took control, angry power swirling inside him. He didn't acknowledge anyone as he ran to the training yard and out the small gate that led into a field beyond the palace where his generals normally ran strategy training when there wasn't an enemy trying to carve off slices of their kingdom.

But Phillip couldn't think of the Gauleans currently residing in a fortress he'd once protected. Not when his heart struggled to beat in his chest. His power exploded from him, sending a nearby tree toppling over, its roots ripping from the ground. A thunderous crash shook him when it slammed into the ground. He turned as the sky darkened, his magic pulling rain from the clouds. It fell around him, but bent out wherever he walked, leaving him dry. He sent the water spinning into a cyclone overhead. Rain crashed against the palace walls, but he didn't stop. He couldn't.

He turned, his palms facing up. Grasses ripped from the earth until the dirt was bare. It turned to mud, clinging to his boots with every step he took.

This was where he belonged. It felt good to let the magic control every action, every thought, letting his mind sink into a blissful blank state.

As each bit of magic seeped from his pores, the anger went with it, leaving him empty, devoid of emotion. His chest heaved, and he pulled back before the last of the power escaped. If he was going to die, it wasn't going to be in a senseless act. It would be for her.

The magic protecting him from the rain collapsed, letting the water crash down on him, mixing with the tears on his face.

He'd always known he wouldn't get to live a life with Aurora, but he imagined them both just living in different times. He pictured her waking to an unfamiliar future where La Dame was her only option. She'd be forced to serve her, having nothing else in her life.

Was this a way to save her from that fate?

His legs collapsed, and he fell to his knees, exhausted from his display of magic.

He never imagined she'd get to know her son. Wulfric was the best part of both of them, and it had killed him to think she'd never see that. She'd never feel his love. Before he'd met her, she'd had nothing, no one who loved her. And it would be like that for her when she woke. No one should have to live like that.

The rain stopped its unnatural fall, leaving with the magic he'd used to pull it forth. A voice that had been screaming through the torrent now grew louder. "King Phillip!"

He lifted his tired eyes to the running form of Renauld Durand, an enemy of Bela by birth. But the Gaulean prince didn't look like an enemy as he stopped moving and sympathy entered his gaze.

"I saw you run out here." He bent over, trying to catch his breath. "I've never seen that much magic. Even living with La Dame... she's so controlled. It was... beautiful."

Beautiful? He'd never thought of his magic as such, but it was now the only thing that could break Aurora's curse. He nodded. That was exactly what it was. Beautiful.

He tried getting to his feet, and as he struggled, Renauld grabbed his arm. Phillip wanted to tell him he didn't need help, especially from a Durand, but it would have been a lie. He could barely stand. Renauld pulled Phillip's arm over his shoulder.

As he helped him back to the palace, he spoke. "My father would love for you to do it."

That answered that question. Renauld had heard about the true love's kiss.

"He'd love for the Basile power to be gone."

Phillip felt like an awful king for not thinking of that sooner. If he did this, the Basile power would be no more. He'd release it out of him, and it would what? Disappear? He wasn't quite sure what would happen. Would Ric not inherit his ancestral right? No, if Phillip died, he had to believe Ric would get the power. That was how it worked, right?

"Do you hope I do it?" He didn't know why he needed to hear the boy's opinion, but he couldn't help the question.

Renauld was quiet for a long moment as they walked back into the training yard. "I don't think it's my place." He paused. "But I don't think the threat of Gaule should factor into your decision. You love her, right?"

Phillip nodded his head weakly.

"I've never loved anyone. Not my father. Not my siblings. But I'm sure if I had someone I cared for that much, I'd do anything for them. That's what life should be."

"Sacrifice?"

"No. Love."

But how were you supposed to choose one person you loved over another? If he did this, he would leave his son to save Aurora.

Renauld stopped at the entrance to the gardens.

"Why did you bring me here?" Phillip asked.

"I've seen you walk this way the past two mornings as if it's the first place you want to see."

The kid was wrong. The first place he wanted to see was anywhere Aurora was, but he wouldn't arrive there without a flower for her. A thought occurred to him. "Why are you helping me?"

Renauld shrugged. "Our families are ancient enemies, but my father... let's just say anyone who hates him has to be good. He's no better than La Dame, and you are an enemy of both."

As the boy walked away, Phillip felt sorry for him. La Dame would eventually leave Bela in peace, but she'd take the prince with her and peace was not something he'd experience at her hand.

CHAPTER THIRTY-THREE

RIC

Wulfric no longer saw Rapunzel in his dreams, and he wondered if it was because his magic had no need of her anymore. It had led him to her in Dracon not only because she was the one who could heal his mother, but also because she had the secret that would change his life.

He loved his mother more than anything in this life... except for his father. He couldn't have one without losing the other. Selfishly, he wanted to keep his father, the parent he knew. That meant never meeting his mother, but he couldn't help the desire in his heart.

Phillip Basile was the king of Bela. If he was gone... Ric wasn't ready to take the crown. He wasn't ready for the responsibility of a kingdom or to be the keeper of the Basile power. What would it feel like? The only magic he'd experienced was his dreams, but the things he'd be able to do with his family's power... he couldn't imagine it.

And he didn't want it. As a boy, the thought of one day being the most powerful man in Bela excited him. He hadn't fully grasped the fact that it would only happen once his father was dead.

He sat outside the palace walls, gazing at the hills across the river rolling down into the village. The people of Bela went on with their lives, having no knowledge of La Dame's presence or the decision their king faced. Many of them were away with the army, but the fighting was over for now. Gaule once again occupied a piece of Bela despite Bela's magical advantage. It would be easy enough to recover, but the generals wanted the Gauleans to feel secure before attacking them.

Footsteps sounded on the dry grass. Ric glanced sideways at La Dame's graceful approach. She was mesmerizing in her dark beauty. A crimson dress hugged her waist before flaring out. The bodice dipped down low, but not low enough to be scandalous. She looked no older than Ric's father, but he knew appearances were deceiving.

He clenched his jaw and focused his eyes on the village once more.

"Darling." La Dame's smooth voice wrapped around him. "What are you doing on your own out here?" She lowered herself to the ground and reached for his hand.

He jerked away from her and jumped to his feet. "Don't touch me."

She pouted. "Your mother and I were dear friends, Wulfric Basile. I was hoping we could be as well."

"You weren't my mother's friend," he spat. "She was your prisoner."

La Dame raised a brow. "I did not force the curse on her family. That was her father's doing."

"A trade. Right. I heard the story. You saved her mother and cursed her. You think that makes any of this okay? What is wrong with you?"

"Now, Ric, you're soon going to be the king of Bela. As the queen of Dracon, we will need to get along."

"He won't do it. My father won't leave me."

She sighed, pity coating her features. "Dear boy, I knew from the moment I met your father that he'd be the one to wake Aurora."

Ric froze. "You never intended for her to wake in one hundred years and join you?"

She laughed as if she thought him adorable. Maybe adorably naïve. "Aurora Rose Brynhild, now Basile, is the most magnificent creature I've ever seen. She's stubborn to the point of stupidity. A thousand years could pass and she'd never willingly stand at my side." She shook her head. "The power she has over your father is incredible. Yes, he will do as I've wanted him to." She stood to walk back into the warmth of the palace.

"Wait," Ric called, running after her. "Why? Why are you doing this?"

"Because, boy, this is the beginning of the end."

She didn't say another word as she walked away from him, throwing up a wall of magic so he couldn't follow. The beginning of the end? What did that even mean?

There was only one person to ask. He changed direction and didn't knock before bursting into Rapunzel's room. She looked up, startled, her features softening when she saw it was him.

"Rapunzel." He could barely choke out her name as his emotions rose to the surface. La Dame seemed so sure his father was going to sacrifice himself. He forgot about La Dame's ominous words about the end and fell into Rapunzel's embrace.

She held him tightly, letting him bury his face in her neck.

"Ric," she whispered, pulling back. "I'm so sorry, Ric." Tears danced in her eyes.

"I don't dream of you anymore," he breathed. It suddenly seemed so important.

"I don't feel your dreams anymore." She brushed a thumb under his eyes.

"I can't save my father." His shoulders dropped.

She shook her head. "No, and you can't change his mind."

"He loves her. As much as I hate the thought of losing him, he wouldn't be who he is if he didn't do this. If he didn't give her everything he had. If he didn't do everything in his power to save her."

She smiled, but there was a sadness behind it.

He leaned his forehead against hers, kissing the corner of her mouth. "I have to save you." He hadn't seen it before, the similarities between him and his father. They'd both fallen for women under La Dame's control. But it was time they broke her hold.

"I barely know you, Rapunzel, but it's like you've been part of me for so long." She had. Every dream made him want her more. He saw her strength, her goodness.

She cupped his cheek, swiping her thumb in slow circles. "She won't let me stay."

"I won't let you go." He pressed his lips to hers. If he was going to lose his father, he would need her more than ever. As he kissed her, he lost himself, pushing all the torment from his mind. She calmed his aching heart, holding him together when he felt like the world was breaking him apart.

He hadn't told her he loved her, but she knew. She knew every part of him.

CHAPTER THIRTY-FOUR

PHILLIP

"I need you to tell me what to do, Aurora." Phillip sat on the edge of her bed, brushing the hair away from her calm face. "Is this how I save you?"

When she'd first fallen into her slumber, Phillip blamed himself. He knew it was an irrational feeling, guilt, but that hadn't lessened the pain inside him. He couldn't free her from the curse. Not back then. He'd thought he had when he used his power to reach inside her, to snap the ties of the magic. Only, it hadn't worked.

Was it because he'd held back? The way to wake her was to do as he'd done then, pushing his power into her every cell, but he couldn't pull it back. Not this time. The magic would leave him, and he'd die. The power would live on, attaching itself to the next Basile meant to inherit it. Wulfric. He was always meant to carry his Basile birthright, but not for many more years.

"He'll be a good king," Phillip whispered, imagining Aurora could hear him. "Our son is a good man." He smiled down at her. "He's the best thing either of us has ever done or will ever do. Honorable, strong. Sometimes, he refuses to see his own strength. The magic he carries can't be used in a fight, but he doesn't realize it's more important than that. He sees things in his dreams, people, that Bela needs in order to remain safe. He brought us Rapunzel to save you."

He rubbed the side of his face. "I wish I could talk to you. You'd know what to do about La Dame. The dark sorceress moves through our halls as if Bela is her kingdom. You knew her much better than I do. What does she want from us? Why does she want you to wake when she cursed you in the first place?"

Was it a way to take down the king of Bela? That made no sense when Ric would just take his place. She'd never control Bela as long as the Basile magic existed. And what of her support of Gaule? She had to have known they'd eventually lose to Bela's magic wielders. They stood no chance.

Even if Phillip died, there were many people with power in Bela. The only reason Gaulean soldiers still occupied the Belaen fortress was because they were allowed to.

Phillip skimmed his hand down Aurora's arm, dipping below the blankets to grip her hand.

"I'll be okay, you know." Ric's voice came from the doorway.

Phillip turned to face his son. Ric's eyes held a sad acceptance as if he'd known all along what would happen. He walked farther into the room. "Father, it's okay."

Phillip shook his head, a lump lodging in his throat. "I can't..."

Ric stepped in front of him, leaning forward to wrap his arms around his father's shoulders. "I love you. I also know you will never forgive yourself if you don't save her." He leaned back. "I get it now. She's everything to you."

Phillip pressed his fingers to Ric's cheek. "Not everything, kid."

A sad smile curved Ric's lips. "I was angry at the thought that you'd leave me, but that was selfish. I know that. You wouldn't be a Basile if you weren't willing to sacrifice everything for the ones you love. Besides, you're never leaving me. I'll always carry you with me. I'm not ready to be king, but when are we ever ready for anything? You inherited the throne the very same night you lost both your father and your wife." He straightened his shoulders. "I want to be like you, Father. I want to make you proud."

"Wulfric." Phillip released a shuddering breath. "You've made me proud every day of your life."

Footsteps sounded at the door, and Phillip's mother entered, tears staining her cheeks. "I was trying to give you two a minute, but I needed to speak with you."

Phillip stood. "Mother—"

She put up a hand to stop him. "I'm not here to change your mind. No mother wants to bury her son, but I have watched you die a little more each day for the past many years. If this final act is how you live again, even for just a moment, then it is what you must do." She wiped her face. "But, Son, we are running out of time. If you are to do this, if Ric is to gain the Basile power, it must be soon. That magic is needed to once again push Gaule from our lands. The people cannot wait any longer."

Phillip wrapped an arm around his son and held the other out for his mother, squeezing them both to him.

It was an odd feeling, knowing his death was imminent. But, maybe it was better. Most people never got to have a final word, they didn't get to say goodbye.

Phillip led them from the room. "There's one more place I need to go."

Both nodded and let him walk off without another word.

Phillip trudged through the palace and out into the courtyard. Life went on inside the castle, people blissfully unaware of the turmoil inside their king. They would find out about his death as soon as Ric showed his ownership of the Basile power. But they need never know their king chose to leave them.

The house belonging to his two best friends came into view at the edge of the village. They'd be there preparing to leave to fight Gaule.

Travis stood outside, kicking a ball up and down the street. He saw Phillip, his eyes widening.

"Your Majesty." He ran up beside him.

"Your father home, Travis?" Phillip stopped at the door.

"Yeah, he's fixing supper."

Pushing the door open, Phillip found his two oldest friends standing near the small stone hearth. Both men looked up.

Alfred crossed his arms over his chest as he glanced behind Phillip. "No guards? That's not safe, Phil."

Phillip opened his mouth, but no words came out. How did you say goodbye to the people you'd known your entire life? Alfred and Chandler had been with him through everything, but there was no time left for the three of them.

As if sensing his distress, Chandler walked forward, pulling Phillip into a hug and thumping his back. "What is it? Is Aurora okay?"

Phillip couldn't answer, but Alfred shook his head. "No, you aren't doing this."

"Doing what?" Chandler pulled back, confused.

"Waking Aurora. He's come to say goodbye."

Chandler's fingers dug into Phillip's arm. "Is it true?"

"I..." Phillip sucked in a breath. "Will you come? Will you be there with me?"

Alfred was still shaking his head, but Chandler didn't argue. "Of course." He pulled him back into the embrace. Before long, Alfred joined them. None of the men spoke until they heard sniffling coming from Travis. Tears tracked down his face and Chandler went to him.

"It's okay, Trav. It's going to be okay."

Phillip hoped he was right. He hoped Bela would get over this quickly and easily. Ric would help them, and Aurora would be by his side. He smiled at the thought of her getting to know her son. She deserved that much.

Grabbing their cloaks, Alfred, Chandler, and Travis, followed Phillip back to the palace. There was no longer a point to waiting. His mother had been right. Bela needed to move forward, and they wouldn't until this was done.

His mother and Ric awaited them inside Aurora's room. To their credit, their eyes were dry. Phillip didn't know if he'd have been able to take free flowing tears. He scanned the faces surrounding him. Every person he loved was there. He'd have done anything to keep each one of them safe. They had to know that. But Aurora was the one who needed him now.

La Dame rushed into the room, a wicked gleam in her eye. Rapunzel and Renauld followed in behind her, both stoic, both sad.

Phillip didn't know much about those two, but he hoped they would escape La Dame. Rapunzel might be her daughter, but anyone could tell at first glance that she held none of the hatred in her heart that her mother possessed. And Renauld... he was not like his father in Gaule.

Rapunzel slid her hand into Ric's, and Phillip smiled at the sight. They'd be okay. He would be the only person in the world who could keep her safe once he had the Basile power.

La Dame clapped her hands together. "We just couldn't miss this."

Phillip didn't trust her. He walked to the bed. "It's time."

He'd said his goodbyes and any more would break him apart. He needed to remain whole, to finish this. For Aurora.

She looked so peaceful in her sleep, completely unaware that her curse was almost over. Phillip would give anything for one final moment with her. Would she wake before he was gone?

He ran his fingertips over her closed eyes, knowing he'd probably never see the blue depths, then down over the curve of her cheek to the corner of her mouth. He'd never hear the sweet sound of her voice as she stubbornly argued with him. He pulled at her bottom lip with his thumb.

He hadn't forgotten a single thing about her, a single moment spent with her. Their time together in her forest cabin seemed like a dream from another life. He'd been injured, sick, and yet happy. He'd fallen in love.

Would she go back there to see the place where they began? Would she only live a half-life as he'd done? "I don't want that for you," he whispered, bending toward her. Maybe if she hadn't been there as a constant reminder of what he'd lost, he'd have been able to move forward, to forget.

At least she'd get that chance. Phillip wouldn't be in a deep slumber within the palace walls. He'd be gone. Dead.

He sucked in air, breathing in the scent that was so distinctly Aurora. It was a smell of flowers and fresh air. He knew it was silly. She hadn't left that room in over eighteen years, but she smelled just as she had the first day he met her. Maybe his memory was playing tricks.

"Aurora," he breathed. "I love you." All noise from the sniffling crowd behind him faded away until all he sensed was his wife. For a moment, only the two of them existed. He'd tried to give himself to the other people in his life, but there'd been so little left to give. Aurora Rose Brynhild owned him, body and soul. He sat on the bed and slid his hands underneath her neck.

All sadness left him as he gazed at the woman before him. "You're going to wake Aurora. You're going to live."

He pressed his lips to hers, holding nothing back. His magic pulsed underneath his skin, waiting to break free. Slowly, he released his control of the power, letting it out in his kiss. Just as he'd done many years before when trying to break the curse, he pushed the magic into Aurora, letting it invade her every cell.

Her body buzzed beneath his, her hair standing on end.

And he didn't stop.

True love's kiss. There wasn't a name more fitting for his actions. With his kiss, he gave her everything he was, the power that made him who he'd become. And he didn't pull it back.

Her skin warmed underneath his touch, and he let himself fall into her, not wanting to let go. As each bit of power left him, his muscles relaxed, weakening slowly. Most magic wielders stopped when strength left them and gave their bodies time to recover the magic.

But Phillip couldn't.

Aurora released a puff of air and a groan soon followed it. Her body shifted, her hands reaching up to hold on to him.

"She's waking up," someone whispered. Phillip didn't know who.

All he knew was he couldn't stop. A tear leaked from his eye, dripping onto her cheek, as his chest crushed against hers. He no longer had the strength to hold himself up.

He felt it leaving him. Life.

Blackness crept in at the edge of his vision, and he gave into it surrounded by the soft cries of his family, with the feel of his wife returning his kiss for the first time in many years.

CHAPTER THIRTY-FIVE

AURORA

Heat enveloped Aurora, snaking down under her skin, filling every part of her. Power. It seeped into every pore, drilling down into her very bones.

Warm lips pressed against hers, and her mind worked furiously. She could feel it. How could she feel it? For so long, she'd laid still, unable to react to the words she heard or feel his touch. Phillip.

Tears leaked from the corners of her still closed eyes, and she wanted to tell him to stop, to take his magic back, but the only thing she could do was kiss him back as her voice refused to come. *Phillip, no. You can't do this.* Their son needed him. Wulfric. Aurora had heard his voice every day of her slumber, but she'd only imagined his face.

Phillip was the king of Bela. He couldn't give that up to save her. Ric was too young to take over the Basile power, to wear the crown. She wanted different for her son even if it meant never once laying eyes on him.

One hundred years. She could have done it. She would have been happy to wake to learn Phillip and Ric had lived great lives and been happy. She'd have served La Dame and not regretted a moment she spent with the love of her life.

Phillip's kiss fell away, his lips leaving hers ice cold in remembrance that he was no longer there. *No.* She tried to force her eyes open, to see him one final time before the light disappeared from his eyes. *Why did you do it?* She'd never have asked him to. She'd known her fate her entire life. It was her curse to bear.

"Father." Ric's tortured voice sliced through Aurora. "Father, wake up."

"He can't, Wulfric." La Dame's dark tone chilled the room. "He has drained himself of all power."

"He's dead?"

"Ric." Aurora didn't recognize the soft voice of the newcomer. "He knew what would happen. We all did."

"I know. I just... my father is dead."

Aurora's eyes slid open slowly. Wulfric and a young woman kneeled over where Phillip's body had slid from the bed to the floor. Aurora swallowed a sob, wishing she could see Phillip's face. She didn't take her eyes from the son she'd only seen in her dreams. She'd imagined him visiting her in her mind, but seeing him now was so much different. A mop of blond hair shielded his face from view. Broad shoulders hunched forward, trembling. He looked so much like his father that a sob broke past Aurora's lips.

Every eye in the room jerked to her.

Ric jumped to his feet, his tall legs making him tower over the bed. He approached her as a man approached a predator, with caution and suspicion. Wiping a hand across his reddened eyes, he shook his head as if not quite believing what he saw.

La Dame clapped her hands together. "Well, isn't this the reunion! It is wonderful to see you awake, my dear."

Aurora scanned the room taking in the familiar and unfamiliar faces. Phillip's mother, Alfred, and Chandler all looked like older versions of the people she'd met. Throughout the years of her slumber, she'd heard them support Phillip. Phillip had talked to her of their friendships and his mother's gardens.

She'd held on to his voice, letting it get her through the darkness.

And now he was gone. Tears clouded her vision as she glanced at the two strangers in the room. A young man and woman hung back, sadness etched into their faces. She trusted them instantly because of their obvious fondness for Phillip.

The only one who didn't look ready to fall apart was La Dame. Glee danced across her eyes. She pushed Ric back and stepped to the side of the bed. "The very first time I met Phillip Basile, I knew he'd be the one to break the curse."

Why would she allow Aurora to wake? Aurora rethought everything she knew about La Dame, every interaction they'd had. What was the thing she wanted even more than Aurora at her side?

The end of the Basile power. The only power that could keep hers in check.

Aurora gathered all her strength to speak. "Wulfric." Her voice rasped.

Ric stepped to her side, staring down into her eyes. "Mother," he breathed. "I always wondered what your eyes looked like."

They would have a chance to process the events at another time. First, she had to keep Bela from falling into La Dame's hands. "Do you have the powers?" She tried to lift her head. "The..."

"Basile powers." He looked down at his hands as if they betrayed him with a lack of magic. "No. If father..."

He didn't need to finish that sentence. His father died, he drained himself of magic. It should have gone to his son.

Fear crept into her heart as La Dame's smile grew.

Ric flicked his eyes from his mother to La Dame. "What's going on?"

Aurora seemed to be the only one who noticed the young woman in the room crouching down beside Phillip. Aurora scrunched her brow and drew La Dame's attention to herself. "You did it."

"Did what?" Ric's voice rose an octave.

"The Basile power is gone."

La Dame laughed. "You were always a smart girl, Aurora. Everything is based on a theory. Facts do not exist in magic. Our theory was that True Love's kiss would wake you. Another theory states the Basile power can only be passed through death."

"But..." Ric's voice trembled. "My father is dead."

She nodded. "You're right, boy. But the last thing he did was drain the Basile magic from him. He did not die with the power inside. He released it into the air where it dispersed, never to be fully grasped again."

Ric fell onto the corner of the bed, his jaw dropping open. "That can't be..."

La Dame shrugged. "Like I said—theories. You don't feel any of the power, though, so that may be evidence enough."

The words shot through Aurora. It was all because of her. Phillip not only gave his life to save her but his kingdom's safety. He'd sacrificed everything. The Basile power protected Bela from the wrath of the other five kingdoms. It sustained them. Without it...

She tried to sit up, but there was little strength in her bones. She wanted to reach for her son's hand, to comfort him in a way she didn't deserve. He'd lost everything he loved because of her.

Muffled voices came from the back of the room, but she didn't hear what anyone else said as her eyes fixed on the boy she'd always wanted to see. His eyes, a sparkling blue, spoke of intelligence and also kindness. She looked for herself in the curve of his cheeks, the arch of his nose, the dimple in his chin. But he was all Phillip.

Her eyes glassed over once more. Ric couldn't seem to look at her, but he reached for her hand, folding it in his larger one.

La Dame flashed them one final smile. "I must be off to make preparations. Renauld, Rapunzel, and I will be leaving with the morning light."

"Where will you go?" Aurora had to know. What came next? Without the Basile power, would Dracon march on Bela?

La Dame paused at the door. "It seems there is a Gaulean force near the border who should know Phillip Basile is no longer a threat." She left the room, whistling as she went.

Dread sat like a cloak over the remaining people. The young man slipped out after La Dame.

"I'm sorry," Aurora whispered.

Phillip's mother looked up from her spot near her son's lifeless form. "Dear, none of this is your fault."

Tears slipped down her cheeks. "He... he shouldn't have..."

It was only then she noticed there wasn't a single dry eye in the room. Alfred and Chandler leaned on each other for support with a young boy between them. The queen mother stilled her trembling lips and approached the bed.

"My son loved you with his entire heart. For that, I can

never be sorry. He chose this path. You did not ask this of him, and I know you never would."

Aurora swallowed a sob. "Never."

Tears flowed more freely down her face. "We will have time to mourn him and welcome you back properly, but right now we must fight for Bela." She turned to Alfred and Chandler. "We must inform our troops that the Basile power is no longer an option. Gaule must still be dealt with. We have other powerful magic wielders that could be of use."

Chandler nodded while Alfred gave Aurora a long indecipherable look before they ushered the young boy from the room.

The queen mother rested a hand on Ric's head. "I'm going to give you some time, but then the kingdom will need you." She looked to where Phillip still lay. "I'll have someone collect him to prepare the body, but right now, I must help protect Bela. Later, I can mourn my son."

She wiped her face and straightened her shoulders. She was still every bit the queen. Sucking in a breath, she stepped into the hall and closed the door.

The young woman Aurora didn't know remained behind. She seemed to be listening for any other footsteps. When none sounded outside the door, she nodded to Ric.

Ric jumped from the bed and dropped to his knees at his father's side.

Aurora struggled to push herself up. The blanket dropped from her chest revealing a silk sleeping gown of the best quality. "What are you doing?"

Ric lifted a tear-streaked face to her. "He isn't dead."

Three words. That was how her heart started beating again.

He isn't dead. He isn't dead. He isn't dead.

She shook her head. No. It wasn't possible. "Wulfric."

"Just trust me."

And she did. Before that day, she'd never looked into his eyes, but she'd known him. She remembered every word he'd spoken to her, believing she couldn't hear him. He was her son, a part of her, a part of Phillip.

"I feel his pulse." Triumph radiated from Ric's words.

"How?" Aurora breathed.

The woman glanced up, kindness in her gaze. "I have healing magic."

"You're Draconian." Aurora's eyes widened. Why was this woman helping them?

"I'm La Dame's daughter, Rapunzel." A scowl marred her features at the mention of her mother. Before Aurora could react, she continued. "I told Ric of True Love's kiss. That's how we got to this point."

Aurora wanted to hate her. She was the reason they were in this situation. But no... they'd said Phillip wasn't dead, right?

"Get to the not dead part."

Rapunzel nodded. "Unconsciousness overtook the king before he could expel the last bits of his power. As soon as he dropped to the ground, I went to him. The magic was seeping out, but I kept his heart beating long enough for his body to draw it back in. Ric didn't inherit the power, not because it was gone, but because it doesn't yet belong to him."

Aurora tried to process the words in her sleep-addled mind. How was it that La Dame's daughter found a way to wake her and save Phillip in the process?

"When... when will he wake?" It hit her then. Aurora would see Phillip again. She'd get to stare into the depths of his eyes, see his brilliant mind spinning. He'd once again argue with her and make love to her, sometimes one right after the other.

Sobs wracked her chest. She never thought it was possible.

"We need to get him off the floor." Ric lifted Phillip by the shoulders.

Aurora scooted over to make room for him.

Wulfric lay him on the bed and all Aurora could do was stare. He was older now but still the same. His face relaxed in unconsciousness, he looked so at peace.

Rapunzel spoke, and it took a moment for Aurora to hear the words. "My healing magic uses the body's own energy. He will wake eventually, but not until he's ready."

Ric grimaced. "If he doesn't wake by the time La Dame leaves, he still won't be of use against Gaule." He paused. "Mo... Aurora, we will talk. I promise. But right now, Bela needs their prince. We will tell no one that he lives, not until Gaule is dealt with. Bela cannot rely on the Basile magic right now." He gave her a lingering look before nodding and walking out the door.

Rapunzel followed him, leaving Aurora alone with the sleeping Phillip. She couldn't help smiling at the irony of the situation. He'd spent so much time with her while she slept.

She reached out, her fingers tentative as she stroked them through his hair, down his cheek. She'd dreamed of touching Phillip again. Of exploring every part of him she'd missed. She scooted toward him, taking his arm to place it around her.

Laying her head on his chest, she tried to pretend as if the years hadn't separated them, as if they were where they were always meant to be.

CHAPTER THIRTY-SIX

PHILLIP

Phillip had been okay with dying. He'd welcomed it if it meant Aurora got to live her life. He knew Bela would be fine. They'd have a new king who would wield the Basile power. Ric, his son. He may not have thought he was ready, but Phillip hadn't been either when the crown was placed on his head.

What Phillip hadn't expected was to ever feel the thump of his pulse pounding in his temples again—the splitting pain of a headache, or a bone-weary exhaustion from using too much magic.

Something heavy pressed down on his chest, and as he forced his eyes open, a head of golden hair came into view, the strands splayed across his shoulder.

His heart-rate kicked up. He was alive. How? True love's kiss should have killed him. It should have taken all his magic and left him an empty shell.

But he felt it. The Basile power. It pooled beneath his skin, drawing all strength to the surface.

The head on his chest moved and mumbled words reached his ears.

Tears pricked the corners of his eyes. Other than occasional groans, he hadn't heard that voice in so long, too long. "Aurora," he breathed.

She stilled for a moment, frozen in time, before tipping her head back to gaze up at him with the eyes he'd never forget. "You're awake." She sucked in a breath.

One side of his mouth curved up. "I could say the same thing to you."

Her mouth opened again, but no words came.

He tightened his hold on her, relishing the way her body felt pressed against his. "Aurora."

"Phillip."

His mind turned rapidly as he slid his gaze over every part of her. She was real. She was awake. His Aurora.

"I heard everything," she whispered, shimmying up so her face rose above his.

"Everything?"

"Every word said in this room for all these years." She touched his face gingerly. "You've loved me every day."

He nodded, swallowing.

"You almost died for me. Do you know what that makes you?"

"A handsome savior?" His lips quirked up.

She shook her head. A tear fell from her cheek onto his, and she wiped it away. "You're an idiot, Phillip Basile."

She kissed him before he could refute her words. Her lips moved over his, fitting like the final piece of an old puzzle, once lost and now complete. The broken parts of him fell back into place as tears fell freely down his face.

He kissed her cheeks, her nose, her hair, and finally her lips again. The years of loneliness, of missing her, drifted away until all he felt was a liberating relief. He'd have gladly given his life for her even if it meant never seeing her again. But this moment... he'd never been more thankful for anything.

True love's kiss broke the curse, but he hadn't needed to give his life for hers. Maybe he'd only needed to be willing to.

Sobs shook Aurora as she broke the kiss. Phillip pulled her against him, holding on as if she'd disappear if he left go. She buried her face in his tunic, her tears making the fabric stick to his skin.

"Aurora," he whispered. "It's okay. It's going to be okay now."

She shook her head. "Nothing is okay."

"What do you mean?"

She lifted her head to meet his stare. "You slept for two days after Rapunzel healed you. They couldn't wait any longer once La Dame left with her daughter and the Durand boy."

"What are you talking about? Where did they go?"

"The border fortress. La Dame's plan was to neutralize the Basile power. If you'd released it all, Ric wouldn't have inherited it."

Phillip shook his head. That wasn't possible, was it? There was so much he didn't know about his own magic.

Aurora continued. "La Dame thinks you're dead. She's aiding the Gauleans in their push farther into Bela. Wulfric left to lead the army into battle against them, but the Gauleans will outnumber him three to one. The generals worry they'll exhaust Bela's magic long before the real fighting begins."

"I have to go to them." Phillip tried to sit up, but Aurora put a hand on his shoulder.

"You're too weak."

He shook his head. "Not for long." Gathering his magic in his fingertips, he pushed it down his arms, through each limb. Little by little, his strength returned to him until he could finally sit up. Not a healing exactly, just a returning of strength.

"Phillip—" Aurora took hold of his arm.

He wanted to stay in that bed with her. To get to know her again. But his kingdom needed him. "You can't stop me."

"I know." She pushed off the blankets. "But I'm coming with you."

He wanted to argue. She'd only woken from her slumber two days before and he wanted to keep her safe, but if she was half the girl she used to be, arguing with her would be no use.

He climbed from the bed and pulled her up to stand beside him, suddenly self-conscious about how young she looked. She hadn't aged a single day.

It wasn't uncommon for men to marry younger women, but he feared he was too different from the youthful boy she remembered.

She reached up, smoothing the crease in his brow. "Are you worried about Wulfric?"

He nodded.

"He's a good boy, Phillip, because of you."

He shook his head and pressed his lips to the side of her head. "No, it's because of him." Inhaling her scent, he reached for the vase beside the bed, pulling the dead flower free.

Aurora took it from his hand. "I smelled these in my sleep."

He kissed her hair again as the door opened and his mother froze. "Phillip."

He offered her a soft smile. "Hi, Mother."

She rushed forward, wrapping her arms around him. "Ric told me you were alive, and I didn't quite believe it.

Even after I felt your pulse for myself, I wasn't sure you'd wake."

Phillip stepped back. "We must join the army, Mother."

"Yes." Her eyes flicked between them.

Aurora slid her hand into Phillips. "I... um... need some clothes."

Her eyes softened. "We kept everything of yours, dear. Come."

They walked the familiar halls to Phillip's room where a trunk sat filled with Aurora's things. He'd been unable to look through it in the years she'd been gone.

His mother stopped at the doorway. "The army has over a day's lead on you. You must leave right away. I will have someone prepare the horses and gather provisions."

When she left, silence hung over the room. Aurora drifted around the small space as if remembering her too-short time there. She walked to the balcony doors and threw them open.

Images assaulted Phillip. He'd never forget holding her lifeless body out on that terrace.

He rushed forward and shut the doors.

She looked to him in surprise.

It hadn't fully come to him yet that Aurora was there in front of him. He expected her to disappear at any moment, for her wide, innocent eyes to close for good this time.

He got his breathing under control and turned his back to pull his tunic over his head. He'd aged eighteen years while she hadn't aged a day. There were scars and years' worth of wear on his body.

As he quickly pulled on a new shirt and his leather armor, Aurora put a hand on his arm, forcing him to turn around. "You're the most beautiful man I've ever seen."

"I'm a man, Aurora. Beautiful isn't the word." One corner of his mouth tugged up.

She smiled, cutting through all his fears with the single act. "I choose my own words." She pushed a hand up under his shirt, feeling the skin beneath.

He no longer had the physique of a twenty-year-old man.

"Every part of you is exactly how I imagined in my dreams." She tapped a finger over his heart. "Time will try to tear us apart at every turn, but we won't let it."

Phillip pulled her into his arms. "Maybe now time can be on our side."

She pressed her lips to his before spinning away from him to fish out a pair of trousers and tight fitting blouse from her trunk. She pulled the wrinkled fabric over her head before tying her hair back.

"Phillip?" Her smile faltered.

"Yeah?"

"I... if I'd have woken up many years from now when you were old and gray, I'd still love you. I need you to know that."

He swallowed heavily, his heart jumping into his throat. "I'm sorry I couldn't wake you sooner."

"You saved me. You don't get to be sorry."

Unable to find the words to respond, Phillip wiped a tear from his eye and handed her a sword belt.

Before they'd even gotten a proper reunion, the two of them were riding from the palace surrounded by guards, hoping they weren't too late for the people of Bela. And their son.

CHAPTER THIRTY-SEVEN

AURORA

A lot changed in eighteen years, and at the same time, things remained the same. Aurora's body remembered what to do as if she'd ridden a horse only yesterday. She didn't ask about her old mule Lea because she knew it must have been many years since she died.

She didn't ask about much of anything on the journey. Longing stares filled the awkward silences. Eventually, they'd have to face the fact that she'd returned, that they'd returned to each other. Aurora's cheeks heated under Phillip's intense gaze.

The years aged him. Gone was the youthful light of the prince she'd fallen in love with. He was a man who'd been through too much heartache in his life. She saw it in his eyes. He didn't trust her presence, guarding his heart against the departure he thought inevitable.

Fine lines creased at the edges of his eyes and his hair, once spun with gold, had darkened. All softness was gone from his face, replaced with hard lines and a cut jaw.

But when she met his gaze, the boy she'd known stared

back at her. When they stopped to rest, they lay together, afraid to let go.

Three days. It took three days to reach the rolling plateau before them. In the distance, the high walls of the border fortress stood stark against the dazzling blue of the winter sky. A dusting of snow covered the ground, leaving tracks in their wake. Smoke billowed in the sky over a battlefield.

"Look." One of the guards pointed to a line of fire snaking through the tall grass. Magic. It had to be.

"We're not too late." Phillip breathed out a sigh and kicked his heels into the flanks of his horse. They crested a small hill. Down below, the Belaen army held siege to the great fortress. Gauleans lined the walls, sending volleys of arrows into the chaos below.

Soldiers screamed as boiling pitch fell from above.

A group of warriors huddled in the small shelter built over the battering ram as they slammed it into the gates again and again. They wouldn't get inside. Phillip's father fortified the walls to be impenetrable. Gaule only captured the fortress by drawing the Belaen garrison manning it out onto the battlefield.

But they wouldn't fall for their own tricks.

A woman darted across the battlefield, her blond braid sailing out behind her. She bent over injured soldiers, laying hands on them before helping them to their feet, whole.

Rapunzel.

That had to mean Wulfric was near. Aurora couldn't imagine the son she barely knew in such a fight. Screams reached her ears as another volley of arrows hit their intended targets. She pulled her sword free. She hadn't woken from a cursed slumber just to watch her son die.

Without a second thought, she squeezed her thighs and gave the horse a swift kick. Phillip's curses followed her and eventually his horse did as well. "Aurora," he yelled. "You need to stay back from the battle."

"Since when have I ever done what you've said, Phillip Basile?" She leaned forward, gripping the reins tightly.

"Bloody brilliant," Phillip yelled. "Eighteen years and she hasn't changed one damn bit."

An arrow sailed for Aurora, but altered its course before making impact. She threw a thank you glance toward Phillip. He hadn't gained the Basile powers until the day she fell into her slumber. But now he was the most powerful man in the world.

The thought had her grinning as she reached the rear of the Belaen forces and slid down. She walked without worry as Phillip's shield protected her.

"We have to find Wulfric," she yelled, searching for Rapunzel who she'd seen only moments ago.

Phillip gripped her arm to slow her, but she shook him off as she caught sight of Rapunzel helping a man with an arrow in his leg.

The Durand boy ran up to Rapunzel offering his aid. Where was La Dame? How had those two gotten away from her?

"Rapunzel." Aurora knelt down at her side to hold the screaming man down.

Rapunzel's eyes widened. "You're here." She lifted her eyes. "And the king."

Renauld fell back, shaking his head as he stared at Phillip. "The king is dead."

"No time, kid." Aurora touched Rapunzel's arm. "Where is my son?"

Her eyes shuttered. She yanked the arrow free and a moment later, the man was able to stand. Rapunzel brushed off her trousers and stood. "In the fortress."

"What!" Phillip rushed forward. "What do you mean he's in the fortress?"

"He went for good faith negotiations."

Aurora snorted, trying to mask her fear. She skimmed the surrounding battle. Yeah, it looked like negotiations were working.

"You can't negotiate with La Dame," Phillip growled.

"Of course not." Rapunzel moved to the next injured man. "But he can stall the Gauleans from marching out and slaughtering us all. As of right now, he's told them you are dead, and he is the new king. My mother would have told them the Basile power is no more."

Phillip tried to say something else, but Aurora stopped him. "He knew you'd come."

Rapunzel nodded. "He didn't know how long it would take you to recover, but he had faith in you, your Majesty."

Rapunzel faced him once again. "Ric was smart. He demanded a trade. Him for me and Renauld—until he returned safely. My mother told me to disrupt the Belaen army in any way I can. And Renauld... she didn't want him near enough the Gauleans that they could identify him. She assumes we are her greatest allies because we have not tried to escape... yet."

"And you're not?" Aurora needed to know if she could trust someone who shared La Dame's blood. "You're her daughter."

Rapunzel stood to her full height and lifted her chin. "I don't want to live in darkness. Not anymore." She met Aurora's gaze unblinkingly. "And I love your son."

Detecting nothing false in her words, Aurora relaxed. She'd spent so long listening to Ric share all his secrets, his worries, with a comatose mother he assumed didn't hear a single word. She probably knew him better than anyone in this world, and she'd protect him with everything she had.

Rapunzel seemed to sense Aurora's acceptance of her words because she stepped closer. "The army's magic is mostly exhausted."

"But mine is not." Phillip took off toward the gate.

CHAPTER THIRTY-EIGHT

PHILLIP

The structure covering the battering ram flared with fire. Soldiers poured out, screaming as the blaze licked up their skin. Phillip pulled water from the earth, drenching them as he ran by. He gathered his magic in his palms, letting it pulse and feed on his anger. La Dame had taken too much from him already. She would not have his son.

The power exploded out of him, slamming into the wooden gates. They splintered and blew apart, showering nearby soldiers in bits of wood. His chest heaved as he stood on the threshold, the dust clearing before him.

Gaulean soldiers gathered in the courtyard, preparing to face an oncoming force. But Phillip didn't wait to see if his men followed him. He sent a wall of power at the foreign army, sucking the air from their lungs as it flung them back.

He pulled the magic back, not letting it kill them. A woman he loved once told him the Gauleans weren't savages, that they had families to return to just as any Belaen. They didn't deserve to be slaughtered in the name of La Dame. She brought them there, convinced them they wanted a piece of Bela—that they could win.

They didn't know Gaule was always going to lose because their kingdom wasn't part of the true game.

He blasted his way through paths of soldiers, slamming them into stone walls or into each other. They fell to the ground and did not rise.

A soldier ran at him and instead of using his power, Phillip ducked his blade, twisting the man's arm until he dropped his weapon. The soldier screamed and Phillip twisted harder. "Where is the prince of Bela?"

"In. The. Hall," the soldier bit out.

Phillip released him, shoving him forward and slamming his head into a wall. The soldier crumpled to the ground.

Ire rose inside Phillip, keeping his magic boiling on the surface. He gave in to his rage, taking it out on anyone who dared step in his way as he tried to get to his son. His control on the power slipped, but he kept going.

The door to the hall was barred shut. Phillip slammed his foot into it, using his magic as a battering ram to burst through. He stepped over the door fragments and stopped.

Sitting at a table along the far wall was Wulfric. He stood as soon as he saw his father, chains rattling around his ankles. Phillip ran toward him, taking in his son's wild hair and the dark circles under his eyes. What had they done to him?

"Father." Relief coated Ric's features. "I knew you'd come."

"Your mother is here too."

Tears welled in Ric's eyes and he nodded. "Both of you. Here. Together." His eyes widened. "We have to go before—"

"Before what, Wulfric?" La Dame's voice reached them from the other end of the hall.

Phillip refused to turn as his magic begged for release. It swirled in him, a living, sentient thing. It wanted to ravage, to destroy this woman who'd hurt so many. But he didn't know how. He knew, without a doubt, he wasn't strong enough to overcome her power. The wielder had to have more rage than Phillip possessed, more darkness inside of them to amplify the magic.

He couldn't risk dying in the attempt. Or worse, becoming something he couldn't come back from.

But maybe, just maybe he could keep Bela safe from her, anyway.

He turned on his heel.

La Dame's jaw went slack when she recognized him, but she quickly covered up her surprise as she jerked her eyes to the door. Sounds of fighting drifted in. The Belaen army was inside the fortress.

Aurora came running in, Rapunzel on her heels.

"Well." La Dame smirked. "Isn't this quite the reunion?" She flipped her palm facing out, and the chains around Ric's ankles disappeared. She pushed her hand forward and his body lifted from the chair.

Ric's scream cut off as the air left his lungs and he slammed into the stone wall.

Rage ripped through Phillip and tried to hold onto the feeling. It screamed for release, and he dropped his control, letting it shoot out of him like a spear aimed directly for La Dame.

She only laughed as she waved it away and sent her own power rolling toward him. He molded his magic into a shield, extending it to cover Aurora as well.

"Did Aurora tell you how it felt to fall into her slumber?" La Dame stepped toward him.

He stepped back, refusing to answer her as their magic

battled. He gritted his teeth, trying to infuse more strength into it.

La Dame seemed to be using little effort. "No, she wouldn't have. Peace. That's what you ripped her from. Aurora lived in wonderful dreams, never having to experience the strife of life in a kingdom that was constantly at war." Her eyes flicked to a frozen Aurora. "It was a relief, wasn't it dear? After the hard life you'd lived, you wanted it all to go away. And meeting your handsome prince only added to your suffering."

Phillip's power weakened as he too turned to Aurora. All these years, life without her caused him more pain than anyone should have to experience. She'd been right in front of him, yet so far away.

But to Aurora... that sleep was an escape?

"Phillip," Aurora cried.

La Dame lifted a chair into the air without touching it and hurled it his way. He ducked, and the wood broke apart when it slammed into the wall.

Whatever the sleep meant to Aurora, she was awake now. And La Dame would not take anything more from him.

"What do you want?" It was the question he'd wanted to ask her for so long. What was the sorceress' goal? Why did she allow Aurora to wake? She wanted Bela destroyed, but how? Now that she knew he still lived, was her plan ruined? No, she had to have other options.

La Dame's lip curled. "What do I want? For Bela to burn to the ground."

"Why?" He glanced from Wulfric to Aurora. They were the royal family of Bela. Destroy them, and it would destroy the kingdom. Then it hit him. The Basile power. Before she could answer him, he spoke again. "You're afraid of the Basiles." He advanced toward her, never dropping his magic shield. Light sparked in his eyes. "We're the only ones who can defeat you."

He pulsed his power out toward her, weakening her defenses.

"Your power is mine," she growled. "The Basile power and the dark power of Dracon are two parts of a whole."

His eyes widened. "You think you can take it back?" Two parts of the same? Dark power curled in his gut, dangerous. He'd always felt the edges of evil in his own magic, but hers? La Dame's was bathed in tar.

"You feel it," she said. "The anger. The hatred. The Basiles aren't the heroes of Bela's story. How does it feel to be just another villain?" She smirked. "I was looking forward to Aurora's service when she woke from her slumber. Her entire life, I watched her, knowing she'd one day be mine. But then she fell in love with the prince and I saw an opportunity, biding my time until you decided her life was worth more than your kingdom."

"Father," Ric rasped, gasping for breath. "Father, it's okay to let the magic overpower you. To lose control. I have faith in you."

His entire life, he'd been taught to gain a tight grip of magic, that it was never allowed to control you. But it had a mind of its own. When Ric allowed his to take charge, it led them to Rapunzel. Maybe it had the same goals as he did. Save Bela. Protect his family.

His pulse hammered in his ears as he lost himself in the current, dipping his head below the surface until he couldn't see anything anymore.

Darkness clouded his vision, and he'd never felt more powerful. His feet moved of their own accord as he advanced. Magic seeped out of his fingertips as he raised a hand, throwing La Dame into the air.

She screamed as her body twisted. He batted away each wave of power she sent toward him as if he'd always known what to do. The black faded from his vision and he saw the scene before him. La Dame slammed into the ground, her body twisted at odd angles.

He saw her healing herself before his very eyes.

Rapunzel gasped, her eyes widening as she flicked them from her mother to Phillip.

His chest heaved from the exertion, but he wasn't finished. He walked forward until he stood above her, searing his magic down into her flesh. Burns spread across her skin as she screamed.

"Rapunzel," she yelled. "Help me."

Rapunzel dropped down beside her mother. Phillip pulled his power back.

The blond girl peered up at him, indecision warring in her eyes. "If you kill her, your magic leaves with hers." Apology flashed across her face.

Phillip's mind cleared as he regained control and heard her words.

Rapunzel wasn't finished. "Her dark magic balances your light magic. It's what she has always taught me—probably to show how superior she was. If you'd died, she could have taken your magic into herself, but that much power in one person would tear out everything they were. If you take hers, you will no longer be the beloved king of Bela, but something darker."

Aurora moved to his side. "And if he doesn't take the power? If he just lets it disappear with her death?" She turned to Phillip. "Do you really need the power if she's gone?"

He looked to her. His sleeping beauty stood by him, her eyes open. It was as if he was seeing everything for the first time. What he'd almost given up for her. His kingdom would have crumbled into ash if La Dame had gained the Basile power. But he couldn't truthfully tell himself he wouldn't do it again.

He listened to the sounds of the fight dying outside the room. The door crashed open, and Alfred barreled through with Chandler and Renauld at his back, their swords raised. They stilled as they took in the view before them.

Wulfric slumped forward, La Dame's magic released him from the wall as she weakened and healed herself. Soon, she'd be strong enough to take everything from them again.

Yet, he couldn't give up his magic. Maybe it was selfishness. Maybe it was a knowledge that Bela would be vulnerable should the Basile power no longer be able to protect them. La Dame wasn't the only evil in the world.

He scanned the faces of the people he loved before meeting Rapunzel's eyes again. "She will live. This time." He turned to his family. "I can't."

"Rapunzel," La Dame rasped.

Phillip froze, turning back on his heel. Rapunzel rested a hand on her mother's chest. At first, Phillip thought she was helping her heal more quickly, but then he saw it. The remaining color drained from the sorceress' face.

"Please," La Dame pleaded.

"What are you doing?" Phillip stepped forward to stop her. La Dame couldn't die.

Rapunzel didn't take her eyes from her mother's face. "I'm preventing her from healing herself." She clenched her jaw and stared into La Dame's glassy eyes. "I will let you live, Mother, but it will come at a cost." She pushed out a breath. "My freedom and Renauld's. We will no longer be under your control."

La Dame coughed. "They've corrupted you. The Basiles."

She turned her head as much as she could to look at Phillip. "You would steal my daughter?"

For the first time, Phillip saw La Dame for what she truly was. Alone. Her blackened heart didn't have the capacity for love. If it did, her own daughter wouldn't threaten her life in order to leave her.

He'd never expected to pity the sorceress.

"I have stolen nothing," he said.

Her gaze landed on Ric who now stood behind Rapunzel as if providing her strength. She closed her eyes, agony twisting her features. "You will pay for this, Basile. For many generations, you will suffer for taking my daughter from me." She sighed, the sound rattling in her chest. "I will give you your freedom, Rapunzel. For my life."

"If you come for her," Phillip growled. "I will use the full might of the Basile power to protect her. She is no longer your child. She is mine." Knowing Ric, he assumed she soon would be. "You will leave this place. You will leave us in peace. We do not wish to fight any longer."

La Dame nodded shortly. "I will not fight you this day, but this is not the end, Phillip Basile. One day, I will destroy you, and your kingdom will fade into nothing. No one will remember you. They will only know an empty land full of ghosts."

Phillip was too exhausted to deal with her any longer. He fully believed she'd live by her word and leave Bela behind. At least for now. His shoulders slumped, and he could barely hold himself up any longer after using so much power.

Aurora grabbed his wrist and looped one of his arms over her shoulders and Ric did the same with the other. The three of them hobbled from the room as Rapunzel finished healing her mother. The sorceress would be too weak from the healing to cause any more trouble before she left.

Out in the courtyard, Belaens recovered from their fight. Gaulean prisoners sat along the outer rim, guarded by their enemies. Phillip wouldn't harm them. Not this time. He planned to send them home to their families.

Blood ran between the stones. It would be a long time before the fortress was worthy of use again. They'd build a new gate, a stronger one.

Aurora tightened her arm around Phillip's waist. He struggled to keep his eyes open.

Outside the fortress, his army began setting up camp, keeping some distance from the bloodstained battlefield. They'd lost too many warriors, too many fathers and sons and brothers; too many mothers, daughters, and sisters. Many would mourn in Bela in the coming weeks.

Alfred and Chandler appeared behind them. "She's gone," Alfred said. "Just like that."

Phillip sighed. "That's good."

"We thought you were dead." Chandler stepped around them to face Phillip. "You died in front of us."

Alfred scratched the back of his neck. "When I saw you in the hall, I thought it was a ghost. Like maybe I was only seeing what I wanted to see."

Phillip shook his head. "I... I'm here." That statement sank into him, causing his knees to buckle. He was there, alive. Aurora was awake. They were together with their son. Every emotion he'd held back because of the imminent danger to Bela hit him in full force. He sucked in a shaking breath. "It's over."

Aurora stumbled forward from the weight of him. Alfred and Chandler took him from Aurora and Ric. He almost protested, but they walked swiftly toward the camp. He needed to rest before he completely fell apart.

He relied on his magic to strengthen him, but he'd used so

much it was no use. Soldiers cheered as they arrived, but the joy held a note of sadness. They'd all lost friends in another senseless battle with Gaule. Many Belaens lost their lives in this feud between the Basiles and the Durands.

Alfred and Chandler led him into a tent and lowered him to a bedroll. He sighed as his body relaxed.

They looked to each other and then to Aurora. "We're going to go help claim our dead."

Phillip nodded. Each slain soldier of Bela was returned to their families. Phillip's father had always been adamant about not letting go of civility in war, of never seeing his soldiers as unknown faces to throw against foreign walls. They each had worth.

Aurora dropped onto the bedroll facing him, but did not touch him.

"Where's Ric?" he asked.

"He went to Rapunzel."

Phillip smiled. "Good. That's good." Another moment passed before he let his exhaustion win, slipping into a soundless sleep.

CHAPTER THIRTY-NINE

AURORA

Aurora didn't sleep. After having her eyes closed for eighteen years, she didn't want to let the darkness in again so soon. The sounds of the camp faded away as night took over. Only the soft chatter of night guards reached her ears. Wulfric checked on his father, staying for a few minutes of awkwardness before returning to Rapunzel. The Durand prince stayed with them rather than returning to his own kingdom and his family.

Aurora heard stories of his cruel father and even crueler brothers.

Alfred and Chandler checked in as well, but no one stayed when they realized Phillip had yet to wake. Only Aurora watched him, noting the soft smile on his lips as he slept. What did he dream of?

In her deep slumber, she'd often imagined him with her, dreaming of a future she'd longed for but never thought they'd have.

With the battle looming, neither of them processed what her return meant. Phillip had a life now. Would she even fit into it? He was the king of Bela, and she was still a nobody who'd lived alone in the forest.

"I can hear you thinking all the way over here." He didn't open his eyes.

His voice sent warmth rushing through her. It had been a constant presence in her slumber. "Not thinking," she breathed. "Just watching you."

"Aurora, you forget that I know you." He finally looked at her.

She crossed her arms over her chest. "But you don't. Not really. We barely knew each other before I fell into the curse, and that was a long time ago."

He pushed himself up, his muscles straining from the effort. "I know you."

She lowered her gaze to her hands, tears threatening to fall. "I wasn't worth you sacrificing yourself." She'd wanted to say the words since waking up to find him unconscious and almost dead.

He scooted from the bedroll and raised up on his knees in front of her. "Aurora, look at me."

She shook her head, golden strands falling in front of her face.

He put a finger under her chin and tilted her face up. "I have spent the last eighteen years in a constant state of suspension, never moving forward, always standing still. I mourned you though you were not dead. Everywhere I went, I looked for your face as if you'd be there smiling at me. I questioned my every decision, imagining they were your words arguing with me."

She started to say something, but he held up a hand, cutting her off.

"Aurora Rose, you're my sun, my moon, and the stars by which I guide myself. You wonder if you were worth it? I'd do it again, giving you every piece of me until there was nothing left. There is darkness in my magic. I know that now. But you, you are pure light." He took her hands in his. "I need you, because without you, I am not whole. For eighteen years, there has been a chasm inside me, widening with each moment you didn't open your eyes."

Tears streamed down her face, but she didn't wipe them away. There are moments in life when everything falls into place. When it's time to stop questioning fate and grab hold of it with two hands. The parts of her that broke apart with the deaths of her parents, her grandmother's demise, and with the impending curse found their way together again, healing as if by magic. Around them, flowers sprouted from the grassy floor, pulled forth by the joy in her power.

And before her, Phillip waited, his shoulders tense.

Aurora leaned forward, pulling him into a soft kiss. She parted her lips, letting his tongue brush against hers.

He growled and hauled her into his lap as he kissed her more forcefully. Aurora pushed her hands through his hair, skimming them down over his neck, his back.

"I love you," she whispered against his lips. "I think I've loved you since the moment I saw an injured soldier in the woods." She pulled back, cupping his cheeks. "Your voice kept me from falling into the dark void of my slumber. It called to me. Every word. I never thought I'd ever get to kiss you again, to see your smile or relax into your arms, but I dreamed of it. I dreamed of you. You're my dream come true, Phillip. And I'm scared. My entire life, I've prepared to lose everything when the curse came for me. Now, it's gone and here I am, still terrified of losing."

"You won't lose me."

She ran her thumb over his bottom lip. "I know." She

leaned her forehead against his. "You and I... we finally have a chance. No more curses."

"No more curses." He kissed the corner of her mouth.

"Just us."

"Just us." He kissed the other corner.

"And Bela. We'll keep our kingdom safe."

He smiled. "Yes. And Bela. They have a queen now."

She sucked in a breath. She'd never wanted to be a queen, but she fell in love with a man destined to be a great king. "Queen."

"I'd say that's an upgrade from sleeping beauty."

"Definite upgrade." When she kissed him this time, she never wanted it to end.

He skimmed his teeth against her bottom lip, consuming her, loving her.

Aurora hadn't had a family in a long time. Now she had Phillip and Wulfric.

No longer the sleeping beauty of Bela, Aurora Rose Brynhild Basile had everything she'd never known to hope for.

CHAPTER FORTY

RIC

Wulfric should have felt guilty sitting outside his parents' tent listening to their conversation, but he didn't. A smile etched across his face. He ignored the guard looking at him strangely and sat back on his heels.

His father had always been his person, his best friend, but even as a boy, Ric knew the pain he lived with. He'd never imagined they could wake his mother.

And it was all because of Rapunzel. A part of him wondered if that was the reason he felt drawn to the woman, but a larger part knew there was so much more to their story.

Rapunzel had invaded his mind, his dreams, long before his heart. She was stronger than anyone he knew besides perhaps his mother.

The two women showed many similarities. Both lived much of their lives under La Dame's control.

In the coming days. Wulfric looked forward to getting to know his mother, but she had his father tonight. Rapunzel had no one. Even Renauld kept his distance, lost in his own pain.

Ric got to his feet and walked across the quiet camp to

where Rapunzel slept under the stars. She'd refused a tent, wanting to watch the world, she'd claimed.

She lay with her head against a log, her eyes fixed on the dazzling sky above. He lowered himself beside her.

"We saw the same constellations in Dracon," she said, her voice soft. "Isn't that strange? All those years in that place looking up at the same sky as you, and yet never knowing the taste of freedom."

Wulfric remained quiet as he let her speak.

Her chest rose and fell with a steady rhythm as she sighed. "Do you want to know something wrong? What am I saying? Of course, you don't want to hear this. But I need to say it, anyway." She breathed in deeply as if looking for strength. "There's this guilt inside of me. It isn't right, but I can't get rid of it. I threatened my own mother's life today, and then I abandoned her."

"Rapunzel—"

"No, please. I just need to speak. You and your father would do anything to protect your mother. I saw that as soon as I told you how to break the curse. I wish I had that. I wish I loved the woman who raised me." Her eyes glassed over.

Wulfric reached out and intertwined his fingers with his. "So, you feel guilty because you don't feel guilty?"

A smile curved her lips. "Yes."

He slid down, lying beside her with their sides touching. Never once did he let go of her hand. "I won't pretend I know what it's like not to have family. I've always had my father."

"And even your mother. She may have been under the curse your entire life, but you could still love her. You knew she was a good person, someone to respect and revere."

He'd never considered himself lucky for his circumstances. To him, he'd always been missing something essential in his life.

He squeezed her hand.

"Have you had any dreams recently?" she asked.

He thought for a moment. When his magic wanted him to find her, it sent the dreams frequently. Since then, it reverted back to the way it was before, just an occasional annoyance, no real power. "No." He sighed.

She rolled onto her side to face him. "I believe in you, Wulfric. You may feel as if your power has no use, but we never know what magic wants from us. It is not ours to own. Sometimes, it is the soul, not the magic, that makes the man."

He dropped his hand onto the curve of her waist, running it along her side. Wide, gray eyes watched him.

"You're not alone, Rapunzel." He lifted his hand to push her hair back, his eyes darting to her lips. "You deserve more than a cruel mother." He skimmed his fingers along the curve of her jaw. "Let us be your family. My parents. My grandmother. Alfred. Chandler. Travis... Me. Our family is sometimes broken. We aren't perfect. But we love each other. Let us love you too."

"What are you saying?" she breathed.

He leaned forward so his lips hovered over hers. "Marry me." Before she could respond, he claimed her lips, vowing to never let them go. She moaned into the kiss, allowing him to take control, to love her the way she deserved.

He'd known she was special since the first time he'd seen her in his dreams. But it was more than that.

His mother's words to his father only moments ago wound through his mind.

I think I've loved you since the moment I saw an injured soldier in the woods. Your voice kept me from falling into the dark void of my slumber. It called to me. Every word. I never thought I'd ever get to kiss you again, to see your smile or relax into your arms, but I dreamed of it. I dreamed of you. You're my dream come true, Phillip.

He'd loved Rapunzel since the first time he saw her. Ric never imagined finding the girl in his dreams or having her love him the same way. His parents loved with an intensity he envied. He watched his father for years, never pitying him for what he'd lost, but only amazed that someone could feel so deeply.

But now he understood.

He felt it too.

He pulled away. "I don't know what the future has in store for us. It'll probably be hard, but I want you by my side."

She wiped a tear from her cheek. "My mother isn't going to stop, Wulfric. I don't know what she'll do, which curse she'll use, but I want this. I want you. I want to be a part of your family, to be loved the way you all love each other." She smiled despite the tears rolling down her face.

Wulfric kissed her again, not gentle this time. He wanted her to know he was hers forever. That she'd never be alone again.

"Is that a yes?" The day had been filled with horrors and death and so much fear, but this, right here, made it all fade into the past.

Rapunzel nodded, and the future grew brighter. Wulfric Brynhild Basile's dreams led him to this point. He'd hated his magic since he was a kid bullied by the other palace children for his lack of abilities. But now he understood. It had a power none of them could see. He'd seen what his future could hold, and he held onto it with both hands, knowing if he let go, it would be the greatest mistake of his life.

He loved Rapunzel as his father loved his mother. Completely. Wholly. Irreparably. And there was no going back.

CHAPTER FORTY-ONE

LA DAME

Unadulterated rage. Complete and utter vengeance.

La Dame knew no other feeling since the Basiles of Bela stole her daughter. They twisted her mind, ripping her from the very woman who raised her.

It wasn't Rapunzel's fault. Phillip Basile and that son of his were tricksters, bewitching their followers with the false light of their magic. What would the citizens of Bela do if they knew their king's power originated in darkness? If they saw the anger burning in his eyes?

She'd seen who he truly was. Aurora was meant to be at her side. La Dame gave that up in hopes Phillip would drain the last of his power, killing himself and leaving Bela vulnerable. His power would then latch onto hers, intertwining its unbreakable embrace.

Only, true love's kiss didn't kill him. He was too strong. She should have seen it coming. He'd let the power control him, gaining ground on hers.

He'd beaten her.

Taken her only child.

She paced the length of the cavernous room beneath her palace. She kept her most prized possessions locked in the space. The door to the cell she'd occasionally kept Rapunzel in stood open, abandoned. Renauld's was just as empty.

What did a Basile king want with a supposedly dead Durand prince?

She shook her head, ridding it of the questions. She had to do something, to take her revenge. Her steps echoed across the stone floor, the sound reverberating along the arched ceilings. Cases of stolen and precious items sat along the far wall. Jewels. Ancient weapons. Relics. One day, she'd have the crown of Bela in this vault. She'd tumble that kingdom from the very cliffs it sat on.

"A curse," she whispered, eyeing Renauld's empty cell.

The Durand prince came from a cruel family. His father and brothers hated nothing more than the Basiles. A smile slid across her thin lips. She pushed her hair over one shoulder and pulled every last bit of her magic to the surface of her skin.

Using magic against others sated her need for anger. But crafting curses was an art that filled her with joy. None other than her knew the true consequences until long after.

She lifted the bottom of her crimson dress and kneeled on the stone, letting her entire body relax into the rhythm of her power. She closed her eyes, rocking back and forth as she molded the magic.

When she spoke, it was only to herself. "The first son or daughter of Basile will be connected to the first of the Durands in each generation. Their lives will intertwine; their very souls will not be whole without the other. Enemies serving enemies. Basile serving Durand. The cursed will be limited and forced into their role. Let it be said that the Basiles destroyed their own kingdom for selfishness." They could have avoided such a curse. Aurora didn't have to wake. Rapunzel wasn't theirs to keep.

As her magic swirled, obeying her commands, La Dame opened her eyes, wondering if she'd just changed the world forever.

Gaule and Bela would now be connected for as long as Bela lived, for as long as Basile descendants were born.

She stood, straightening her dress. Now, all she had to do was wait for their destruction.

For La Dame never aged. She couldn't die. She would have the pleasure of watching everything she'd done play out.

And it would be glorious.

CHAPTER FORTY-TWO

AURORA

Aurora stood atop the palace walls watching life happen below her. Wulfric and Rapunzel married two months before. They stood amidst the flowers in the queen mother's gardens and pledged to love each other forever.

Each moment Aurora spent with her son was another that reminded her of what she'd never thought she'd have. He was an easy man to love, open, honest, and good. Just like his father.

Arms wound around her waist from behind, and Phillip rested his chin on her shoulder. Being the wife of Phillip Basile was like a new adventure every day. He reveled in showing her how much he loved her, and she tried to do the same for him. But she knew nothing could match the power of what she truly felt.

"Renauld is leaving soon," he whispered. "We're wanted in the courtyard."

Word reached them of the death of the Gaulean king days ago. Aurora was proud of Renauld as he planned to return home and claim the crown for himself. She didn't know how his brothers would react. Most likely, he'd end up living as an outlaw within Gaule, but he'd rightfully claimed he couldn't just abandon his kingdom.

Aurora sighed and followed Phillip down the steps. In the courtyard, Renauld faced off against Rapunzel. Each held a wooden practice sword aloft.

"One last spar." Rapunzel grinned.

She'd only returned to the palace with Ric the day before after some time away, but they'd spoken of their sparring matches within the palace of Dracon.

They shared the kind of history no one should have to experience. It bonded them.

Renauld gave her a short bow before circling her. He lunged forward, and she twisted out of the way, ducking his sword in the process. A laugh burst out of her.

Aurora liked her son's new wife. Without the threat of La Dame hanging over her, she radiated joy. In her slumber, when Aurora heard the words spoken in her room, she couldn't remember hearing any laughter. She got the distinct impression it had been missing from the palace for a long time.

Phillip's mother sidled up to her. "Aurora." She smiled, kind eyes sparkling.

"Come to say goodbye to Renauld?"

The queen mother nodded. "He is our hope for peace with Gaule." Her brow creased. "At least for a while. We've had peace before, but it never seems to last beyond a single king. The Basiles and Durands are fated to be at odds, I'm afraid."

Aurora took in her words, hoping there was no truth in them.

Rapunzel ran forward, bringing her practice sword down

across Renauld's back. A scream pierced the air, but it didn't come from Renauld.

Wulfric's knees buckled. He rubbed the area of his back where Renauld was struck. Aurora's eyes narrowed. "Ric, what's wrong?"

"I..." He pushed out a breath. "Nothing."

"Rapunzel." Renauld met her eyes in silent communication. "Hit me again."

Rapunzel didn't hesitate. She slammed her closed fist into his stomach.

Wulfric bent over, holding an arm across his front. "Ugh, that hurt."

"Again, Rapunzel." Renauld braced himself.

She slapped him across the face with the back of her hand. Wulfric rubbed his face.

Rapunzel ran to him, shaking her head violently. "No. No. No."

"What?" he wheezed.

Renauld joined them. "A curse. It has to be."

"But what does it mean?" She asked. "I've never seen a curse where a person feels another's pain."

Renauld only lifted his shoulders in a helpless shrug.

Phillip gripped Renauld's arm. "More reason for you to leave. We need to get you far away from Wulfric if he is indeed tied to you. Distance may be the answer."

Renauld nodded shortly as a stable boy led his horse forward. His few belongings hung in the saddlebags. He gave Rapunzel and Ric one final look before climbing on. "Thank you, all of you, for what you've done. I will not forget the generosity of the Basiles." He kicked his heels into the horse and thundered through the gates followed by the guards Phillip had provided him.

Wulfric dropped to his knees, a cry dead on his lips as he clutched his chest. "Father, it hurts."

Aurora watched helplessly as Rapunzel tried to heal Ric, only able to easy some of his suffering. She'd use her power and within half an hour, he'd be screaming in agony again. Eventually, he fell unconscious, not making another sound.

And Aurora couldn't do a damned thing about it. She couldn't help her son. Not even Phillip with all of his power found a way to help.

All they could do was watch him writhe in pain.

RAPUNZEL CAME to Aurora after two weeks of Ric groaning and screaming in his sleep. "He's not getting better." She plunked down into the chair beside Aurora. "We've received word of Renauld's arrival in Gaule. He has taken the throne. One of his brothers challenged him to a fight, but Renauld won despite reports of his illness." She bit her lip. "He writes of pain not unlike Ric's."

Aurora nodded, but Rapunzel's next words chilled her to the bone.

"We have to go to him."

"To the king of Gaule?" Aurora shook her head. "No." She'd worried it would come to this. They all saw what was happening to Ric.

Rapunzel reached forward, taking Aurora's hand in hers. "You saw as much as I did. The sparring with Renauld. What happened as he left. It's one of my mother's curses. It has to be. Ric and Renauld are connected."

Aurora didn't want to believe the words. Her father had been selfish in dealing with La Dame to save her mother. It stole much of Aurora's life. Phillip had some of that selfishness, willing to risk anything to wake her. He hadn't made a deal with the sorceress, but he'd angered her.

And then Rapunzel decided to stay, her own daughter.

It was enough to drive anyone mad.

"She's taking my son," Aurora whispered. Just like Aurora took her daughter.

Phillip walked toward them, pain etched into the lines of his face. He looked from Rapunzel to Aurora. "Wulfric told me your decision." He dropped into a chair at the table and put his head in his hands. "My son is going to serve my enemy."

Rapunzel's eyes softened. "Renauld won't make him serve him."

"They're connected," Aurora started. "When Renauld felt pain, Ric felt it too. Do you think..."

"Their lives are connected as well," Phillip finished. "La Dame is nothing if not cruel."

Rapunzel stood. "Ric cannot live like this much longer. We leave tomorrow."

As she walked away, Aurora moved to sit in Phillip's lap and clung to him. She never thought by gaining her life she'd lose her son.

As the sun rose the next morning, a wagon left the palace surrounded by trusted guards. Chandler and Alfred would only go so far as the border. Travis ran after them, screaming Ric's name. The boy didn't yet understand. Then again, neither did Aurora or Phillip.

This time, she didn't cry. She held her head high as the people of Bela watched their prince leave, his life no longer his own.

It was then she realized, La Dame won. She would always win.

For Aurora and Phillip there would be no happy ending.

EPILOGUE

Persinette Basile had never been in charge of her own life. That was what her father was telling her.

"Do you understand, Etta?"

How could she understand? She was a kid and only days ago her mother was murdered by the very people hunting them now. Magic. The life force inside her was newly illegal in Gaule. For most of her life, the descendants of Bela lived in peace in Gaule. Their kingdom was long destroyed, but the magic lived on.

Then the purge came. The king of Gaule outlawed magic and hunted down all those carrying its power. Her father, Viktor Basile, had once been his greatest friend, crafting wards around Gaule to keep those with magic in or out. Really, he just wanted to keep one magic-wielder out. La Dame. The villain from stories Etta was never supposed to hear.

She snapped her attention back to her father. "What?"

He sighed, stilling his hands on the log he'd been cutting. He worked tirelessly building a home for them, but it would never be home without her mother.

Her father fixed her with a stern stare. "Child, the curse will fall to you on your eighteenth birthday." He shook his head. "Not even I can save you from it. Your life will be connected to that of the young Durand prince."

"Alex?" She didn't see what was so wrong about that. He'd been her friend since she was small.

"He's no longer your friend," her father growled. "The Durands are enemies of the Basiles. I lost sight of that and now look at us? Forced to hide in the woods near the palace. Even being this far causes me unimaginable pain." His lips drew down.

She'd seen the fog of pain in her father's eyes but didn't understand what it meant. "Can we leave? Find a far corner of the kingdom."

He put a hand on her shoulder. "You didn't hear a word I said. I cannot go far from the king. As the first of a Basile generation, I am tied to my counterpart in the Durand family. One day, you will need to find a way to stay close to Alexandre."

"That's easy." She shrugged. "He likes me."

Her father slammed his fist down on the log. "Hear me, daughter." His voice held a dangerous tone. "When you one day return to the palace, Alexandre Durand will not be your friend. Remember that always. You will be drawn to him, but that is only La Dame's magic. Now go to the river and fetch us some water. You've learned enough family history for one day."

Family history, Etta scoffed as she swiped the wooden pail from the ground and walked in the direction of the river they'd found the day before. They weren't the only magic wielders who'd escaped the purge among the trees. Her father had warding magic. He'd crafted wards to hide them from the rest of Gaule.

Etta knew little of her family. As far as she knew, it was now only her and her father left of the Basile line. They were descended from the royal line of the ancient kingdom of Bela. Bela was now only a vacant land.

She laughed at the image of her as a princess. Etta preferred running through dank tunnels under the palace, scraped knees and all, to sitting down to tea with the queen as her mother once made her do. She'd rather be covered in dirt than tiaras. It didn't help that the princess of Gaule was such a brat.

No, Etta was meant to be nothing more than a common girl.

She reached the river only to find she wasn't alone. A beautiful speckled horse dipped its head to drink.

"Hello." She set the bucket down, scanning the surroundings for any sight of saddle or rider. There was none. A smile split her lips. "Are you out here alone?"

The horse lifted its head as if it understood her words. Brown eyes bore into hers, seeing right into her soul. It took a step toward her.

"Are you a boy or a girl?" she asked. "Silly question. I'm going to call you a boy because I don't get along with girls so well." She flashed him another smile and bent to fill her bucket.

Before she knew what was happening, a nose nudged her forward. She lost balance, her arms flapping wildly as she soared toward the water and hit it with a splash.

She sputtered, getting her feet under her in the shallow water. Standing, the water dripped from her clothes. She crossed her arms. "That wasn't nice at all. What if I drowned, you big oaf? I can't die. Apparently I have to fulfill some stupid ancient curse."

Tears came unbidden to her eyes as she climbed the bank

and sat with her back hunched. Sobs burst out of her, and she couldn't stop them. Etta wasn't a crier. She may be a kid, but she was tough.

Yet, as her father's revelations rolled through her mind, she couldn't help but feel her emotions slip beyond her control.

Alex apparently wasn't her friend, yet she'd spent most of her life at his side. How was she supposed to return to the palace where her mother was killed?

Every emotion she'd suppressed since finding her mother rose to the surface. It wasn't until she felt the same nose that had pushed her into the water nudging the side of her head that she let herself breathe.

She reached out without hesitation, just needing a friend as she curled her fingers into the horse's matted mane. No one had been taking care of him. That much was evident. Maybe they needed each other.

She met his understanding gaze. Had he lost as much as her? He rubbed his long nose along her cheek, and she finally calmed. "You need a friend too, huh?" She shook her head. "I don't know how long I'll be here. I'm cursed, see, not in control of my own destiny."

She wiped her face and stood, turning to face him. "I'm going to call you Vérité. Truth. Because, friend, that's what today has become about. Truths my family hid from me, truths about the world." She leaned in. "But can I tell you my own truth?"

Vérité snorted.

Etta grinned at her new friend. "I don't react well when someone gives me an ultimatum. That's what a curse is, after all. La Dame may be powerful, but she doesn't know me. I'm going to break her curse. Her magic can't hold me. She won't break me."

She filled the bucket and straightened up to walk back to her soon-to-be home. "Because I am Persinette Basile. Descendent of a great line of kings and queens. Daughter of the cursed. Friend to horses everywhere." She grinned at that part. "I am a Basile and the Basiles always have greater battles to wage."

HAVE **you read the series from the beginning? We come full circle as we come back to Etta's story in Golden Curse. If you're an advanced reviewer who is just now coming to the series, email me and I'm happy to send you a copy of book 1!**

ABOUT MICHELLE

M. Lynn is a USA Today bestselling author of love. Yes, love. Whether it be YA romance (Under Michelle MacQueen) or fantasy romance, she loves to make readers swoon.

The great loves of her life to this point are two tiny blond creatures who call her "aunt" and proclaim her books to be "boring books" for their lack of pictures. Yet, somehow, she still manages to love them more than chocolate.

When she's not sharing her inexhaustible wisdom with her niece and nephew, Michelle is usually lounging in her ridiculously large bean bag chair creating worlds and characters that remind her to smile every day - even when a feisty five-year-old is telling her just how much she doesn't know.

See more from M. Lynn and sign up to receive updates and deals!

www.michellelynnauthor.com

ALSO BY M. LYNN

Fantasy and Fairytales (Written as M. Lynn)

Golden Curse

Golden Chains

Golden Crown

Glass Kingdom

Glass Princess

Noble Thief

Cursed Beauty

Legends of the Tri-Gard (Written as M. Lynn)

Prophecy of Darkness

Legacy of Light

Mastery of Earth

Redefining Me:

The F Word

The N Word

The C Word

The Invincible series:

We Thought We Were Invincible

We Thought We Knew It All

The New Beginnings series

Choices

Promises

Dreams

Confessions

ACKNOWLEDGMENTS

"I can no other answer make but thanks, and thanks, and ever thanks."

-William Shakespeare

This is my favorite part of a book - when I get to see just who all is responsible for taking me on a journey. When you're a writer, you get to be the one to showcase how many special people had a hand in crafting the story. There's no better page in the book.

I write because God has given me the opportunity to pursue my dreams. Without the challenges he's given me, this book wouldn't exist.

So many people supported me throughout this series. My parents, sisters, brother in-laws, niece and nephew.

Friends who provide me with constant inspiration.

A cover designer in Covers by Combs who is a brilliant artist, and an editor in Melissa Craven who is a sculptor of words.

I've been lucky enough throughout the past year to experience the true generosity and kindness of the reader community as they have rooted for these characters. I couldn't ask for better people to surround myself with. So, thank you. I wrote this one for you.

Made in the USA
Columbia, SC
17 January 2020